T0166989

Readers love
the Bad to Be Good series
by ANDREW GREY

Bad to Be Good

"This book had it all, amazing characters, suspense and an absolutely adorable little boy."
—Paranormal Romance Guild

"Grey has a plethora of passages that convey the essence of his characters and the storyline."
—Love Bytes

Bad to be Worthy

"I am a huge Andrew Grey fan but this one surprised me. I think this is one of my favorite series by Andrew Grey IF I had to choose."
—TTC Books and More

By ANDREW GREY

Published by DREAMSPINNER PRESS
www.dreamspinnerpress.com

By Andrew Grey (cont.)

Published by Dreamspinner Press
www.dreamspinnerpress.com

BAD
TO BE
NOBLE

ANDREW GREY

DREAMSPINNER
PRESS

Published by
DREAMSPINNER PRESS

5032 Capital Circle SW, Suite 2, PMB# 279,
Tallahassee, FL 32305-7886 USA
www.dreamspinnerpress.com

This is a work of fiction. Names, characters, places, and incidents either
are the product of author imagination or are used fictitiously, and any
resemblance to actual persons, living or dead, business establishments,
events, or locales is entirely coincidental.

Bad to Be Noble
© 2021 Andrew Grey

Cover Art
© 2021 L.C. Chase
http://www.lcchase.com
Cover content is for illustrative purposes only and any person depicted
on the cover is a model.

All rights reserved. This book is licensed to the original purchaser only.
Duplication or distribution via any means is illegal and a violation of
international copyright law, subject to criminal prosecution and upon
conviction, fines, and/or imprisonment. Any eBook format cannot be le-
gally loaned or given to others. No part of this book may be reproduced
or transmitted in any form or by any means, electronic or mechanical,
including photocopying, recording, or by any information storage and
retrieval system, without the written permission of the Publisher, except
where permitted by law. To request permission and all other inquiries,
contact Dreamspinner Press, 5032 Capital Circle SW, Suite 2, PMB#
279, Tallahassee, FL 32305-7886, USA, or www.dreamspinnerpress.
com.

Mass Market Paperback ISBN: 978-1-64108-254-9
Trade Paperback ISBN: 978-1-64405-914-2
Digital ISBN: 978-1-64405-913-5
Mass Market published March 2022
First Edition
v. 1.0

Printed in the United States of America

This book is dedicated to Karen and Martin for taking me to Longboat Key and helping to get my imagination running.

Prologue

IN THE past twenty-four hours, the old man who had protected the three of them had died, and now their entire future was uncertain. The man who would one day take the name Terrance knew it as soon as he heard the news that Harold Garvic had passed away. It took a matter of hours for his son, Junior, to consolidate his hold on power.

"What are we going to do?" Terrance asked, plopping his muscular body into one of the chairs in the office of the club they used as a home base. The club was closed; it was one of those hours of the early morning when the rest of the world was asleep.

Richard sat next to him, legs spread, leaning back in the chair. "We're going to prepare ourselves. We've made a lot of money and never cheated the family." They skimmed off the top, but that was expected… as long as the family got their share. "I'm already hearing rumblings from a few contacts that Junior has decided that he isn't going to taint himself by getting rid of us himself. But he intends to see to it that we go down one way or another." His eyes and voice were steady as a rock. Richard had always been the leader. He ran the clubs. Gerome was the financial wizard and idea man.

Terrance was the muscle. No one intimidated him, but for a moment, Terrance let the pure fear that welled up from inside show in his eyes and then tamped it down. Fear was useless. They needed to think and plan.

"What are you saying?" Gerome asked. "I've had things in place for years for all of us. We disappear, wait a few years, and then we all have enough to live on for the rest of our lives."

Richard leaned forward. "Can you add to it? Say in the next few hours? Time is of the essence here. I'm not sure when Junior will make his move, but we need to beat him to the punch if we want to survive."

Terrance knew that he meant that in the most literal of terms. If Junior intended to push them aside, he would do it down the barrel of a gun. It wouldn't matter how strong they were, a bullet would kill each of them just as easily as it would anyone else.

"Sure." Gerome shrugged. "There is plenty of money lying in a myriad of accounts that could be pooled and sent off as soon as the banks open." He was probably already planning how he was going to pull this off. He was smart—whip smart. Terrance sometimes wished he was more than just the muscle. Not that he was dumb, but he didn't have the talents the other two did.

"Then do it. And make copies of the most incriminating things we have against Junior and the rest of the organization. Lists of associates, crimes, dates, places, everything." Richard's expression was as serious as a mob hit. "We're going to do something we said we would never do. We're going to go to the feds with enough evidence to take everyone down."

Terrance swallowed. That went against everything he believed. No matter what, you didn't squeal. If someone hurt you, then you and your friends hurt them back. That was the law of the street and of the business they had been a part of since they were teenagers. You handled things inside, with the support of the organization. "The feds. Are you fucking kidding me?" He nearly jumped out of his chair.

Richard shook his head. "This is death to us. Junior wants us gone, permanently. Harold appreciated what we did and understood that business was business. Junior got religion or something." He shook his head slowly. "The fact is that he doesn't want any part in our gay businesses, so he's going to pull all his money, then take us down, and I suspect that means we'll wake up to guns pointed at our heads and that will be it."

"But…," Terrance sputtered. "I'm no squealer." He had never been one, and he sure as hell had no intention of starting now. This went against everything Terrance believed, even if he knew Richard was right.

"We're loyal," Gerome added.

Richard got to his feet. "To what? Loyal to someone who wants us gone? Who sees us as nothing but animals to be put down? No matter how much money we make, he doesn't want to have any part of us, and Junior is not going to let the three of us exist on our own. We have to join up with someone against him—you both know that. And the best way for us to be safe is if we take Junior down." Richard was as passionate as Terrance had ever seen him. "Gerome, you get as much money out of here as you can. Take it all. Hide the trail, and then we gather all the evidence we can. Hard evidence. Between the three of us, we have enough to put away a ton of people, including Junior, and that's what we're going to do. Hit them before they hit us."

Gerome hesitated and turned to him. Terrance hated doing something like this, but Richard was hardly ever wrong, and Terrance trusted him with his life.

It looked like that trust was going to be tested.

Gerome broke first. "Okay. Let me get busy. I have a lot of work to do to make sure our activity can't be traced." He pulled a small laptop out of his case and attached a cellular network connection, completely separate from the club's network, and got to work.

Terrance nodded his agreement, sealing their fate.

Richard left the small room, most likely heading to the office he used. Terrance had no doubt that they were getting together information that they had gathered for years as a sort of insurance policy. Gerome was great with numbers, Richard was an amazing leader, and Terrance made sure no one messed with any of them. That was his role, and he was damned good at it. The three of them were closer than brothers. They were part of a whole, and that was more important than anything else in the world.

"What can I do?" Terrance asked.

"Let me handle it for now. I have to do this in such a way that everything runs through without me actually being there to make it happen." He was already deep into his computer work. "I need to set up timed transfers that will all happen over the next few days, sending the money on a wonderful journey where it combines with other accounts and then continues on." He worked quickly, his fingers flowing over the keyboard. With each keystroke, Terrance knew they crossed farther over the point of no return, and the consequences of what they were doing sank in. There would be no turning back.

Gerome worked for hours to get everything set up, staring at the screen and muttering under his breath. Richard gathered and organized paperwork, making sure they had as much financial evidence as they could in order to implicate the rest of the organization. They had plenty of it, and Terrance placed it in file folders and slipped them into Gerome's bag.

"Check this out," Gerome said. Terrance moved behind him and looked at the screen. "These numbers match, correct?" He hovered his mouse over the final transfer details, the button that Gerome said would start everything, cursor blinking on the blank field.

"Yes." Gerome's arms shook slightly, and Terrance placed his hands on Gerome's shoulders. "We're all in this together," he said quietly.

Gerome sighed. "Within a matter of hours, large sums of money will move, some laying a trail that leads right back to Junior, and the rest disappearing into the ether of international banking, only to end up eventually in our accounts in the islands." For him it was easy, but all Terrance could do was nod. He trusted Gerome and Richard with his life. With one additional confirmation, Gerome set everything in motion, then shut down the laptop and slipped it into his bag. Only then did Gerome breathe a sigh of relief before getting up.

The official club computers held nothing out of the ordinary, and they left them to possibly be found. "Let them go through the computer. The real data is on the laptop in my bag, and that can be wiped or destroyed in a matter of seconds if necessary."

Gerome and Terrance found Richard in the other office, pulling materials from under the floor and stuffing the papers and photographs into their bags. "The clock is running. It's only a matter of time before someone figures out that things aren't right and starts asking questions." Gerome checked the clock on the wall, and Terrance pulled his phone out of his pocket and held out his hand. Both Gerome and Richard handed him theirs, and Terrance set the three of them on the floor. He removed the SIM cards and used the hammer kept in the bottom file drawer to smash them to small pieces, taking a little of his uncertainty out on the small electronic chips. Then he smashed the phones themselves, poured water into the trash can, and dumped all of the pieces inside. There was no way in hell that anything there was going to be useful to anyone.

"Do either of you have anything else electronic?" Gerome asked.

"What about your laptop?" Terrance asked. He figured Gerome would have a plan to ensure they couldn't be traced.

"It gets the same treatment as soon as I verify that the transfers are complete. I already have a flash drive of the important data hidden away," Gerome explained. "I only need it for that and then the laptop is history."

Terrance wasn't sure how he felt about what they had decided to do, but it was too late now. They were on a path that they couldn't turn back from.

Richard looked around the office to make sure it was as they wanted it. Then he pulled a locked box from the hiding place in the floor and handed them driver's licenses and other identity information, including credit cards. "These are prepaid with a grand on each. Now we go into hiding and watch the fireworks... literally. Once the funds are all transferred, we make a deal with the feds and tell no one about any of it."

Terrance took over as Gerome and Richard left the office.

"What is he doing?" Gerome asked as Terrance emptied the contents of all the files onto the floor, spreading the paper everywhere. Then he went out to the bar and got a couple bottles of Everclear, 190 proof, that they had bootlegged in. It was nearly pure alcohol and would burn beautifully. He saturated the papers with one bottle and left the other open nearby to add fuel.

"Making sure that anything we might have missed goes up in smoke, along with everything else. The fireworks should be spectacular." Richard seemed pleased. They waited until Terrance was done and had joined them, closing the office door behind him.

"I set the timer for thirty minutes. There will be no one here, and there should be nothing left of the office."

They exited the building and climbed into Richard's Lincoln. They had a few final stops to make, at their apartments and then finally to see his mother. Terrance sat in back, watching out the window as the lights of the city streamed past. He wiped his eyes once at the thought that this could be the last time he saw her before their lives changed forever—and just how much, none of them could begin to comprehend.

Chapter 1

"ARE YOU coming to the Driftwood tonight?"

Terrance took a break from pricing weed whackers to answer Gerome's question. He sighed and placed the yard implements on the shelf. "Is it Wednesday already?" Not that he hated getting together for what amounted to a weekly family dinner with Richard, Gerome, and their families, but he was now the odd man out. They had partners, and each had an important little boy in their lives. Both boys had him wrapped around their little fingers, but Terrance found the happiness grating. Richard and Gerome were paired off and did more and more things as a family. Not that he wanted to push his way in, but it left him feeling a little like he was on the outside looking in.

Terrance had grown up with Richard and Gerome on the rough streets of Detroit, fast and hard. They were his brothers under the skin since age nine—his family. Together they ended up running the gay vices in Detroit for the Garvic family. When things had blown up and they'd had to save themselves, they first ended up in Iowa in witness protection, and after they broke WITSEC rules to see his mother before she died, the three of them were moved to Florida. It had taken a lot of negotiating in order to keep them together, but they were family, even if the marshals didn't think so.

Lately, though, it seemed his family was moving on. Granted, most of what he was feeling was probably in his head. The guys didn't do important things without him. He was always invited and included in gatherings. The boys called him Uncle Terrance, and he loved both of the kids as well as Gerome's and Richard's partners.

"Yes, it's Wednesday," Gerome said, cutting through his thoughts. "And it's Joshie's birthday." He lifted the bag he was carrying. "I brought over a few things he wanted the last time he was in the shop. I thought you could pick what you wanted to get him."

Terrance grinned. The Gerome he knew growing up was hard as nails. Lately Gerome had turned into a doting uncle, and it was almost comical to watch. "You couldn't let me pick out his gift on my own?"

Gerome looked around. "He already has a chainsaw, and he doesn't need a weed whacker," he joked. "You could get him a shovel, but he'd dig up the entire yard looking for buried treasure or dinosaur bones." He handed Terrance the bag filled with dinosaur figures.

"Perfect. Thanks," Terrance said. "He'll love these." He closed the bag and placed it next to where he was working.

"I was intending for you to give him one."

Terrance rolled his eyes. "How am I supposed to stay the favorite uncle with just one?" He grinned, and Gerome shook his head. Terrance loved to win. "I appreciate you looking out for me." It was what they did for each other.

"Maybe after the gifts, Joshie will stop asking why Uncle Terrance is grumpy?" Gerome hit him with a glare.

"I'm not grumpy, I'm—"

Gerome didn't look away. "What? Short-tempered? Surly? Been in a bad mood for the last three months?" He crossed his arms over his chest, and Terrance did the same, staring Gerome down. "Glare all you want, but it doesn't change the facts. You need to figure things out and decide what you want."

"Like what? A kid and a boyfriend? What you and Richard have?" He shook his head. "I'm doing just fine. I like the store, and I get to work with Richard at the Driftwood on the weekends. Unlike you two turkeys, I'm free to do whatever… and whoever… I like."

Gerome turned to walk away. "You keep telling yourself that." He patted Terrance on the shoulder and headed for the exit. Terrance swore under his breath and went back to stocking the shelves, putting more muscle into the job than was really needed.

AFTER HIS shift, Terrance returned to his apartment, where he showered and changed clothes. He wrapped the gifts for Joshie before leaving the building.

When they'd first moved to Florida, all three of them had small apartments in this same complex. Richard was the first to leave, moving into Daniel's condo with him. Gerome followed, moving into a larger apartment with Tucker. Joshie lived with Cheryl just across the hall from them. That left Terrance the last one in tne building, in his furnished apartment. Most of the time he tried not to think about it, but it was lonely. He was used to having the guys around. Hell, for years they were in each other's back pockets, doing everything together. Now their lives were more distant, and he was the one getting the short end of the stick.

Still, it was time for dinner. He left the apartment and drove the short distance to the Driftwood.

Everyone was already there, with Coby, Daniel's son and Richard's stepson, and Joshie hurrying over as soon as he arrived. Coby gave him a picture he'd drawn of Terrance on a boat. "I'll put it on the refrigerator when I get home." He got a hug from each of them as well as from Tucker, Gerome's partner, and Daniel before sitting down and giving Joshie his gifts. He tore open the bag and then ripped into the presents, bouncing in his seat at the dinosaurs.

"You need to eat your dinner before you play with them," Tucker said.

Joshie looked at him with an expression of exasperation that only a five-year-old could muster.

"What are you going to have?"

"Mac and cheese and french fries," he answered like it was obvious. Terrance had to admit it was what the kid had every week. "Daddy Gerome got a cake too." He eyed the box sitting on the table that had been brought over to accommodate them all.

"What about you, Coby?" Terrance asked as he sat across from him.

"A hamburger and fries, and salad." He leaned over the table. "Daddy says I have to have salad." He made a yucky face. Not that Terrance could blame him—salad wasn't one of his favorite things either.

"I'll show you how to make salad taste really good." He said it like he was sharing a secret, and Coby grinned like they were being naughty. "Tell your dad that you want ranch dressing. It's really good and you'll like it." He winked, and Coby grinned back.

"What are you two conspiring about?" Daniel asked as he slid into the booth with the boys.

"Salad," Terrance answered, and Coby giggled and shared a smile with Joshie.

"No causing trouble," Richard said as he sat down as well. "Does everyone know what they want? Annie will be right over to take orders for food, and I got you a beer." He slid the mug in front of Terrance and set down two smaller mugs of root beer for the boys. As usual, everyone settled down around the extended table, conversations flowing between them.

Annie took their orders, and like any Wednesday night, they all laughed and talked like the family they were. It reassured Terrance. This was his family, the only family he had, and he felt a little stupid for ruminating on how lonely he was becoming. Richard and Gerome would always be there for him, just like he would be there when the two of them were in trouble. And judging by their history, it was only a matter of time before that happened again.

When Richard met Daniel, they had all worked together to get Daniel out of a scrape. The same could be said of Gerome with Tucker. Granted, those scrapes put

Richard and Gerome on the paths to the guys they fell in love with, but Terrance had had to do plenty of things in order to see to it that they came out right on the other side. Not to mention the fact that they had managed to hurt the remnants of the Garvic organization while remaining anonymous. It had been a delicate dance and one that he had had a major part in. Terrance would do it all over again if he had to.

"Can we have some beers here?" a man called over the humming conversation.

Terrance turned away from the family toward a group of bikers in the corner. They were loud and waving their glasses around. Terrance turned to Richard and nodded. He slid out of the booth and approached Alan, Richard's business partner in the Driftwood, who stood behind the bar.

Terrance didn't even need to speak to Alan; just a small nod and a glance in their direction was enough for him to know exactly what to do. He veered over toward the table.

Gerome appeared beside him and took his arm. "Terrance, just don't kill them like you did the last time." He said it loudly enough that the men at the table could hear clearly. "It took forever for Alan to have the mess cleaned up."

"What's this shit?" the big meathead asked, getting up from the table, his hands at his hips, chest puffed up and pressed forward. Terrance had seen guys like this many times before.

"This… is about your manners. You be nice to the servers and behave yourself." Terrance saw the swing coming a mile away. He dodged it and smashed his fist into the guy's nose.

The guy getting blood all over his leathers grabbed his nose, and Terrance manhandled him right out the front door. "You see how fast things turn around?" Terrance wasn't going to stand for anything from the likes of him. He knew that if he took care of the ringleader, the others would fall into line. "You have a choice. I can call the police, and they'll gladly put you in jail because you swung at me first. Or you can stay out here and wait for your friends. Got it?" Terrance knew how to use his voice, and the guy snapped to attention at the knife-edge he added to the question. "Answer me," he said without raising his voice.

Still holding his nose, he groaned. "Yeah. I got it."

"Good." Terrance clicked his teeth. "I didn't even hit you that hard, ya big baby." Then he turned and went back inside.

The table with the bikers had quieted down immensely, and one of the guys hurried out to look into their missing member. Terrance checked with Annie and the other servers to make sure they were okay.

He was about to return to his seat when his eye caught on a small man wearing a faded blue polo shirt, sitting in the center of the banquette seat where the bikers were. He looked about as out of place as a nun in a whorehouse. "Let him out," Terrance ordered, and the bikers slipped out of the booth.

"We were just talking to him," one of the guys said. "He was sitting here all alone, so we were keeping him company."

Terrance knew that game too. Find some guy sitting alone, join him, box him in, scare the shit out of him, and before he knew it, he was paying the bill just to get them to go away.

The smaller guy with huge blue eyes and curly blond hair that flopped forward almost to his eyes slid out of the booth without saying a word. He turned his back to the others and then looked up at Terrance, biting his lower lip like he expected to be hit at any second and was just trying to steel himself so he could take it.

"Fucking hell," Terrance muttered under his breath, wondering what some son of a bitch had done to this kid. "You okay? Did they hurt you?"

"No. Just trapped me and started ordering stuff," he said, lowering his gaze.

"I see. And did you know that they were gonna get you to pay?" Terrance asked. The kid shrugged. "And you didn't have any money."

"Just enough for what I was gonna order," he said softly. "And that…."

"I know. That went to a round of beers because you thought they'd leave you alone." Terrance ground his teeth for a second. He'd seen that kind of shit plenty back in Detroit. The kid nodded. "Don't worry about it. Go on over there to that table. The guy right there is a partner in this place, and the one across from him is Gerome. They're my oldest friends. Go sit down, and I'll be over just as soon as I take care of something."

He waited until the guy had taken a few tentative steps away before approaching the group of assholes.

"What's the problem?" the new spokesman for the group asked. He looked just as stupid as the guy Terrance had thrown out.

"It seems you like pressuring people into buying shit for you. So pay up and get the hell out. Your patronage isn't appreciated." He motioned Annie over. "Make up the bill for these gentlemen and be sure to add a very generous tip for yourself. They'll be settling up… now." He turned back to the table. "Either you pay or you'll deal with me." He gripped the edge of the table. "Whatever shit you think you're gonna pull, forget it right now. I broke your friend's nose, and I can break a hell of a lot more than that." He wasn't going to take any crap from these people, and the restaurant's customers shouldn't have to either.

Annie brought over the check, and Terrance collected the money and handed it to her. "Now get out."

"But we got change coming and…."

What a douchebag. Terrance cracked his knuckles and any protests dropped away. All four of them got to their feet and headed for the door.

"Don't come back. Ever. In fact, I suggest that you get off the Key and back to the highway. None of the folks out here need any of the trouble that comes from the likes of you. Do I make myself clear?" He waited until they were out of the bar and had gotten on their bikes before returning to the table.

"Uncle Terrance got mad," Joshie said.

Coby nodded. "He punched someone." They looked at each other.

Terrance groaned. "They were really bad men and they were being mean to people. Don't either of you go hitting anyone." He glanced apologetically at Daniel, Cheryl, and Tucker. "The only reason I hit him was because he tried to hit me first." He hoped he hadn't set a bad example.

"We don't go hitting people," Daniel said, with Tucker echoing it. "No matter what Uncle Terrance has to do. Okay?"

Both boys nodded solemnly.

Once Annie began delivering their orders, the incident seemed to be forgotten soon enough over hamburgers and bowls of macaroni and cheese.

"Go ahead and order," Terrance told his guest. "Annie will bring you whatever you'd like."

The man nodded and placed an order for a hamburger and salad with ranch dressing. Terrance shared a conspiratorial look with Coby.

"What's your name?"

"He's Ashton," Gerome answered.

"You know him?"

Gerome nodded and reached over the table to shake Ashton's hand. "You remember those blown-glass pumpkins and snowmen we had at the store? He's the guy who made them." Gerome smiled and introduced everyone. "And the guy who saved the day is Terrance."

"Um… thank you. I didn't know what to do to get away." He seemed like a deer with the most incredible eyes ever, caught in the headlights. "I appreciate you getting me away from those guys. I didn't know what they were going to do."

Terrance accepted his plate from Annie, who turned to Ashton. "Yours will be out in a few minutes. I asked the kitchen to rush it for you." She refilled their glasses and brought Coby some extra ranch dressing. It seemed Coby had found the joys of the stuff—he looked about ready to drink it.

"Thank you," Ashton told her and then turned to Terrance. "I don't know why you're doing this. You don't owe me anything. I was the one stupid enough to be caught by them."

"Bullshit," Terrance said, offering Ashton some of his fries while he waited. "Those men were looking for someone to take advantage of. I'm just sorry that it was you. And you need to eat. This is sort of a family dinner night. It's Joshie's birthday, so we'll be having cake later." He was hoping to entice the cute guy to stick around for a little fun.

"Yeah. It's chocolate cake," Joshie interjected as though that alone was worth just about anything. "And Uncle Terrance got me dinosaurs for my birthday. You can play with them if you're sad."

Ashton actually smiled, the darkness evaporating from his features in an instant. Damn, his smile was radiant. Terrance swallowed hard. It had been quite a while since something that simple turned his head, and he found himself wondering all kinds of things he probably shouldn't be thinking about. At least not in front of the kids. "I'm good, thank you—and your uncle," Ashton said as Annie placed his plate in front of him.

Terrance ate his fish while the others talked and brought everyone up to date on their week.

"I arranged for a boat to take us fishing next Wednesday," Richard said. "Can everyone get the day off? I thought we could all go, take the boys out for the day."

"Fishies," Coby and Joshie said together.

"Yes." Richard beamed. "We can catch some fishies and have a great day out on the Gulf. The long-term forecast is good, and the water is just cool enough that once we get away from shore, the air should be fresh and breezy. What do you think?"

Daniel was already nodding. Tucker and Cheryl agreed, and Gerome said he'd ask for the day off. Terrance wasn't scheduled, so he was clear.

"Ashton, do you want to go?" Gerome asked. "It's a lot of fun. The captain takes care of the boat, so we drink, fish, eat, and have a day out on the water."

"It sounds like fun," he said softly. "But…." His gaze shifted to each of the guys. Judging by Ashton's gaze and the way his back stiffened, Terrance thought he might be afraid.

"You don't have to come if fishing isn't your thing," Terrance said. Something about Ashton piqued his curiosity. "It would still be fun, though."

"I appreciate that, thanks." He lowered his gaze to the table and ate his food while the conversation continued. Terrance found himself listening to them as he watched Ashton. Each bite was deliberate and slow, like he was savoring every morsel. "I really can't afford something like that." He never looked up.

Terrance understood. How many times when he was growing up had he watched others getting whatever they wanted while he had to make do with clothes from the Salvation Army and shoes that barely fit him? Once when he went to school, one of the other kids had pointed and said that Terrance was wearing his older brother's old clothes that had been donated. Terrance had wanted the floor to open up and swallow him.

Of course, at recess, he made the kid wish he had kept his damned mouth shut.

"It's already rented, so if you'd like to come, you'd be welcome," Richard said. Terrance knew he understood as well.

"Ashton," Gerome said, putting on one of his huge smiles, "I just thought you could come along and have a little fun. A bunch of my customers have been asking for more of your work, and I thought we could talk about it."

Ashton lifted his gaze. "Really?"

"Yeah," Gerome told him. "I got a request just today and called the owner, who told me to get in touch with you. We need some fresh items for this time of year. There are plenty of people passing through, and some of them want more than a dolphin bottle opener that says Florida on it to take home with them."

Ashton grinned. "That's pretty awesome. Since the snowbirds left, it's been hard to get people to buy my work." He sighed and returned to eating his dinner, finishing the last of his food. Then he dug into his pockets and pulled out a few bills, which he set at the edge of his plate. "I need to go, but thank you for saving me from those guys." Finally his gaze fell on Terrance. "I really appreciate it. But I need to get back home."

Gerome stood and shook his hand. "We understand. I have your number at the store. I'll call you about going out with us on the boat, and you can tell me what you have so we can bring more of your work into the store."

"That will be great," Ashton said, pausing to look at Terrance. Terrance thought Ashton might have something to say, and he leaned forward as if pulled closer by an invisible force, waiting. "Thank you again," Ashton said just above a whisper, and then turned and hurried toward the door.

"What are you up to?" Terrance asked Gerome as soon as the door closed behind Ashton.

Gerome rolled his eyes. "Oh, come on. I saw the way you kept watching him, and how he held his head down but watched you from behind those long lashes of his. The eye-fu—" He cleared his throat before he could finish the word in front of tender ears. That was another change in their lives—swearing was now completely out the window. Jesus fucking Christ, what a pain in the ass that was. "You know what I mean. He's a nice guy. Maybe a little shy, but…."

Terrance glanced at the boys, who were sharing some kind of secrets, giggling as they ate and not paying attention to them. "I don't need you or anyone playing Marva Matchmaker." He rolled his eyes. "I was just helping Alan out and trying to make sure that one of his customers isn't scared off forever." He glared at Gerome. "So back off."

"Fine," Gerome hissed softly. "So you don't want me to call Ashton in a few days and remind him about the boat trip? Or I could just tell him that something came up and that we had to cancel. Then we could all go out and you wouldn't have to worry about seeing him again."

Terrance shook his head. "Who says I'm worried?" he countered, a little too fast.

"Just relax and go with it. You like him, and I think he likes you back." Gerome finished the last of his fish and leaned back in his chair like he'd just won or something.

"You're a blind as a bat. That guy is half scared to death of me," Terrance countered. One thing he definitely knew was fear. And Ashton was afraid of him. The thing was that Terrance actually cared. Fear was the tool of his trade, and damn it all if he didn't want Ashton to not be afraid of him. How was that for a kick in the shorts?

Gerome smiled. "We'll see." He sat up straight and grinned at Joshie. "Now who's about ready for cake?"

Using the kids to cut off a perfectly good argument was so unfair.

Chapter 2

ASHTON WELLER paced his small apartment. Well, maybe not paced as much as turned in circles. There wasn't really enough room to pace, but he was doing a good impression of it. Gerome had called on Friday to talk to him about what he could bring into the store, and he was coming over in a few minutes to see what he had.

The apartment was tiny and in the back of the building, with north-facing windows, so it got very little light and reminded Ashton of a cave. But with the money he saved, he could afford the garage space next door that he used as a studio. It was barely big enough for the items he needed, but he made it work because he had to. He'd already set out all of the finished pieces

that might work for the shop. He had some sea creatures, including a few urchins and even a seahorse. That
was one of his favorites. Ashton had also created some
delicate glasses and bowls. They sat on the bar counter
that doubled as a table in the small space.

It had taken just about everything he had in order
to put together his glass studio, and he really needed
to figure out a way to make it pay. Making trinkets for
tourists wasn't the way to build a career, but he needed
to start somewhere.

A knock on the door stopped his pacing, and Ashton opened it. Gerome stood just outside, with his huge
friend Terrance right behind him. Instantly Ashton's
tension rose to the ceiling. Terrance was handsome, and
his dark eyes promised all kinds of things that Ashton
wondered about all the time. But Terrance was huge
and strong as an ox. That was both enticing and frightening as all hell.

Ashton tamped down the urge to run and stepped
back to let both of them inside. "I set out some of the
things I've been working on." He swallowed hard and
tried to concentrate on the task at hand, but it was hard.
Terrance fascinated him—the guy had actually helped
him and had been nice.

Ashton needed to stop stereotyping. Not all big
guys were going to try to hurt him or take advantage of
him. They weren't all like Frank.

"These are beautiful," Terrance said, cradling one of
Ashton's dark blue anemones in his huge hands, gently
turning it so he could look. "The light dances off it."

"I have a number of sea creatures and things like
that. I even made a few manatees. But I didn't want to
just make things that were touristy." He held up one of
his floral pieces. "I wanted things that could be artistic

as well as beautiful." He set the delicate lily back down and stepped back.

Gerome looked over each of the pieces, smiling. "I love them." He pulled out his camera and took pictures. "I'd like to send these to the owner so she can see them as well." He fiddled with his phone and got an answer pretty quickly. "Okay. We have two ways we can go. The first is that we buy them outright, provided that we can arrive at a price that works. The other is a consignment agreement. We put these in the store, set a retail price, and you get 75 percent."

Ashton told himself to take a step back. He could really use the money if he sold them all, but the consignment deal was probably worth more in the long run. He did some quick math regarding what he had in his account.

"You don't have to give me an answer right now. Think about it," Gerome told him.

"Are there more?" Terrance asked, still looking over the collection of his work.

"Yeah. There's some that I haven't put out here. This is a sample. I've done more of the holiday items in preparation for fall, and I'm working on some new designs." He went to what most people would use as a linen closet and gently pulled the door open. He had lined it with shelves, and that was where he kept his stock.

Gerome smiled, but when Ashton turned to Terrance, he seemed mesmerized. He grew even more so when Ashton turned on the lights.

"What are those?" Terrance asked, pointing to three of the larger pieces Ashton had on the lower shelf because it had the most clearance.

"Some pieces that I did to enter the local art shows. They jury their pieces very closely, and I was trying to get in. It's in one of the big parks. I've been trying for three years. The pieces I showed you weren't good enough, but I'm hoping these will get me in."

"What are they?" Terrance seemed itching to touch, moving his hand forward, but then he pulled back.

"The one there is a ceiling fixture. What you see on the shelf would be attached to the ceiling and would light from behind. The other pieces next to it would hang down, and the whole thing looks like a cloud with glass pieces to catch the light as rain. I'm really proud of it." He smiled as Terrance gawked. "The other two are artistic pieces. That's a stylized stand of irises, and that one is daffodils. They're intricate, but neither one is meant to be strictly realistic." Ashton loved talking about his work. "I have another couple of pieces in the works. One is a shade to go on a lamp base. I finished it yesterday, and it's in the annealer finishing up. If it works, I should be able to make a few more. I'm hoping to have those for the show, if they accept me."

"Why wouldn't they?" Terrance asked. "Is this one of those things where it's who you know?" He stepped away from the closet and put his hands on his hips.

"No. They're very fussy when they put the show together. They look at each submission and then take into account all of the artists who submit. The work has to be high-quality, unique, and have artistic merit." He was pretty sure that they were looking for artists with names as well. He shrugged. "It is what it is."

Gerome nodded as Ashton closed the door.

"I'm working most days to make some more, but it gets really hot in the studio, and I can only work for so long. Mostly in the early morning before the heat builds. Then I get the work into the annealers to slowly cool down." He desperately hoped the store would take his pieces. What he really needed was an outlet where he could sell them and a place he could meet people rather than having them come to the house. "I'm putting together a website for my work. Once we come to an agreement, I'll add links to your store so people know where they can go to buy them."

"That's great," Gerome told him, smiling. He glanced at Terrance, who seemed to have grown quiet as well. Finally Gerome nudged Terrance's side.

"Yeah, sorry. Look, the boat trip is still on, and I wondered if you were still interested in coming. It will be fun, and the entire group that you met at the restaurant the other day will be there, including the kids. They love going out on the water and always look for the dolphins."

"I'm not really much for fishing. I never catch anything," Ashton admitted. He hadn't been out on the water at all in the time since he'd moved here from Chicago a few years ago. After his move, he had been determined to rebuild his life and try to not repeat his mistakes. Terrance's appearance made him think that maybe he could be doing that with him, but he couldn't let Frank determine the rest of his life. Frank was thousands of miles away. Besides, Frank was never nervous, and Terrance seemed a little jumpy.

"If you'd like to come, you'd be welcome," Terrance finally said with a surprisingly disarming smile.

"Okay, I guess it could be fun." He needed to get out of the house and away from his own circular thoughts. A boating excursion might be just the thing. He had never been out on the Gulf, and there would be plenty of people to talk to if things with Terrance didn't work out... or something. Part of him screamed to just stay inside within the boundaries that he had set up for his life. But the rest of him said it was time to get out of this cocoon he was building, and Ashton knew that the longer he took to break out of his shell, the harder it was going to be. "Where should I meet you?"

APPARENTLY FISHING and boating were things that started before the sun came up. Ashton brought a very light jacket, not because of the temperature, but because he figured he might need it in order to keep dry at some point. He needn't have worried. Ashton hadn't known what to expect as far as the boat was concerned, but he hadn't expected a forty-foot cabin cruiser. He grabbed his bag of snacks and the cooler of food and drinks he had brought to contribute and got out of his old Fiesta.

"Ummm… is this the right place?" he asked Daniel, as he got out of his car with Coby following behind like some sort of half-asleep zombie.

"Yeah. The boat is my father's, and he's letting us use it. The original plan was to rent a boat, but Dad came through, so we have this one for the day. Come on." He strode toward the boat, holding Coby's hand, and Ashton followed.

The boat was beautiful, with a gleaming deck and a box for fish on the back, sleek padded seats, and built-in coolers on deck, with a cantilevered roof over part and an awning that extended over the rest. "Where should I put this?"

"Come on." Daniel led him down into the cabin, where they put the broccoli salad and drinks Ashton had brought in the refrigerator and stowed the rest of the snacks. "Excuse me," Daniel said softly and disappeared behind an accordion screen at the bow of the boat. He came out a few minutes later. "I put Coby on the bed to rest."

Judging by the sounds from up above, the others were arriving. Richard joined them with Joshie and put him in the bed with Coby. "Everyone else is here," Richard whispered.

"Okay. I'll help get everything stowed and we'll shove off."

Ashton joined the others on deck as Daniel took charge. It seemed he was their captain for the day. Ashton took a seat under the canopy, and Terrance sat next to him.

"Have you done this before?" Terrance asked.

He shook his head. "I was out on Lake Michigan once. It was choppy and I got seasick. I already took a pill so I don't have a repeat."

"This is something special. We've always rented a boat before, but this one is really sweet." He grinned like an excited little boy, which helped calm some of Ashton's nerves. He was always jumpy in new situations and with new people, a remnant of the life he'd left behind two years ago. He should be over it by now, but it was hard. The ghosts of his former life seemed to follow him everywhere.

"It's really nice." He returned Terrance's smile and received a soft bump on the shoulder.

"Okay, everyone," Daniel said. "Here's the deal. We made arrangements and have licenses for everyone for the day, so all of us can fish. There is a limit of five snapper or grouper per person, and that includes the boys. The smaller ones we'll throw back, along with the sharks and anything else we might catch." Daniel turned to Richard. "Today is meant to be fun. There will be no repeat of the last time, where certain bets were made and Gerome ended up being tossed into the water." Ashton wondered what the story behind that incident was. "There is a prize for the biggest fish, but any sort of bets or side wagers will be dealt with severely."

Richard slipped his arms around Daniel's waist. "We already agreed that we'll be good." He leaned close, and Daniel snorted and then turned this lovely shade of beet red. "Let's go."

Daniel swallowed and nodded, clearing his throat. "Okay, then."

"Was he talking dirty to him?" Ashton asked Terrance, who nodded. "What could he have said to make him turn that color? I mean, it's just talk...."

Terrance leaned close, and Ashton got an amazing whiff of soap with a touch of cologne, but under it all was the incredible scent of summer tinged with testosterone. "If you don't think talk can be sexy, then you just haven't been doing it right." The words were innocent enough, but the tone and resonance sent a zing racing through him, and it took a few seconds for him to realize it was desire.

That part of his life had been on hold since he'd gotten to Florida. The truth was that Ashton wondered so many times if he would ever feel anything for anyone again. He pondered if it was possible... and then if it was something he could ever take a chance on again. He had spent two years trying to figure out how to put his life back together once again. "Maybe I haven't been doing it at all." God, that was the truth.

"Then it sounds to me like you need a little practice." Terrance smirked, and Ashton realized Terrance was flirting with him. He turned away but smiled nonetheless, watching as the sky slowly grew lighter.

The boat engine roared to life, and under Daniel's direction, Richard cast off the lines and they were free, rocking slowly side to side as they glided forward.

"How long have you lived here?" Terrance asked.

"Two years. I was in Chicago before I moved down here. I studied there under a few glass blowers who moved with the Renaissance Faire circuit. They did some interesting things, but I wanted to do more. So I learned what I could from them and rented some time at their glass studios."

Terrance nodded slowly. "We're from the Midwest and moved down here about four or so years ago. Do you miss it?" There was a note of nostalgia in his voice.

"A little. Mostly in the summer when it's so hot here. I can't work during the day then because the studio is just too hot to work safely. I have to sleep during the day and work at night. Even then it's too hot a lot of the time, and air-conditioning a studio where you have to keep the furnace hot enough to work glass is problematic at best."

"How do you work, then?" Terrance leaned closer as the boat cleared the marina and they rounded the point into more open water.

"I have to work for a while and then step into the air-conditioning to cool off and rehydrate. It limits what I can do and is really frustrating sometimes. The glass is unforgiving." So many times he had gotten to the end of a piece only to find a flaw he hadn't seen or to have it fall off the punty. He never liked to hear the ring of glass crashing to the floor. He shifted on his seat to look at Terrance. "See, the glass has to be a certain temperature in order to be workable, and it only stays that way for a short period of time before it has to be put back into the furnace to heat up again. But it has to be done right. If a more delicate portion of the piece gets too warm, then it will weaken and even melt away." He shrugged. This was one of the things he'd had to learn very early—how to heat the part of the glass he need-ed to work. "When making pieces to attach, I need to make sure they are close to the same temperature or one can shatter the other. It's a really delicate balance." He realized he was almost bouncing in his seat. Sometimes he got so excited about his work.

"I guess I never thought about it." Terrance seemed to ponder a minute. "You know, I don't think I've ever seen anyone blow glass in person before. I think I might have seen it on TV or something."

"Glass is amazing. It's a liquid and it stays a liquid. Even when it cools and looks solid, it's still a liquid. That's why old glass becomes wavy. The molecules are still moving, just very slowly." Ashton swallowed and grew quiet. He needed to remember that not everyone shared his passion, and sometimes he needed to tone it down a little.

"Your pieces were amazing, especially the ones for the show. Have you heard from them yet?" Terrance asked.

"Not yet. Hopefully soon." He turned to look out over the water, the sun shining across the waves as it drew higher in the sky. "It's beautiful out here." He took a deep breath and let it out slowly, watching all around them. When he looked toward Terrance again, he found him staring back.

Ashton's anxieties, which had slipped away, seemed to return in force, and he had to tamp down his instinct to move away. Not that Terrance had been anything but nice—it was just that he wasn't sure what the large man wanted from him.

"We're going to be about half an hour before we reach the fishing areas," Daniel said as they cut through the water at what Ashton hoped was top speed. The slight bouncing of the boat had his stomach rolling a little. He hoped the pills he'd taken earlier kicked in soon. He didn't feel sick exactly, just a little queasy.

Terrance got up to rummage in one of the coolers, then returned with a bottle of water that he put in Ashton's hand. "Drink that, breathe evenly, and keep your eyes on the horizon."

"Huh…."

"You're looking a little green. Just relax. The feeling will pass pretty quickly. There are some crackers here too if you need them."

Ashton nodded and drank some of the cold water. "I took the pill right when I got up." He drank a little more.

"It needs to get into your system. I took mine last night and then one more this morning," Terrance said.

Ashton turned toward the huge man. He hadn't expected Terrance to admit to any kind of weakness. Frank certainly never had under any circumstances.

Ashton drank water and looked out over the waves toward the horizon. The queasiness in his stomach and the lightness in his head passed, and by the time they stopped at the first place to fish, he felt pretty good.

The boat rocked with the waves as Daniel and the guys got out the fishing gear and set it up. The boys were still down below. When Ashton checked his watch, it was only seven thirty in the morning. "I take it you've never done this before," Terrance said as he helped Ashton get into position. "Okay. I'll bait your hook." He cut a piece of a small fish and placed it on the hook. Then he showed him how to lower the line using his thumb to keep it from tangling. "Once the bait reaches the bottom, click it up a few times and there you go. The fish we want are about eighty feet down, and they'll find the bait fast if they're here." Terrance stood near him and lowered his own line.

"I bet I get a fish before you," Gerome teased Terrance.

"No betting," Daniel scolded immediately. "I'll push you overboard myself." He had his hands on his hips and glared at Gerome like he'd taken a dump on deck. "Don't make me warn you again."

"Oh, come on. I didn't make a wager," Gerome countered.

"That's how it always starts. First it's that comment, then a wager, and before long you've started some sort of pool. After that there's threatened shark bait, the kids get upset, and someone ends up in the water. I decided whoever starts it ends up in the drink and then it'll be over. Is that what you want?"

Daniel might not have been a big guy, but Gerome laughed and promised no more bets just as Ashton's line tugged and then the pole bent.

"That's good. Reel it in," Terrance said from right next to him. "Take it slow and easy. That's it." Terrance got the net and scooped the fish out of the water as soon as it broke the surface. "That's a beautiful grouper." That was not the word Ashton would use to describe the mean-looking brown fish. He got it off the hook and helped Ashton hold it so Daniel could take pictures. Then he put it into one of the fish lockers.

"That was pretty awesome." Ashton practically bounced as Terrance rebaited his hook.

"Beginner's luck," Richard teased before patting him on the shoulder. "You did really good." He returned to his line as Gerome and Tucker talked softly.

Daniel stood next to Richard, the lines going still, but the others seemed to just enjoy being together, looking out over the water. Gerome pulled in his line and set the pole aside, holding Tucker around the waist. It seemed like both couples had slipped into their own worlds. Ashton glanced at Terrance, who had been watching them as well, but he pointedly turned away, returning to his line.

"Sometimes it's hard watching others be so happy," Ashton said softly. Terrance glanced at him and nodded, sighing gently. "Have you had a boyfriend recently?"

Terrance shrugged, his incredible eyes filling with pain for a second and then it was gone. "I was seeing a guy a little while ago. Well, more like I liked him, but he wasn't really interested. I saw quite a few guys before I moved down here, but things are different here." He reeled in his line, but all he had was an empty hook. He rebaited the line and set the end of the rod on one of the holders. "Starting over really sucks most of the time."

Ashton had to agree. There were opportunities to starting a new life in a new place. But it was also hard as hell. He didn't know a lot of people here, even after two years. A lot of the people he did meet were only down for part of the year and then they were gone. "I suppose it takes time to meet people and find a place where you fit in."

Terrance nodded. "Have you found yours?"

Ashton shrugged. He wasn't going to admit that he felt like a total loser a lot of the time. "Not really. I had a few contacts in the art glass community in Chicago, but I haven't found anything like that down here yet. How about you?"

"I moved here with the guys, so I always had them with me. We had to adjust together, so it wasn't like being all alone." He turned to where the other couples still stood, talking so quietly, pressed together in that intimate way couples had to let you know that they were just happy to be together. "But sometimes it feels like I'm on the outside looking in."

For Ashton, that was the story of his life.

Chapter 3

"I THINK your friend is having a good time," Richard said as Ashton disappeared down below to use the head. Daniel was explaining how to use the facilities properly. Nothing like bathroom lessons in the morning.

"I hope so. He's nice," Terrance said. "But there's something going on with him. His story seems a lot like ours."

Richard drew him toward the back of the boat. "What do you mean?"

"I know he came down here from Chicago and talked about starting a new life. He mentioned how hard it was to make friends and things like that. But you know how we never talk about anything specific regarding stuff in Detroit? He was the same way about Chicago. Maybe I'm reading a lot into it, but I get the feeling that there's a lot more there."

Richard scoffed. "Dude. Guys don't lay out their entire history, hopes, and dreams in five minutes." He rolled his eyes.

Terrance growled. "I know that." At times Ashton seemed almost afraid of him, but he'd come out on the boat anyway, as though he was determined not to let it get the better of him. That intrigued Terrance. He knew he could be intimidating as all hell. That was a trait he sometimes went out of his way to accentuate.

He also thought Ashton was adorable when he got excited. Terrance made a note to get Ashton to talk about his work some more. Excited Ashton was pretty interesting. "But… we have something to hide, and I guess I recognize that in someone else."

"Then find out what it is if you can. Maybe Daniel can take a look into his background to see if there's anything there, if you like." Richard didn't seem overly concerned, but Terrance shook his head. It seemed like a violation of Ashton's privacy. Terrance didn't want to go there. He liked the idea of finding out things about Ashton on his own.

"Maybe you're right and I'm just being paranoid." Being in witness protection and already having two close calls, maybe paranoia was par for the course. After all, they were hiding from people who would think nothing about having them killed. Though as more time passed, Terrance hoped that the urgency around locating the three of them would slack off. Especially since their little group had grown to include a lot more than just Gerome, Richard, and him. It now involved Daniel, Tucker, and Cheryl as well as the boys. They had all agreed that they would do whatever it took to protect their families. No matter what.

"Just relax and have a good time."

"Let's pull our lines in and we'll move to a new location," Daniel said, and they all got ready as Daniel revved the engine to move them. He watched the fish finder and a readout of the bottom of the Gulf.

Ashton rejoined Terrance. "Are you feeling better now?"

"Yeah. The meds must have kicked in." He was munching on a few crackers and sat down next to him. "You know, I almost chickened out this morning and didn't come."

Terrance raised his eyebrows. "Why?"

Ashton turned to look out over the water. "I guess I'm not really great at meeting new people, and...." He turned back to him. "You're not the most approachable guy."

Terrance scowled for a second and then smiled. "Is that your way of saying I'm intimidating?"

"Yeah," Ashton agreed.

"I guess that's my role. I'm a bouncer and the first guy my friends call when they need to move furniture.

"You're more than just muscle," Ashton said. "I saw the way you looked at my work. You appreciated it for more than just because it was pretty. I liked that. I put some of myself in each thing I do."

Terrance nodded. He had understood the real beauty of those pieces and the loving hand that went into making them. Especially in something like the manatees—they showed a beauty and an artistic sentiment in each one. No two were alike, and they had personality. "I try to be more than just this big guy who goes around threatening people."

"Are we there yet?" Coby asked his dad as he came up on deck, wiping his eyes. "I wanna catch the fishies."

Daniel cut the engine. "We just got to what I hope is a good place. Why don't you fish with Papa? He'll help you get the hook baited." Coby nodded. "Where's Joshie?"

"He's still sleeping," Coby said. He went to Richard, who gave him a hug and then helped get the line ready. It was cute watching Richard with the little boy. Back in Detroit, none of them would have given a moment's thought to being a parent, but here Richard was, Coby's papa.

"Ashton already caught a big fish," Richard told Coby. "He'll show it to you when we catch a fish of our own."

"Are we gonna catch a bigger one?" Coby asked.

Terrance snorted and turned away. It seemed Richard's competitive nature had found fertile ground in Coby. Terrance could just imagine Daniel was not particularly happy with that.

"We're gonna try. Your daddy said there was a prize for the biggest fish."

They all got their lines in the water, and Daniel kept the boat in position. Terrance got a bite, but the snapper was too small, so he tossed it back. The excitement of the stop occurred when Ashton caught a small reef shark. Coby wanted to see it, so Ashton and Coby posed for a picture with it before putting it back in the water.

Joshie came up on deck, and he, Tucker, and Gerome fished together.

"Do you ever wish you had a family like that?" Ashton asked. Terrance was tempted to slough the question off, but he found himself nodding anyway. "Me too."

"What about your family?" Terrance didn't often talk about his blood family.

Ashton bit his lower lip. "My mother died when I was twelve of an overdose. She had been using for a long time, and I had been in foster homes since I was nine. I got to see my mom a few weekends a month—at least that was how it was supposed to work, but she didn't always show up." Damn, that must have been hard as hell. Terrance knew that kind of pain through his friends, and how it made you feel like you weren't good enough. "Then I heard that she was dead. By then I hadn't seen her in almost six months. I guess I was lucky. The foster family who took me in… they adopted me after she was gone, and they're my real family."

"Are they in Chicago?"

"They were. Mom and Dad were older when they took me in. Their bio kids were out of the house and Ellen missed having kids, so they took me in and then made it permanent. They were almost seventy when I was adopted. They saw that I got through school and took me everywhere with them. She was a retired schoolteacher, so she homeschooled me for three years and we traveled all over the country. Then Roger got sick and we stayed close to home." He swallowed hard and turned away again. "Roger passed away two weeks after I graduated high school, and Ellen passed away a year later. So basically, my family is gone." The pain that rang in his voice was almost palpable. He breathed deeply and grew quiet before picking up his pole and starting to fish again.

Terrance understood so much of what Ashton had said. He'd been lucky in that he had his mother through his childhood and until he was an adult. Richard and Gerome had either lost their parents or had absentee families, so his mother had stood in as family for both of them. They had even broken the rules of WITSEC to contact his mother before she'd passed away. That decision had precipitated their move to Florida. "The guys are my only family too."

Ashton nodded and reeled in his line. Terrance re-baited the hook, and Ashton returned to fishing. "Did you grow up with your mom or dad?"

"My mom. She was a mother of sorts to all three of us." Terrance couldn't give out any details, so he grew quiet. "I miss her."

Ashton nodded, still looking out over the water. "Ellen was the closest thing I had to a real mother, and losing her really set me adrift." They lowered their lines into the water, and Terrance stayed quiet to let Ashton talk. He didn't think this was the kind of thing Ashton spoke about very often, any more than he spoke about his own mother, except occasionally to the other guys. But even then, he didn't like to bring it up. The subject was still too raw. "But I have to get it together and move forward."

"When did you discover working with glass?" Terrance asked. He was really curious how someone came to work in that field.

"About three years ago. I…." He sighed. "I had gotten myself in some trouble, and one of my foster parents' friends had a son who needed someone to help him work the glass booth at the ren faire. He cared enough to try to help me, and I needed the work. When I was there, I was fascinated with what he was doing, and eventually I got the chance to help him. I was good at it, and Clive taught me the art and let me use his studio for a while to do my own work. From there, I moved on to what I'm doing now."

Terrance got a bite, and he reeled in a fish that was big enough to keep. The boys all wanted to see it before he put it in the box with the huge grouper, which both Coby and Joshie agreed was really ugly. Grouper definitely weren't going to win any beauty contests, but they were very tasty.

"I'm going to move again in a few minutes. Once we're in position, we can get out the food and have breakfast," Daniel said. They pulled the lines in, and Daniel revved the engine until they found a new spot. Then he set the engine to keep them on location and they all worked to get out the food and set up the large table under the canopy.

"This boat is something else," Ashton said.

"Daniel's father is a bigwig with one of the banks," Terrance told him.

"My father and I didn't get along for quite a while. Meeting Coby changed things between us. My father and I came to a truce of sorts, and my parents get to see Coby, which my mom is tickled pink about. My dad is over the moon at being a grandpa. So maybe things will work out after all." He put one of the baskets on the table and began pulling out a number of dishes. They were all cold, but as usual, it was wonderful. Daniel had made cinnamon rolls, and once everything was set up, he went below and returned with a warm quiche.

"Wow. This is amazing," Ashton whispered. "I only brought a few snacks and things."

Terrance lightly bumped his shoulder. He didn't want Ashton to feel bad. "Daniel loves to cook, and he's really good at it. We'd all think something was wrong if he didn't go a little overboard." Terrance caught Daniel's gaze. "Not that any of us are the least bit sorry he does. Daniel's food is always a treat, especially to a guy like me who can burn water." He made sure Ashton got his plate and then got some food for himself. His mama would be happy that he remembered his manners.

"You all have been friends for a long time," Ashton said to Richard.

"Since we were kids." Richard shared a pointed glare in Terrance's direction, probably wondering what Terrance had told him.

"In Detroit. Terrance told me. And I thought growing up in Chicago was tough," Ashton commented. "I bet that must have been really hard." The way he said it made Terrance wonder if he had told Ashton too much, but as he went over what he'd said, nothing came to mind. "I understand." He ate a few more bites and then looked up once again. "How did you get past it? I mean, stop looking at everyone the way you did when you were living on those tough streets?"

Suddenly what Ashton was saying made sense. He was searching for answers. "All of us had each other," Gerome chimed in.

"And they met us," Tucker interjected. "Daniel and I didn't grow up that way. Granted, we haven't necessarily had it easy either. I was homeless when I met Gerome." Tucker leaned against his lover's arm, looking at him like Gerome hung the moon. "And don't let any of these guys fool you—there are still plenty of rough edges." He smiled and leaned closer. "You come to appreciate them. It's part of who they are."

Terrance rolled his eyes. "Excuse me. It's getting way too sappy. I'm going to go heave my breakfast overboard." He set down his fork with a clang.

"My point exactly," Tucker commented without missing a beat, and everyone laughed.

"Seriously, it takes some getting used to. Not everyone is out to get us, and we don't feel like there's a threat around every corner," Richard explained. "But we have each other's backs and we stick together. When we moved here, we were a family of three, and now we're a family of eight with room to grow." Richard held Terrance's gaze.

"But… you don't act tough all the time," Ashton said.

"That's what happiness looks like. They don't need to be tough all the time, but they can be, believe me. You saw it at the bar the other night."

Ashton paled slightly. "That's what I'm trying to get my mind around."

Richard nodded and leaned over the table. "We're tough when we need to be." He put his hand out over the table, and instantly Terrance put his on top, with Gerome following. "And we look out for each other and what's ours." Coby and Joshie added their hands too, which Terrance thought adorable. Then Tucker and Daniel did the same. For a second, Terrance knew exactly where he belonged, and the alienation that had been plaguing him for the last little while slipped away. They drew their hands back and returned to their breakfast.

Daniel leaned closer to Ashton again. "Look, they can tell you anything they want. But it's Tucker and I that have softened them up. Being happy has changed them. I think it changes everyone."

"But… how do you stop feeling so scared all the time?" Ashton whispered. "I moved here because I thought it was a quiet place and that maybe I could get to know people, stop looking over my shoulder all the time, and have a chance to breathe. But I constantly wait for something to happen. Living in Chicago was like holding my breath all the time, waiting for something to happen. I thought that maybe I could breathe easier here, but…."

Terrance took Ashton's hand without thinking about it. "It will go away eventually. We've all lightened up since being here." That was true to an extent. But they were also on their guard all the time in case trouble should make itself known. It had happened twice before, and Terrance figured it was bound to show up again. It was only a matter of time.

"So basically, you don't have answers either," Ashton said flatly.

Terrance looked at the others and shrugged. "I guess not. Maybe this is one of those things that you have to find your own answers for."

Ashton held his gaze and then laughed. "You know, that's what everyone says when they don't have the answer."

Terrance thought for a second. "You're probably right, but it doesn't change anything. So let it go and have some fun."

"Yeah, have fun!" Joshie threw his hands in the air. "I have toys. We can play and have fun." He went back to his breakfast.

"Yes, you do, but don't let any of them go overboard or the fish will eat them," Terrance told Joshie.

"No. It's littering and it's wrong," Joshie said seriously. "And Pop says I need to keep my toys in the boat or they will make the fish sick." God, he was adorable.

"Marcie told me that fish pee in the water."

Joshie scrunched up his nose. "I swimmed in fish pee?"

"Ewww," both boys said, then broke into a fit of giggles.

"Eat your breakfast," Tucker told both of them. "Then we can fish some more."

Terrance waited for some comment about there being less fish pee in the sea, but thankfully the boys went back to their breakfast.

Ashton grew quiet, and Terrance finished his own breakfast before helping Daniel put the disposable dishes in the trash. Once the food was cleared away, they returned to fishing, the boys having a good time trying to catch their fish.

The day was gorgeous and sunny until just after noon, when clouds formed on the horizon, growing darker. "We're going to head back in," Daniel announced, and everyone pulled in their lines in as he revved the engine and headed back toward the shore. "The forecast didn't call for rain, but the radar is showing something building."

They raced back toward land, with Tucker taking the boys under the overhang while the others stowed the gear. Then they gathered together as the storm drew closer.

"I hate storms," Ashton said, sitting next to Terrance up toward the front, well under the cabin roof. "Never liked them, not even as a kid."

"I always loved them. We lived this this apartment building on the top floor," Terrance answered.

Ashton snickered. "The penthouse?"

"You could hardly call it that. It was the fourth floor in a building with no elevator or air-conditioning. In the summer the place roasted like an oven. I used to go up to the roof to watch the summer storms get closer. They usually heralded cooler weather, and in the summer that was always welcome. I used to lie awake in my bed most nights, sweating up a storm, wishing for any breeze through the open window. A storm meant wind, and it cleared out the stale air from the place."

A clap of thunder split the air, and Ashton jumped. The wind picked up just as Terrance had been talking about, blowing forcefully through the cabin.

"How much longer before we make the marina?" Richard asked Daniel, who stared intently ahead.

"About half an hour. I have it opened full and this is as fast as we can go, but if the seas pick up, I'm going to have to slow down to cut some of the choppiness." He glanced at the instruments as Ashton looked around, biting his lower lip.

"It's going to be fine. The storm is getting closer, but we don't have that far to go."

Ashton sighed. "I know. It's just that I hate these things." Another rumble of thunder split the air, and Terrance looked at his phone. He was back in range of cell service, so he checked the radar. According to the GPS, the storm was only five to ten minutes away, but they were moving ahead of it.

"Take the boys below and get them settled. When the rain hits, it's going to be something fierce, and they need to stay dry." Daniel didn't look away as Richard, Gerome, and Tucker herded the boys down into the cabin. Terrance made sure the deck was clear and that everything was well battened down.

Behind them, the clouds seemed to reach all the way to the water, which Terrance had learned was the line of rain sheeting out of the clouds. He turned toward the front windows at the land getting nearer.

"Are we going to make it?" Ashton asked.

"Probably not," Daniel said. "But we'll be close enough that it should be just rain and wind. "Once we're through into the inlet at the key, the waves will die away. There shouldn't be anything to worry about at that point. But if we were still way out in the open water, we'd get tossed around." Daniel seemed at ease, and Terrance put an arm around Ashton to try to comfort him.

"It's going to be fine. Daniel knows what he's doing."

The rain broke over them right then, and Daniel had to slow down as it sheeted over the boat, pelting the uncovered portions of the deck with buckets of water.

"I can barely see," Daniel said. The wipers' attempts to sluice the water off the front windows did no good at all. He slowed the boat down further, the engines quieting. "It's going to take longer to get into port than I expected. Go on below with the others and stay dry. This wind is whipping the rain everywhere." He pointed, and they hurried below, closed the hatch, and took seats around the small table.

The boat pitched and rolled as they moved. Tucker and Richard sat on the bed built into the point of the bow with the boys, holding them as they continued toward port and shelter. The waves rocked the boat from side to side, and they all held on until suddenly the movement ceased. They must have passed the spit of land that protected the marina, because the rocking ended and their motion became smooth, even as the rain continued rolling past the porthole windows.

"It's okay. It's just some rain and wind, and we're all fine," Tucker whispered. "There's nothing to be scared about."

"But it was scary," Joshie said.

"Don't think about that too much. Remember the fun we had fishing and being with Coby, playing with your toys, and catching fish." Joshie nodded. "We'll do it again and it will be fine."

"We were going to sink?" Coby asked.

"No. We came down here because we didn't want you to get wet. That's all. We can go back outside if you want." Terrance wanted to get the kids out on deck so they could see what was happening.

"That's a good idea," Tucker said and helped the boys up to the deck. The rain had let up a great deal, and Terrance and Ashton followed them out as Daniel pulled the boat into the slip. Terrance tied up the boat as the last of the rain ended.

"See? Everything is fine," Terrance told both boys. "We're back and everything is okay. Daniel knows what he's doing, and we were never in any real danger." He knew that wasn't necessarily true, but he didn't want the boys afraid of the water and boats. "It was just a little rainstorm, that was all." Terrance lifted Joshie into his arms. "I can't wait for you and me to go out fishing again. Would that be okay?"

Joshie nodded. "No rain?"

"I hope not." He hugged Joshie and set him back down, then hugged Coby as well before starting a tickle fight. The boys laughed, and without thinking, Terrance shifted to Ashton, and damned if he didn't fill the air with laughter. It was a joyous sound, and while Terrance didn't tickle him for a long time, it was wonderful. To his surprise, Ashton retaliated and tried tickling him.

"Come on boys, help me," Ashton called, and soon Terrance was set upon by all three of them. He laughed and let them play, even though he wasn't ticklish, just because they were having so much fun.

"CAN WE go back out fishing?" Joshie asked about an hour later, when the sun stayed out. They were still on the boat having lunch. They had decided that since everything was there and they had the boat for the day, they might as well make the most of it.

"I don't think so," Gerome said gently. "There are still storms forming, and we don't want to get caught out in one again."

"How about after lunch, we take the boat out again, but just for a ride?" Daniel offered.

"Yay. Boat ride!" Coby said.

"Do you want to come?" Terrance asked Ashton. "I'll understand if you have something else you need to do." Terrance hoped that Ashton would come with them, but he couldn't blame him if he chose not to. He also didn't want Ashton to feel as though he had to stay. Sometimes Ashton reminded him of a rabbit, ready to bolt at any second.

"If I'm welcome," Ashton answered without looking up from his plate.

"Of course you are," Daniel said before Terrance could answer. "Now, let's finish up our lunch and we can go out for a joyride." He sipped some of his Coke. The other adults were drinking beer, but Daniel wasn't about to drink and boat.

After casting off the lines a half hour later, they enjoyed what turned into a glorious afternoon. There were no signs of more storms, the breeze was perfect, and the sky remained blue and clear.

"This is better than anything I could have imagined," Ashton told Terrance. They were sitting side by side toward the back, engines humming as the land passed along the port side.

"Yeah." Terrance held Ashton's gaze, his intense blue eyes shining in the light reflecting off the water. The jolt of attraction that went through him was unescapable, and Terrance had seen Ashton watching him on more than one occasion. Before he could ponder the consequences, he leaned in closer, his eyes half lidded, lips slightly parted—

"Uncle Terrance," Joshie said as the boys hurried over.

Terrance straightened up. "You shouldn't run on the boat," he told them gently, holding back his frustration.

"Dolphins," Coby cried, pointing as a pod of them played in their wake.

Terrance tried not to huff as he broke the gaze with Ashton.

"Aren't they fun?" Ashton said, his gaze once again locking on Terrance's for only a second, and then he turned to the boys. "Do you think we might see a sea turtle too?"

"We did once, but way out when we were fishing," Coby explained. "Daddy said it was coming up for air and then it went back underwater and was gone." He seemed so proud. "It was really big, and I asked Daddy if I could ride it like a merman and he said that I couldn't and I was sad. I really want to ride a turtle and see what's at the bottom."

"Maybe when you're older, you and your daddy can take diving lessons and then you can see what's there," Terrance offered.

Coby brightened and hurried over to where his father was piloting the boat. The expression Daniel flashed him clearly demonstrated that Terrance's suggestion was not one he particularly appreciated.

Terrance hoped that maybe he and Ashton could have a few minutes alone, but Joshie settled onto the seat next to him, telling them about all the sea creatures he had seen the last time they went to the aquarium and when they went fishing. He had been so shy and quiet when Gerome had first brought him and Tucker into their lives. Now little Joshie was outgoing, happy, and in every way a normal little boy. "Where's your daddy?" Joshie asked. "I have two now, Gerome and Tucker, as well as my mommy."

"My mommy and daddy died a long time ago. Now I just have me," Ashton said.

Joshie patted Ashton's knee. "It's okay. They're looking down from heaven." He went over to where Gerome sat and climbed on his lap.

When they were growing up, Terrance would never have thought of any of them as a parent. Now he was a little jealous of the families his friends had.

Terrance turned to Ashton, who looked blankly toward the deck. Terrance swallowed, not knowing what to say. "I remember them. It was so long ago, and unfortunately the memories seem to have faded over the years. I don't have any pictures of them. When I was taken into foster care, they said that some of my parents' things would be saved for me, but when I asked for them, they couldn't find them." Ashton lifted his gaze slightly.

"Damn…," Terrance said and pulled out his wallet. "This is the one picture I have of my mother. She hated having her picture taken. But we convinced her to go to

Sears and get it taken once." He showed it to Ashton. "I'm sorry you don't have any of your mom." He swallowed hard. "What was her name?"

"Lorraine. Lorraine and Denton Weller. Those were their names, and that's about all I have of them." Ashton sighed, and Terrance put his arm around his shoulder and held him gently. Ashton stiffened at first and then relaxed, leaning slightly against him. Terrance didn't move in case something broke the spell. He liked the way Ashton felt against him. "No one has touched me since I left Chicago. Not like this."

Terrance swallowed hard. "Not anyone?"

Ashton shook his head. "I bet you've had lots of guys that are interested in you."

Terrance did his best not to preen a little and failed. "I've had a few. But they were just… well… you know. There hasn't been anyone who was more than a passing interest." That was the truth. He wasn't sure what, if anything, was happening between the two of them. He felt more protective of Ashton than he had of anyone other than the guys. It was new for him. Usually the men he went out with—and by that he meant took somewhere for sex—were bigger guys like him. Terrance tended to like his sex rather on the athletic side. But just sitting with Ashton, his arm around him, sent ripples of heat running through him stronger than the intense rays of the sun. He had never thought he'd be interested in a guy like Ashton, who was way more on the cute side than on the hunky side, but still….

"How many is a few?" Ashton asked.

"I don't know. I haven't kept count. It's not like I have a rollicking social life. Most of the time I'm with the guys. I work at the hardware store and some evenings at the Driftwood to make sure the rowdy element stays away." He smiled slightly. "By the way, I'm sorry for those guys bothering you the other night. But in a way, I'm glad, because I would never have met you otherwise."

Ashton scoffed. "I'm not sure whether that's a good thing or not."

Terrance leaned back, and Ashton broke into a wry grin. "You're teasing me."

"Of course I'm teasing you. Those guys were being assholes, and you sent them packing and came to my rescue. That was very nice of you, especially on your day off and all. At least I assumed it was your day off, with the way you were sitting with everyone else."

"It was. We get together every Wednesday. It's our version of a family dinner. The boys look forward to it, and it's a chance for all of us to see one another. Everything keeps getting busier and more hectic all the time. Coby is in school now, and he wants to take tennis lessons and play baseball. Joshie says he wants to play soccer."

"And that affects you because…?"

Terrance scrunched his brow. "They're family. Daniel is an IT specialist and works from home. You know that Gerome works at the gift shop. Tucker and Richard work at the Driftwood, and all of us have peculiar schedules and commitments, so sometimes I take the boys to school or to their activities." That was what family did.

Ashton leaned closer to him. "You know, when you said you all were a family, I thought that was in the sort of close friend way, but you really are. One huge, different-looking family." He sighed. "Can I ask a question?"

Terrance nodded slowly. "Of course."

"How do I get one of those for myself?"

That was the one question Terrance didn't know how to answer. Part of him wanted to give Ashton a real chance to see if he might fit in, but there was a secret that bound all of them as well, and Terrance had to tread lightly. They had been lucky with Daniel and Tucker, but would that kind of luck hold for someone Terrance was interested in? He had no idea and wasn't sure if he could take the chance.

Chapter 4

THE AFTERNOON on the water was great, and by the time they pulled back into the marina at the end of the day, the boys were run out and were napping in the shade. Everyone except Daniel, who was acting as captain, sat at the table with a drink, until they had to secure the lines. Then Daniel joined them, the boat engine silent, with only the sound of the water against the dock and the other boats to break up the night.

"The boys are zonked, but they're going to wake up soon enough," Daniel said, popping open a beer and drinking most of it. "I don't know what we're going to do for dinner, but I'm not cooking, and someone else is going to be doing the driving. I'm done for the day."

"I've already called the Driftwood. Alan is making up dinner and he's going to have one of the guys bring it over for us, so we don't have to move for a while," Richard told them. "Alan says he knows us well enough to put together a good dinner." He sat back, and Ashton relaxed as the shadows continued to lengthen and the sky grew darker, the sun having just set.

Terrance opened one of the coolers, pulled out a few bottles of beer, and placed them on the table. He handed Ashton one. "Or would you like something else?"

"This is great. Thank you." He still wasn't sure what to make of all this. Terrance had been really attentive all day.

When the food arrived, the boys woke and joined them at the table. They passed out the food, and Terrance made sure Ashton got a burger and some salad. A massive amount of food had been delivered, but it didn't last long. Still, there was plenty for him, and Terrance sat right close, occasionally resting his hand on Ashton's arm, a gentle and caring gesture.

"Is everything okay?" Terrance asked. "Did you get enough?"

"I'm full, thank you." He chuckled. "You don't have to worry about me. I'm not going to starve, believe me."

"With this group? They do a great impression of a cloud of locusts," Terrance teased.

"You did more than your fair share of sucking up the food," Gerome teased right back and patted Terrance's belly. "You seem to have been overeating, getting a little belly on you."

Terrance growled. "You aren't the one to talk." He patted Gerome's belly. Both men growled at each other and glared.

"Do we need to get out the rulers?" Tucker quipped.

"What rulers? What are you going to measure?" Coby asked. "I have a ruler at home."

Daniel and Tucker both glared at the two men. "Now see what you've done." Daniel turned to Coby. "Uncle Terrance and Uncle Gerome are only picking on each other."

"That's mean. You should say sorry and shake hands. Picking on each other is wrong." Coby put his hands on his hips.

Ashton turned away to try to keep from chuckling. It was cute beyond all measure, and danged if it didn't go to the hearts of these men, including Terrance.

"Yes, it was," Terrance agreed and scooped Coby into his arms, tickling him and eliciting giggles that rang through the evening. Ashton realized he could learn a lot about someone by the way they treated children—especially other people's children.

They continued talking as it grew darker. The boys became restless, and everyone got their things ready to go. Gerome, Tucker, and Joshie left, as did Daniel, Richard, and Coby, with him and Terrance near Ashton's old car. "I should go home, but thank you for the fun and the bit of adventure today."

"Nature provided the adventure part. I didn't have anything to do with it, I promise." He smiled.

Ashton nodded. He wasn't sure what to say other than good night and thank you. "Ummm…." He felt Terrance's heated gaze, and it drew him closer. His feet took small steps, almost on their own, and then Terrance leaned closer. Ashton wasn't sure if he was actually going to kiss him until Terrance's lips met his.

Warmth spread through Ashton in a quarter of an instant, and he drew even nearer, wanting more.

Terrance tasted a little spicy from dinner, but under that, warm and rich. Ashton expected to be engulfed in Terrance's huge arms and nearly crushed against him with the big man's strength, but Terrance only touched his cheek with the tips of his fingers, adding to the energy of the kiss. Ashton wound his arms around Terrance's hips, holding him to keep upright.

He ended the kiss and pulled back slightly, his vision a little out of focus, mind drawing inward slightly in order to assess what had just happened. Fortunately, before his mind could travel too far down the rabbit hole, Terrance kissed him again, this time with more energy.

Ashton's blood thrummed in his ears, and he pressed to Terrance, giving over more of himself as Terrance softly cupped his cheek.

When Ashton pulled away this time, blinking and trying to remain steady on his feet, he smiled. "I'll see you soon, I hope." They hadn't made any arrangements for another date or anything, but he wanted to let Terrance know that he hoped there would be more. Then he turned and got into his car.

He slowly pulled out of the lot, his heart still racing… which it continued to do all the way home. He probably should have gone inside for the night, but he was too keyed up, so he did what he usually did when his mind refused to shut down. He went into the small studio, started up the equipment, and sat at his desk to plan how he was going to complete the piece that flashed into his mind as the equipment heated up.

HEAT ROLLED out of the furnace as Ashton blew into the end of the rod, slowly inflating the glass at the other end while he turned it back and forth. The shape was forming. After adding a little more air, he heated the glass once more until he finally got the size he wanted. He then shaped the glass to the exact curve he needed. Then he set it aside and made the other pieces to attach.

At times like this, he wished he had an assistant, because glass was a time-sensitive material. But he had done this sort of thing before. He got the pieces attached, creating a freeform piece that represented his angst, with writhing swirls of color all blended and moving through and past one another, some pulled out into strands that went nowhere, while others flowed out and then back onto themselves. It reminded Ashton of those intricate carved Chinese puzzle balls, but with layer upon layer of glass, representing his fears that never seemed to go away.

The piece came off the punty successfully and went into the annealer. After closing the door, Ashton got some more glass, colored it, and started blowing multicolored balls that he could sell at Christmas time. He wasn't ready for bed, even though it was well into the wee hours of the morning, and he needed something easy and repetitive.

Once he had finished half a dozen, he had used up the remainder of his raw glass. It was time to put his materials aside. Ashton made sure the annealing process was set so that the temperature in the oven would reduce slowly and his pieces would remain intact.

Usually this kind of work freed his mind and helped Ashton to see things clearly. But it hadn't worked this time. As soon as he stepped out into the night, thoughts of Terrance, their kiss, and their day together flooded over him.

He reminded himself that Terrance wasn't Frank. Ashton had left him behind for the chance to start a new life, and if he let his old life and decisions color everything he did here, then he wasn't going to have a life of any kind. For the past two years, he'd lived in fear, watching over his shoulder, unsure whether Frank would follow. And he had seen nothing of him. It was likely Frank had moved on and found someone else to dominate, someone else whose life he could take over until there was nothing left of them but what Frank wanted. Two years of expecting Frank to step into his life at any moment, and yet… nothing.

Ashton knew he should be grateful that he'd managed to disappear so completely. But now, what he wanted more than anything was some sort of normal life, and that meant sticking his head up once again in order to be part of the real world. Ashton was willing to try. He just hoped he didn't get it shot off in the process.

Ashton went inside his small place, stripped down, and headed right for the shower. After drinking a lot of water, he fell into bed.

He blinked himself awake and checked his phone. It was well after noon, and he rubbed his eyes and got out of bed and stumbled to the bathroom, where he shaved and cleaned up before ravenously attacking his refrigerator. Not that he had all that much inside, but an apple and some cheese took away the hunger. He wondered if the Driftwood was open for lunch and briefly thought about taking a walk, but a rumble of thunder changed his mind.

Instead, he detoured to the studio and checked the annealer, which had finished its cycle. Opening the door was always one of those moments. Just because a piece made it inside didn't mean that there wasn't a fatal flaw that could result in a pile of glass shards. However, he found all his glass balls and the piece he'd spent so much time on still intact.

Ashton removed the balls and set them in bubble-wrap compartments of a box before taking out the piece he was really interested in. He held it in his hands, examining the perfect flows of the glass. But when he held it to the light, he nearly dropped it. The effect of the colored glass interior surrounded by the layers of clear glass had a prismatic effect that mixed and shimmered the colors together into different combinations when he moved it. What he had meant as an expression of his knotted and twisted worries and fears had turned into this stunning thing of beauty he had never expected.

Ashton wrapped the piece in bubble wrap, carried it back inside, and added it to the closet along with the items for his potential art show booth. What he needed was a spectacular way to display it. He closed the closet as a knock sounded on his front door.

Ashton opened it to an agitated Terrance, who stepped inside. "Are you okay?"

Ashton stepped back at the snap in Terrance's tone. "I'm fine. I slept in late. But why are you here?"

"I tried calling you. Richard is working the lunch shift. This huge guy came in, ordered food, and asked if anyone had seen a man. He flashed a picture of you. Only he said your name was Carter West." Terrance's hands went to his hips. "What's going on?"

"Did he say anything?" Ashton was already trying to figure out how quickly he could pack and get the hell out of there.

"No. Richard is cool, and he knows trouble when it walks in." Terrance held his gaze. "So who is Carter?"

"That's me. Ashton is my middle name and the one I used when I came down here. I changed my name to Ashton Weller after I moved here, but back in Chicago I was Carter West." He swallowed.

"Richard covered for you and then made sure the guy from the bar left. But he called me, and I'm here because I need to know what's going on." The gentleness that had been present in Terrance's posture all day yesterday was gone. "Who is this guy?"

"He's Frank Petrano." Ashton stepped back to let Terrance inside.

"What does he want from you? What is he to you? Why is he here?" Terrance's questions came quickly. "Are you in some sort of trouble?"

"Hold on. Frank is my ex-boyfriend and the man who wanted to control my life. I was with him in Chicago, and he was the reason I left." Ashton looked around his pathetic apartment filled with other people's furniture. "I had to get away. He was dangerous, and I knew I couldn't stay with him."

"Dangerous... how?" Terrance asked as he checked the front window.

Ashton waited until Terrance turned back to him. "Why are you asking me these questions? I need—"

"You need to give me the answers so I can figure out what we're going to do." Terrance grabbed him by the arm and sat him on the sofa. "Tell me the truth, no bullshit."

"He was my boyfriend. I thought things were okay until I started to meet his friends. Scary men, hoods... creeps... and God knows what. He was always talking about moving up the ladder and that I was his and that no one was supposed to know about us." Ashton shivered. Terrance was acting a lot like Frank. All he wanted to do was get the hell out of there. "I left two years ago, changed my name, and tried to start a new life in the middle of nowhere." He glared at Terrance and pulled his arm away. "Don't manhandle me. I've had enough of that to last the rest of my life. And now that Frank is here, I need to figure out what I'm going to do. Probably pack everything I have into my car and move on again. I can't let him find me."

Terrance lowered his hands. "Okay," he said calmly. "Richard said that he hadn't seen you and asked a couple of the guys, who agreed with him. They suggested that Frank might try Sarasota or something. Apparently he told him that everyone knows each other here. He said that Frank seemed discouraged and left in a huff."

"Fine. But you don't know Frank. Something must have led him here, and he won't be put off. He may move on for a while, but he'll come back because this was the last information he had." Frank was a threat not only to the life he had built, but to his very life itself.

"And you haven't done anything wrong?"

Ashton was done with this shit. "Yeah. I really wanted my life turned upside down by a controlling asshole who decided he had the right to run my life, decide who I could see, who my friends were, where I could eat, what I could eat. You get the damn picture. Yeah, I did something wrong—mainly dating Frank in the first place. I packed up everything and got out of town. I even had to leave behind my car—which was no great loss—change my name, and cut up my credit cards. The only things I took were my clothes and the equipment I could fit in the new car I bought in a different state." He was so wound up he began to pace. "And now my tormentor, who I thought I had shaken and I hoped had given up, is here where I live. That's just fucking awesome." He glared daggers at Terrance. "And you have the nerve to ask me if I did anything wrong." His voice rose by the second, and he blew out a deep breath.

Terrance took a step back and put his hands up. "Okay. I get you."

Ashton was shocked into silence. That was not the reaction he had been expecting. Frank would have raised his voice and either shouted Ashton down or simply walked away to ignore him until Ashton did exactly what Frank wanted him to. "What's that supposed to mean?"

"Hey, I didn't mean it as an accusation. I just needed to know where you were coming from. Richard stuck his neck out for you, and Gerome and I will do the same, but I need to know what I'm sticking my neck out for. Between the three of us, we can lay a pretty good trail that should lead Frank away." Terrance crossed his arms over his chest.

"How?" Ashton asked.

Terrance shook his head. "Just promise me that you aren't involved in anything illegal."

"I wasn't! But that doesn't mean Frank isn't and that I'm not guilty by association. He did a lot of shit, I know he did, and he hurt people all the time. For a while I turned a blind eye, but I couldn't do that any longer. I wasn't involved in any of his dealings."

Terrance nodded and seemed thoughtful. "But did you know any of the details about them?"

Ashton shrugged. "Nothing specific. We used to go out to dinner. I suppose I could tell you the names of the guys he ate and hung around with." He bit his lower lip and decided it was best to keep quiet. That wasn't exactly the truth, but he had told himself over and over that he was never going to speak about what he'd seen. All he wanted was to get out and have a life of his own and not have to live under Frank's shadow or influence.

"Okay. Let me talk to the guys and we'll see what we can do to send Frankie Boy on a wild goose chase." He grinned, and Ashton got the idea that this wasn't the first time Terrance had done something like this. Maybe Terrance really could help him.

"What do you want?" Ashton asked. "No one does something for nothing. What's your price?" He was damned well going to know what he was getting into. One mistake of not knowing the price for a favor had nearly cost him everything, including his freedom.

Terrance growled and shook his head. "I'm going to remember that Frank treated you like shit and take that question as a symptom of your nervousness." The fire in his eyes told Ashton that he had judged the situation all wrong.

"Sorry." He needed to remember not to paint Terrance with the same brush as Frank.

"I offered because I thought I could help you. I didn't do it because I want something from you. I don't treat people that way. Do you really think I'm the kind of guy who would do a favor for someone so I could get in his pants or something?" Terrance actually blushed.

Ashton grinned. "So, you're saying you want to get in my pants?" He tilted his head slightly. Terrance was a hunk and a stud. There was no doubt about that. And to see the guy look like he'd just been caught with his hand in the cookie jar was kind of fun.

While there was no arguing that Terrance was hot, what Ashton wasn't so sure about was whether he wanted to act on the attraction or resist it and keep Terrance at arm's length. That would be the smart thing to do, and yet very few guys had actually offered to help him without strings attached.

"I didn't mean it that way. I was just saying that…." Terrance huffed and didn't seem to know what else to say. Maybe Ashton had hit on the real heart of the matter. "I meant that I'll try to help you."

"Because you like me." He couldn't resist.

Terrance growled once more. "Yeah, I like you. I wouldn't have kissed you otherwise. I…."

Ashton nodded. "You're kind of noble, then."

Terence chuckled softly. "I wouldn't go that far. No one is ever going to mistake me for a fucking prince. I'm rough around the edges, and a lot of the guys I've been out with tell me that I'm an asshole who spends more time with his friends than I do with them. They see me for a few weeks and then get pissed off and leave."

"Because they can't understand your family? What kind of jerks have you been seeing, and where do you find them so I know where not to go?" This was kind of fun. Keeping Terrance a little off-balance was rather telling.

"Maybe. But they tend to be a little superficial." Terrance held his gaze, and Ashton didn't want to look away. Being held under that look was surprisingly enticing. He liked the idea that Terrance wasn't looking for a guy with big muscles and a brain like a box of rocks. "You'll be surprised that I'm looking for someone I can talk to and who has a sense of humor. A pretty face and a built body aren't enough." He got all growly once more.

"Why not? I would have thought that would be the kind of guy you'd go for." It certainly wasn't a skinny, scruffy guy from Chicago who could barely afford to get his hair cut and whose nose had been broken and healed a little off-center.

"So would I," Terrance countered. "Then Richard met Daniel, and Gerome met Coby, and the guys I dated for years seemed a little dim and boring. I tried just dating them for their... obvious assets...." He sighed. "God, they were boring as dirt *and* terrible in bed."

Ashton chuckled and turned away. "I see. So you think that just because I'm smaller and not good-looking that I'd be good in bed?" He took a step forward. "Because... well... it seems you'll have to find out. Maybe... eventually."

Terrance rolled his eyes. "You're funny. I like a guy with a sense of humor." The heat in Terrance's eyes grew, hotter than Ashton's furnace. That was a reaction he would never have expected. It was fun teasing Terrance, and he had thought Terrance had been teasing him in return... just playing. But maybe there was something more. The idea sent excitement racing through him because Terrance was hot... and smart... funny, with a quick mind. Now *that* was attractive.

"Okay," Terrance said softly. "Stay inside for a few days until we can figure out what we need to do. I'll talk to the guys, and we'll see what we can come up with."

Ashton nodded, all joking and teasing put aside. "I'll ask you again. Why would you do this? Frank isn't a nice man in any sense of the word. Why put yourselves in harm's way?"

Terrance drew closer and leaned forward. "I don't intend for him to know we're involved." He kissed Ashton, pouring residual heat into the few seconds of the kiss. "Just stay out of sight. I'll call and let you know what's happening later."

"How are you going to do something like that?" Ashton grew nervous, not just for himself but for Terrance. Maybe it would be best if he just got everything into his car and left. But starting over yet again…? He was just beginning to be able to make a living, and there wasn't much left of the money he had been able to squirrel away in Chicago and bring along with him. He was stuck. All he could hope for right now was that Terrance was what he claimed to be. Otherwise Ashton was going to be in big trouble.

Chapter 5

"YOU WANT us to do what?" Gerome asked. "Lay a trail so this Frank Petrano leaves Ashton alone? What if he's trouble and we're getting pulled into it? We've already had two close calls. A third is going to get us all moved." They sat in Daniel and Richard's living room. Cheryl had taken the boys to play in the park.

"What do any of us know about Ashton or this guy that's after him?" Daniel had already gotten up and was heading to his computer. In the past he had been a world-class hacker, and that skill had saved them on a few occasions. It had also been the source of the troubles that had ultimately brought him and Richard together. "Knowledge is power, so let's see what we can find out." He started typing.

"This is a huge chance you're asking us all to take," Gerome continued. "And it isn't just us anymore. It's our families and the kids. Did you even think before you offered our help?"

Terrance was on his feet in a second. "We all helped you when you needed it, so shut your face before I put out a couple teeth."

"Knock it off," Richard said, getting between them. "You didn't tell him anything about us, did you?"

Terrance shook his head. "Only that we could try to create a trail of some sort that would lead this Frank asshole away." He took a deep breath and sat back down. Richard was right. He needed to get his feelings under control. "Look, there's something going on here. I got a feeling about Frank from the way Ashton described him."

"Look at this," Daniel said. "It seems there's a Frank Petrano in Chicago, and he's suspected of having underworld dealings."

"What site are you on?" Gerome asked.

Daniel scoffed. "A law-enforcement database. Don't ask questions. Anyway, he's a suspect in a number of killings as well as for prostitution and running drugs. Though the information they have seems to be a few years old. There's nothing recent in the database." He turned the screen. "Is that the guy from the Driftwood?"

"Definitely. And he was asking for Ashton, but under a different name." Richard crossed his arms over his chest, and Terrance relayed what Ashton had told him.

"That checks out," Daniel said a few minutes later after more furious typing. "Ashton has no record, and what I can find details a pretty normal kind of life."

"So what we have is a picture that matches what Ashton told me. And it seems that we have a member of the Chicago mob hanging around looking for Ashton. Sending the guy on a wild goose chase is in all our benefits. What if he has contacts in Detroit?" It wasn't a stretch for these guys to know one another. They often traveled in the same circles or did business. Nothing was local any longer, not even mobsters.

"That's an even more important reason to lead him the hell out of here. We need to keep our families safe, and keeping him away from this part of the country will do that."

Terrance leaned forward. "So we're selfish enough that we'll do what's right to keep ourselves safe, but not Ashton? We all liked him, and you saw his work."

Daniel got up from his computer, came right over, and hugged Terrance lightly. "Of course we'll keep him safe. These two are being dicks and they know it." The look he gave Richard was as cold as winter in North Dakota. "Coby and Joshie liked him, and you know they're better judges of character than either of you." He released Terrance and whirled around. "So yes, we'll help Ashton, but he can't know how we're doing what we're doing or any of the details. We all have too much to lose. What I'm going to try to do is plant some activity on one of Ashton's old credit cards in California. The transactions will be declined, but it should be enough to get someone's attention. It's on the other side of the country, and that should pull their attention away from us."

"Can you really do that?" Terrance asked.

"Of course I can," Daniel said quickly. "It's easy, and because the transaction will be denied, there's no harm done. But if Frank is watching for some kind of slipup to find Ashton, then this will do it for him. He'll see the transaction and be off on a cross-country journey." He seemed pleased.

"Is that all?" Terrance asked.

Daniel shrugged. "Sometimes less is more. Just trust me." He went back to the computer and got to work. "There we are. Transaction made and denied at a small store in Fresno. It's local, so it means that he had to be there. No muss, no fuss. Now all we need to do is make sure tall, dark, and dim is truly gone. Can you help with that?" he asked Richard.

"How am I supposed to do that?" Richard asked.

"Did you string him along, get some info out of him when he was in? Maybe ask where to contact him if you saw the guy he was looking for?" Daniel shook his head when Richard shrugged. "And you call yourself a self-respecting former mobster."

"I didn't get that, but I did pick the guy's pocket when I came around the bar to wipe up the front." He handed Daniel a card. "Here's where the guy is staying."

"Now that's the man I know and love. Stealing a matchbook."

"Hey, I only do it to help people." They had long ago switched to walking the straight and narrow.

"Yeah, yeah, you're fucking Robin Hood," Daniel teased and then kissed him. "That's why I love you."

"I know. I'm bad, but for a good reason." Richard smooched Daniel. "And I was careful. Don't worry."

Daniel sat on Richard's lap. "I know your heart, and you're a good man." Daniel shared a moment with Richard before turning to Terrance. "And you... I'd say you like Ashton."

"I do, but it's way too soon for me to be taking this too seriously." Terrance needed to explain. "I'm not going to fall in love at the drop of a hat. Ashton is a nice person, and you know we all don't meet that many of them. My past, our past, is one of harshness, muscle, and threats. It's what we all grew up with. Ashton is different."

"We understand," Richard said.

Gerome glared at him for a few seconds and finally nodded. "Just don't do something stupid."

Tucker lightly smacked him. "Be good. Remember that these two helped you and me when we were figuring our shit out. So stop being cynical. Terrance needs his chance at happiness just like you had. Whether Ashton turns out to be the man for him or not, you still need to support him, just like you helped support me and Joshie when we needed you most." Tucker spoke so softly, and Gerome nodded.

"Sorry." He cleared his throat. "What do you want us to do?"

Terrance had no idea, but having his brothers behind him was all he could ask for. "We protect each other, so let's do that. We need to get Frank away from all of us, and then we need to move forward with our lives and make sure he doesn't find Ashton. Because if he does, then he finds us as well."

"Okay," Gerome agreed. "Since he hasn't seen me, I'll be the one to go over to that hotel and see if he's still there." He picked up the matchbook and put it into his pocket. "One way or another, this guy needs to get out of Dodge." Tucker sat down, and Gerome leaned forward. "What is it about this guy that got to you?" He seemed so serious and gentle, a combination that Terrance rarely saw in him.

"He grew up like we did. Though he didn't have Mama. He ended up in foster care." He swallowed. "When he told me his story, it was a lot like ours. I think Ashton is a kindred spirit." He shifted his gaze to Richard. "You know how hard we all had it. So did he, and once he was starting to build his own life, Frank crossed his path." He sighed. "The thing was that I saw myself in Frank—the way we were before we left Detroit." Terrance had spent hours late at night thinking about this. "We can say what we want, but before we left, we weren't Boy Scouts. The three of us did whatever we needed to in order to get what we wanted and to make money. We hurt people and used them. I think I have to do something to atone for that."

"Bullshit," Gerome spat. "We did what we had to do to survive. There was no one around to look after us or fight our battles for us. Mama did the best she could." He seemed angry, but his voice was scratchy. "And when we were able, we took care of her. She was our atonement. Your mother was the one who saw to it that all three of us had something to eat and shoes on our feet, even when she was working hers off doing whatever she had to. Helping her was all that was required, because she was the only one who helped us." He stood and set his beer on the counter that separated the rooms, a small amount of foam bubbling out of the bottle and running down the side.

Richard nodded, but Terrance wasn't so sure. "We ran roughshod over a lot of people, and I…." It hit him in a strong way. Gerome and Richard had usually been the ones running the business or developing other ways to build on what they had. Terrance was the muscle—he was the one who had done the dirty work. He was good at it. But he'd also been the one to see the pain they caused. The others could close their eyes to it; he couldn't. "I did the dirty work. So maybe I have more to pay."

"No," Richard snapped. "It was all of us. We did what we did together, and if the good we've done isn't enough to make up for it, then…."

"How can it be?" Terrance asked, suddenly seeing things clearly for the first time. "Yeah, we helped Alan and Daniel and Tucker, but that was helping ourselves too. It kept us all safe. And in the end, helping Ashton is to keep us safe too." He settled back in his seat. "I guess I'm wondering if we can do anything that isn't for ourselves." Maybe he was getting older and more introspective. Lord knows he never thought about this shit when they were back in Detroit. He just did what he had to do. "I know, I know, I'm probably spending way too much time thinking about crap and I need to let it go."

Richard and Gerome shared a look that Terrance didn't understand. "Our lives are different here, and that's going to have an effect on all of us. None of us is the same as we were when we arrived here. This has become our home, and the people in our lives our family." He snickered. "Who would have ever thought that?"

"Yeah, I guess we've all changed," Gerome agreed.

"Not that much," Daniel told them. "All three of you can still be pains in the ass." He dramatically threw his hands in the air. "Look, all of you, stop this mushy shit. It's scaring me. I get that you're getting older and introspective, but God… it's frightening."

Richard chuckled. "Okay. We'll all do our best to be the rough, self-centered assholes we were when we first met you." He leaned close to Daniel's ear, and color rose in Daniel's cheeks.

"How long are they staying?" Daniel asked.

Richard chuckled, and Daniel went into the kitchen and got himself a glass of water.

"I think Daniel's right. That's enough of this touchy-feely stuff." Terrance had spent way too much time mulling this over the past few nights, and he didn't like it. "There is something I'd like to ask. Do you think it might be possible to get at some of the money that's stashed away? I'd like to be able to move out of the apartment I'm in, find a place like this that can be mine." Maybe get a car that he didn't have to pray would start every time he turned the key. He didn't need much, but it would be nice if there was something.

"We can't," Gerome said. "Not for years yet. The money is the result of criminal activity, and if they trace it back, then we could lose everything. I figured it would need to stay where it is for ten years or so. Then we could use some of it and bring it back over time."

"I see." That was what they had agreed to, and Gerome knew best, but Terrance was getting anxious. He was tired of the crappy apartment and shitty car. It wasn't like he wanted to quit his job and do nothing all day, but with the job at the hardware store and at the Driftwood, he was just making enough to keep his head above water and that was about it. It sucked, especially with the others moving forward when he seemed to be stuck.

"It has to be this way," Gerome explained. "If we could bring the money back, then we all could get better places and nicer cars. Then people would start to ask questions. If someone began to look into our backgrounds…."

"I know… I know…." He'd only been hoping. "I'm going to go." It had been a long day already, and he had to be at the hardware store when they opened in the morning. He had only had a single beer, and he grabbed a water out of the refrigerator and downed it before saying his goodbyes and leaving the condo. He waved to the kids and Cheryl, who were on their way back, and then drove off. Sometimes it sucked being the odd man out.

"IT SEEMS that Frank has left town," Terrance told Ashton early the following evening. "We figured out where he was staying, and he left about noon. Apparently in a bit of a hurry." At least that was what Gerome had reported. Maybe Daniel's little trick had worked. "I'd suggest you stay inside and out of sight for a few days just to be sure, though."

"How did you do this?" he asked. "I know I asked before, but it seems like a lot to do for someone. You barely know me."

Terrance nodded. "Maybe I know you better than you think, because your story is a lot like my own. And we don't know for sure if he's gone. Honestly, it wasn't hard to lay a trail to the other side of the country." He hadn't been nervous with another guy in years, yet asking Ashton to dinner had his belly full of butterflies. Like he was jittery and scared of what Ashton would say. It was wonderfully strange. "Anyway, I thought that once we're sure he's gone, maybe you and I could have dinner somewhere. Maybe we could go Sunday. I'm off at the hardware store, and the Driftwood is usually slow that night, so I can get the night off." He swallowed hard. "Maybe we could go to Tampa for a nice meal."

Ashton didn't move at first, and he didn't respond, which made Terrance even more nervous. God, he both loved and hated this feeling so damned much. "You really want to go out on a date?"

"Yeah," Terrance answered with a smile. "Do you have any idea how long it's been since I went on a real date? Maybe since I was fourteen years old. The guys I saw were hookups. A few of them lasted a week or so, but then that was it."

"And you don't want to hook up with me?" Ashton asked.

"No."

"I see. But then why take me to dinner if you don't find me attractive or… whatever." The light from Ashton's eyes dimmed.

It took Terrance a few seconds to understand what Ashton meant and what he'd said. "I didn't mean it like that. I meant that you deserve more than a hookup, and maybe I deserve that too. So instead of a 'wham-bam, thank you, and don't let the door hit you on the way out,' we can go to dinner, have a real date, walk on the beach, talk a little, and see what might happen." Part of Terrance was excited about the idea, and another part wondered if he was as crazy as a loon. He decided to listen to the first part and told his old self to take a hike. If he wanted to be happy in his new life, then he needed to leave parts of that old self behind. Gerome and Richard had, and they were happy. Maybe Terrance needed to take a chance, and this was it.

"You really mean going out on a *date* date. Like a real date."

"Of course. That's what I'm saying. Okay?" He smiled as Ashton nodded. "Not that I have experience with this sort of thing. So you'll have to tell me if I do something wrong." Terrance checked his phone. "I'm sorry, but I need to go to the Driftwood. Alan and Richard gave me enough time to talk to you, but I need to get back." Terrance kissed Ashton on the cheek—also a first for him—and then hurried down the walk to his old car. Maybe it was true that his feet barely touched the pavement.

THE KNOCK on his door startled him. Terrance turned down the television and hefted himself up off the sofa to let Richard and Gerome inside. "What's going on?"

"We came to drink your beer." Gerome went to the refrigerator, grabbed a couple bottles, and headed for the sofa. "No, really. We came because we never come here anymore."

"Is this a pity visit?" Terrance asked.

"Don't be a pain in the ass. We stopped by the hotel where Ashton's ex was staying, and he's definitely cleared out. Daniel found where his car passed through a tollbooth in Texas, so he's headed out to California. Daniel added slightly to the trail today, and that should keep him busy looking for a ghost. Hopefully he'll give up after his little wild goose chase." They clinked bottles, and Richard settled into one of the chairs. "What's the next step for the two of you?" Richard asked.

"Have we all turned into gossipy old biddies now?" Terrance challenged. "I have a date with him Sunday evening. Is that a big deal?"

"Nope. It's the same with him as it was for the two of us. We need to be careful about who we trust, and with Frank's appearance, he could bring us closer to the brink than we've ever come before," Gerome said in his usual cynical manner.

"Look. Just be careful. Frank is connected. Like, really connected. Daniel did some more digging and found out Frank was in Detroit a few months ago. He got picked up for speeding on 75. The ticket is in the system," Richard explained.

Terrance nodded. "And it's for damned sure that Frank wasn't there for his health or the freaking weather." The only reason someone like Frank Petrano would be in Detroit was on business. It was likely that he was meeting with the remnants of the Garvic family. They still held sway, even if it was diminished.

"Exactly."

"I should back away?" He finished off his beer, set the bottle on the counter, and grabbed another.

"We didn't ask you to do that. Not that you would any more than we would. Just be on the lookout and be careful."

He didn't need to be told that. Terrance had already run interference for both Richard and Gerome, and he had taken care of business without anyone knowing it was him or that they were pulling the strings.

"Keep a lookout. Not that we expect him to return, but you never know. And we don't know very much about Ashton. Be careful and find out what you can about him."

Terrance shook his head. "God, when did we get to be so sanctimonious and judgmental?" He took a huge drink of his beer.

"We aren't judging him. But a Chicago mobster followed him here and could put us all in danger. Why? You said that Ashton left two years ago, but what changed all of a sudden? This Frank guy had plenty of time to track Ashton down, so why now?" Richard cocked his eyebrows. "I have to admit that I like the guy. The boys liked him, and that says a lot."

"Guys, you want me to spy on him?" Terrance asked.

"Hell no. Just listen, that's all. Be careful, and for God's sake have fun." Gerome smiled. "And don't mind either of us. We're probably being overcautious assholes anyway. We all know that sometimes shit happens. We just don't want it happening to us."

"You're a fucking comedian," Terrance deadpanned. "And you're definitely a couple of assholes." He sipped his beer and settled in. He didn't have to be anywhere, so he figured he could tie one on and let his mind float.

The three of them bullshitted each other as they usually did. In some ways, it felt like old times, before their lives had changed completely and everything they knew was ripped away. For a few hours, things felt like they had then.

But it was only an illusion, a temporary condition, and he knew it. Everything was temporary and had been for quite a while. The only constant was the three of them.

Chapter 6

SWEAT ROLLED down Ashton's cheeks and the back of his neck, his clothes plastered to his skin, but he was too close to stop. He inserted the gentle curve of glass carefully back into the heat and grabbed a cloth. He wiped off the sweat and wished for the millionth time that he had someone to help him. Working glass was usually a two-person job, but there was no way he could afford anyone to help him, so he did it himself. Tasks would be easier with help, but he did what he had to. The story of his life.

Tossing the cloth out of the way, he pulled out the glass and worked it into the next stage. He had decided to make a vase this time, but not one for flowers. This was to be a showpiece, with the flowers on the vase itself. He needed it as large as he could make it without—

He nearly dropped the entire thing at a knock on the door. He put glass back into the heat and turned it. "Come in." He continued the rotation as Terrance came inside.

"I heard the rush from the flame and…. Jesus Christ." Terrance stepped back as a wave of heat welled up when Ashton pulled the piece from the fire. "How in the hell can you work in this?"

"Lots of water." Ashton sat down to shape the glass. He had just been thinking he needed an assistant and here Terrance was, strong and available. But his help could backfire and Terrance could break something without much effort. "Put on those huge gloves and come over here and sit down. I'm going to put the glass back into the oven to warm. Then I'm going to pull it out again. I want you to slowly rock it back and forth just like I'm doing now. Then put the glass into the oven and turn it. What you have there is the base, and I need to make the top. What you're doing is buying me some time."

"Okay," Terrance said, "but I have no idea what I'm doing."

"Just follow my instructions," Ashton said calmly. "This is going to be a dance with poles and hot glass. That's it, keep turning. You're doing wonderfully." It occurred to him that Frank would never do this in a million years. Letting Ashton take the lead in anything was beyond him. Terrance seemed like he might be enjoying helping with his art. "Now put it back into the heat, the pole on the stand, and turn it. Then take it out." Ashton got some more glass on a punty, and when Terrance pulled his piece out of the furnace, he put his in. He heated the lump, then removed it and quickly formed an ovoid. He heated it quickly again, expanded the glass by blowing into the end of the rod, and turned it before heating again and again.

"Heat yours once more for just a few minutes," he told Terrance while he worked. "That's great, just keep turning it slowly. Okay, remove it." Terrance did. Ashton had to give him credit—there was no confidence in Terrance's movements, but no fear either and maybe a touch of fascination. He followed Ashton's instructions until the elongated bubble was the size he wanted. "Okay, hold yours still. Perfect."

Ashton touched his bubble to the top of the glass base, marked the glass, and held his breath as he tinked the punty, which dropped away, leaving Terrance with the whole piece.

"That's heavy," Terrance said, but he held it as Ashton set the used punty aside and took over for Terrance. "But beautiful."

Now the heating was more delicate. He needed to keep the base warm but not too hot, or the place where he joined the pieces would melt. He needed the piece in the right place so the weak spots didn't melt but got hot enough to work at the same time.

"Please keep the gloves on and stand near the door. Open it if you want to let some of the heat out." Ashton sat at the bench and worked the glass to just the perfect graceful curve with a slight flare at the top. He gave the edge of the top five indented flutes and pulled the center of each flute to a slight point to mimic a flower petal. Then, after one final heating before completing the last details, he checked it over, warmed it slightly, and called Terrance over. "Place your gloves under the piece and keep your body away. I'm going to release it. It will drop into your hands, and then I'm going to open the annealer. Place the piece on its side and step back."

"Okay," Terrance told him without hesitation. Ashton looked into Terrance's eyes and expected to see fear or concern. What he saw was determination. "Let's do this." He got into position, and Ashton marked and separated the piece from the punty. It dropped slightly into Terrance's hands, and Ashton opened the annealing oven.

"Perfect. Lay the piece down and step away." He closed the door as soon as Terrance was out of the way. Only then did he breathe again. "Now it's out of our hands."

"I don't think I've ever held liquid fire before," Terrance said softly.

"Not many people ever do. It's heady, isn't it? Something so beautiful, so malleable, can be deadly if it touches you at the wrong time. Yet once it's cool, it can shine with all the light of the sun." Ashton shut down the furnace, and the room grew much quieter as he made sure everything was set for the night. "Come on inside."

The night was still warm, but the air felt cooler against his superheated skin. He closed and locked the studio doors and led Terrance to his apartment, where he pulled bottles of water out of the refrigerator. "Not that I'm not happy to see you, but what brings you here at this time of night?"

"I saw the lights and wondered what was going on." Terrance drained the bottle of water in a few gulps.

Ashton followed his example, then got them each another water. He needed to hydrate after a session like that. "I work at night." He sat in one of the old wooden chairs. "Have you been watching me? Have you been passing by my place each night to check up on me? Or is it something else?"

Terrance swallowed. "I drive by here every night to make sure you're okay. Usually the lights are off but your car is parked in its spot. Then I go by that damned hotel to see if Frank's car has turned up again. It hasn't. Tonight your lights were on and I heard the roar of the furnace, and I wondered what you were working on."

"You scared me. I thought you might have been Frank." He smiled. "But then if it was, I'd at least have had a weapon. Still, you helped me a lot. I could have done what I needed to, but it would have been difficult and taken a lot longer."

"Is that for your booth at the fair?" Terrance asked.

"If I get in. I still haven't heard. I suppose no news is good news." He got up. "Can I get you something to eat? It's late, but…."

"I'm fine." Terrance finished his second water. His shirt clung to his skin, every muscle outlined in the light blue fabric. "But if you need something to eat…?"

Ashton didn't, and he absently shook his head, gaze glued to the dark skin that peeked through the now partially translucent fabric. Damn, Terrance was stunning. "Are you always up and about at this hour?"

"Sometimes. The bar closes late, and after all these years, it's become second nature. The hard part is when I need to get up for an early shift."

"Or fishing," Ashton teased. "I had to peel myself out of bed that morning. It's way too hot to work during the day and only bearable at night, so I sleep late most of the time and work after dark. It helps some and allows me to open the doors and let the heat escape."

"That makes sense. But I didn't see you working the last few days."

Ashton threw away the water bottles and grabbed a Gatorade. He drank half of that down as well. He hadn't realized how thirsty he was until he began drinking. "I was designing the piece. I don't generally just go into the studio. It does happen, but usually I plan the piece ahead of time. Tonight I finished the base of the vase, and tomorrow I'm going to make the stylized flowers that will decorate the outside. Then I'll put them all together with a special adhesive that chemically bonds with the glass.

"Will the flowers have color?"

"No." He shook his head. "If this works the way I'm hoping, the color will come when the light shines through the prisms of glass that will make up the petals. Most vases are for putting flowers in, but this one, the flowers will be on the outside. If it works, it will be an art piece. If not, it will be a pretty piece of glass and I'll have to figure out what to do with it." He shrugged. Sometimes things worked out as he expected, and other times they didn't. "Are we still on for Sunday?" He checked the clock and realized it was already Saturday. "I guess tomorrow." He was so tired and stifled a yawn. His skin had cooled and now he shivered a little in his damp clothes.

"Yes. Of course. I'll pick you up here at a little after five, if that's okay. I thought we'd drive into Tampa for the evening." Terrance got up. "I'll see you then."

Ashton saw him to the door and watched as he got in his car. He closed the door once Terrance's taillights made the turn onto the road. He was still a little unsure how he felt about Terrance watching his home. Part of him was flattered that he seemed to care enough to watch over him, but it also seemed like something Frank would do, and that bothered him. He didn't want to think of Terrance the way he thought of Frank, yet there were just enough similarities to make him nervous.

There were also significant differences, and those were why he was going out with him tomorrow night. Ashton locked the door before turning out the lights and going right to the bathroom, where he turned on the shower to wash away the sweat and grime of the studio. He needed to get clean and he needed a chance to think. He hated the reservations and doubts that kept popping into his mind. What he wanted was the chance at a life free from fear and worry. Ashton hoped that kind of dream was possible for him. He guessed the name of the game was caution.

THE CLOUDY day was a blessing. Ashton checked his watch after putting the last flower piece for the vase in the annealer. He closed down his equipment for the night, made sure everything was as it should be, then went inside to shower. When he checked the clock, he wondered where the time went. He had fifteen minutes before Terrance was supposed to show up. He washed quickly and dressed as fast as he could, then hurried to the living room to check out the window before grabbing his shoes and socks.

Ashton had no idea what type of date Terrance had in mind. He wished he had better clothes to wear. Frank had bought him all kinds of expensive things, including silk shirts and designer pants, but he'd left all of that behind. In his bid to get away, he took only what was his and left many of his clothes in the hope that Frank wouldn't figure out that he was gone quite as quickly.

Once he had his shoes on, he checked out the window again and grabbed his keys and wallet, making sure he had everything ready. Then he sat in front of the television.

Ashton checked his watch again. Terrance should have been there a half hour ago. He checked out the window once more and looked at his phone to see if there were any messages. He found nothing and sighed.

Maybe he'd been stood up. That sucked. Terrance had been nice, and Ashton had hoped that he would be different from Frank. But then, maybe not.

Chapter 7

TERRANCE SAT on the wrong side of one of the bridges that had been up for the past fifteen minutes with no sign of movement. The damned thing was stuck, and he was boxed in on both sides. No one was moving. He tried backing up to turn around, but the roundabout way to get onto the key was just as bad as staying where he was.

Terrance reached for his phone to call Ashton, but it was dead. When he opened the console, he remembered that he'd brought the cord inside because his other one had broken.

Alan had asked him to make a run into Bradenton to pick up some supplies for the bar, and he'd expected to be back an hour ago. He had planned to drop the supplies off at the Driftwood and then go right on to Ashton's.

Terrance swore and pounded the steering wheel in frustration as the bridge began to lower. "Finally," he breathed as it continued going down.

The gates lifted and traffic moved forward. He crossed onto the key and continued moving with the long line of traffic, wishing it would speed up. Bypassing the restaurant and bar, he went right to Ashton's, where he hurried out and knocked on the door.

Ashton pulled it open, his eyes a combination of anger and hurt.

"I got caught on the other side of the bridge," Terrance explained quickly. "My phone died, and I didn't have a charger." Ashton definitely deserved an explanation.

"I was starting to think…." Ashton trailed off, and Terrance was well aware of what he was thinking. He disliked it when others were late, so he hated not being on time himself.

"You look really nice," Terrance said, changing the subject. "I know I'm late, but are you ready to go?"

"Let me get my keys and things. I'll just be a sec." He went inside and returned after a moment. Terrance hated that Ashton seemed to have been waiting for him—the things he grabbed were right next to the door. "Ready." Ashton smiled, and Terrance opened the car door for him. "You don't need to do that."

Terrance said nothing, closed the passenger door, and went around to his before sliding into the old seat. Terrance really didn't like this car. He wished he had something nicer. Terrance was taking Ashton out on a date, and his car looked like something he'd used to haul fertilizer. Still, it was what he had.

Terrance pulled out of the parking area, made his delivery at the Driftwood, then headed north toward the bridges, hoping they were operating now.

"What restaurant are we going to?"

"It's a small, out-of-the-way restaurant that I found a little while ago," Terrance offered. "They have wonderful Spanish food and tapas. When I was there, I ate out on the terrace, but as warm as it's been, they have indoor seating too. I asked for a table by one of the windows." He crossed the Sunshine Skyway and drove on into the city.

"But won't that be warm too?" Ashton asked. The air-conditioning in the car strained to keep out the heat. Terrance was really coming to hate this car.

"That's the most wonderful part. One of the restaurant owners is a gardener, and the grounds are a tropical paradise with tons of shade, even a pond and waterfall." He had wanted to take Ashton somewhere special. Terrance had hooked up with a few guys since he'd been down on the key, and a few times he'd wanted to impress them in order to get the dude to drop his pants. Most of the time he took them to the Driftwood or to the Beach House, but that wasn't what he wanted for Ashton. He deserved better, and Terrance wanted to create more of a memory.

He continued driving, shaking his head as he wondered what the hell had happened to him. Back in Detroit, he was tough and feared. Now he had romantic notions about where he wanted to take Ashton on a date.

"Are you all right?" Ashton asked. "You were grinding your teeth."

"I'm fine." He forced his jaw to relax.

Ashton shifted in the seat. "We don't have to go if you don't want to." He touched Terrance's leg, and heat spread instantly. "I don't need to be taken to a fancy place."

"Of course you do, and this is really nice." He wanted this to be special.

"I really don't. Frank used to take me to all kinds of expensive restaurants, and he'd order what he called special food. Usually it was awful and really strange, but it was supposed to be a delicacy, so he'd glare at me until I ate it." Ashton shivered.

"That's awful. I guarantee there will be nothing out of the ordinary here, and you can choose whatever you want yourself." He was really getting pissed off about this asshole Frank. "I promise."

Ashton nodded and left his hand where it was. The heat easily worked its way through Terrance's pants, and he had to force himself to concentrate on the road because Ashton's touch threatened to draw all of his attention. "I'm sorry I keep thinking of Frank. I know you aren't him and that you're just trying to be nice. I was fine until he showed up. I'd really thought he had forgotten about me and had just let me go."

Terrance humphed. "Guys like him never let anyone go. They think they own and control other people. You leaving only made him determined to find you. Some guys just get off on control. They love lording it over other people. Like at those restaurants. It wasn't that he liked the food—it was that he could make you eat it." Terrance had known guys like Frank his entire life. They started out as the bullies on the playground and ended up as the predators who ruined other people's lives.

"How do you know?" Ashton asked.

Terrance wasn't sure how to answer. "Because I've dealt with plenty of guys like that. I've been a bouncer for a number of years. Most of the time there are the guys who just drink too much, but then there are the real assholes who like to push and see what they can get away with."

Ashton smiled. "What's the craziest thing you've seen?"

Terrance chuckled. "Before I got here, I was working in a club in Detroit and I saw this guy come in. He thought he was the cat's meow. You know the type, swagger, great looks, gets everyone's attention. At first I noticed him because he was something else, but then I saw that he kept watching one of the guys behind the bar. He worked his way over and the two of them eyed each other up." Terrance paused.

"Were they trying to hook up?" Ashton asked breathily.

Terrance shrugged. "I kept an eye on them as I moved through the club. Then Mr. Hottie sort of disappeared. I looked all over for him and headed to the bar. The bartender was still filling drinks. But something wasn't right. I peered over the bar and there's 'hot and bothered' giving the bartender a blow job right there in the middle of the club from behind the bar... and he was *talented*."

"I see...," Ashton said with a soft chuckle.

"Yeah. See, the bartender needed to keep working so he didn't blow his cover, and it seemed that every time he popped open the drawer on the register, hottie there sucked harder and grabbed some cash. I suspect that when things came to their inevitable conclusion, his pockets would have been full and the club out a lot of money."

Ashton was quiet for a second and then broke out laughing. "That gives a whole new meaning to being sucked dry."

"You better believe it," Terrance told him. "Anyway, I had to take care of both of them. The bartender was fired, and 'hot and bothered' ended up out in the cold." Quite literally. No one stole from them, and Terrance had made an example of him. But there was no need to go into that part of the story. "There were also the numerous times I broke up liaisons in the men's room or guys going out into the alley." The last thing any of them wanted was to draw police attention. "What about you?"

Ashton shrugged. "My funny stories ended a lot quicker than I thought they would. Frank was so serious, and he could suck the fun out of a room like a tornado. It wasn't always like that. When we first met, he took me to a Cubs game. We sat right down the first base line, front row. Some of the players even said hello and waved to us. It was special. People knew him, and they stopped and talked to me. I actually felt important. Frank even got a gallery to take on some of my work." He grew quiet for a few seconds. "I thought he loved me, but he didn't. I was just a guy to have on his arm, an ornament… someone to control and to make him feel important and powerful."

Terrance made a few turns and pulled into the restaurant parking lot. "I'm sorry he did that to you." He had never terrorized anyone like Frank had done to Ashton. He protected his family and their interests, but once the threat was over, he walked away.

"This is where we're eating?" Ashton opened the door, and Terrance stepped out into the middle of a tropical garden paradise with orchids and multicolored flowers lining the path up to the door. The grounds were breathtaking.

"Yes. We have ten minutes before our reservation." They wandered the cobbled paths between the plantings and around to the back of the building.

"It's so pretty. I don't think I've seen so many orchids before." Ashton smiled and took his arm as they walked. "I love this. Growing up, I used to like to make things grow. At Frank's I planted everything and made the yard into a showplace." Ashton turned away. "Why does everything remind me of him? I hate it. The guy was a jerk and a half, and I need to be able to leave him behind."

Terrance knew that leaving shit behind was a lot easier said than done. He and the guys had been in Florida for nearly three years, and it was still difficult not to long for what he had had before. "Let's go inside and have dinner." He didn't know how to help and hoped distraction would work. "And don't worry about anything." If anyone was going to do something wrong at dinner, it was Terrance.

He loved his mother greatly, but growing up, he'd never ever set foot in a fancy restaurant. Heck, a lunch counter had been a huge treat for him. Maybe once a month, his mother would give him enough money that he could go to the movies with the guys and be able to get popcorn. But that hadn't lasted, and he'd quickly learned how to sneak in to watch any movie he wanted. Mama could keep her money, and he got to see the movies. It had been a win-win for everyone except the theater owner. Terrance tended to think of food the same way. When he was hungry, Terrance found a way to get what he wanted, and he ate it quickly to hide any evidence.

The hostess inside the restaurant showed them to their table, and it was just as Terrance had asked for. They sat next to a window overlooking the flowers they had walked through earlier. Terrance hoped Ashton liked it. The hostess handed them both menus and excused herself.

"You order what you want. Each item is small, so we can get things to share. It's what tapas are about," Terrance explained. He had asked Daniel about it before making the reservation. Daniel had smiled and told him everything he needed to know.

"I've had it before. Frank used to like a place in Chicago, except I never got to choose anything," Ashton said darkly.

"Get anything you want. I like the sausages and the potatoes. They're really good. They also have bread and croquettes. They're supposed to be really good too." He wanted until the server took their drink orders before telling him what he wanted. Ashton added a few dishes of his own, and soon their feast arrived. Dishes came out when they were ready, one or two at a time, and they split them, with Ashton smiling at each new item.

"This is so good," Ashton said as he finished the last of a green bean dish that had been amazing.

"We can get more." Terrance intended to order another portion as the server approached with their croquettes. Ashton nodded and turned toward the server, but his fork caught the edge of his plate and sailed through the air before tinging to the floor and sliding under a neighboring table.

Terrance smiled and was about to ask for a fresh one when he noticed that Ashton had gone still, his pupils wide and filled with fear. Then he rubbed his wrist and slipped his arms under the table. Terrance wasn't sure Ashton even realized he was doing it. Shit and damn, what had that ex of his done to him? "It's okay," Terrance said and requested a new fork for him.

It took Ashton a few seconds to relax, and Terrance did his best to pretend he hadn't seen his reaction. Whatever was going on, color had risen in Ashton's cheeks, so Terrance simply offered him some of the croquettes and then took one himself. "These are wonderful."

Ashton nodded. "I'm sorry." He drank his water and sat back in the chair. "Frank would punish me if I did something like that. He always said I was way too clumsy. That only made me more nervous around him, and I tended to drop things. I work with molten glass that's hundreds of degrees and I have no problem. I don't drop things in the studio and can control a substance that can burn or kill. But with Frank I couldn't make it through a meal without something ending up on the floor." He rubbed his wrists once again, and Terrance got a pretty good idea of the kind of punishment Frank had inflicted. The thought of him hurting Ashton made his blood boil even more.

"Let's talk about something else," Terrance offered, and Ashton sighed and nodded. "What sort of pieces are you putting together? Have you heard about your art fair application?"

"I have this idea for a piece. It's a floriform light. Not a lampshade but a light itself. I think it will be interesting." His expression lit as his lips turned upward. "I also have this idea for a hanging light fixture." The light that shone in Ashton's eyes was intoxicating as he talked about his work.

"What about the fair?" Terrance asked. He hoped that Ashton had heard something.

"I emailed yesterday to ask, and they said that they were making final selections and that I was still in the running and they would let me know in the next few weeks. That's so exciting. Apparently they have already sent out rejection letters to some they have decided not to include, so I'm hopeful but scared too. I have to have this body of work to sell in the booth, but if they don't accept me, then I'll have to sell that work someplace else. I'm a little nervous about that."

"Don't be. The pieces you have are stunning. I'm sure you can find a gallery that will be willing to take them." He was pretty sure the art pieces were too expensive for the gift shop that Gerome ran, but there had to be places in town. Maybe if Ashton didn't get in, Daniel could ask his family. They traveled in expensive circles and might know someone to help. "Your work will get noticed, and people are going to love it."

Ashton groaned. "That's what I'm worried about. What if Frank and his people recognize me? I want to be able to make a living at what I do, but if I get too good, maybe he'll be able to find me that way. It really sucks being this afraid all the time."

Terrance knew exactly how he felt. "There's nothing to be afraid of here," Terrance told him with a smile.

Some of the tension left Ashton's shoulders as he smiled again. "I know that. But it's taken some time." The server brought more of the beans, and they settled in to finish their dinner.

"When you first came over and got those guys to leave me alone, I thought I had fallen out of the frying pan and into the fire. But then you brought me to the table with the rest of your family. It was so surprising to me. The way the kids and everyone seems to get along. How could I be afraid of someone like that?"

"Just because I'm big doesn't mean I go around beating everyone up," Terrance said. He used his size sometimes to intimidate, but he didn't hurt people. Not since he'd moved to Florida.

"I guess not. But you're still intimidating. You have this look, though."

Terrance tried to seem innocent. "What look?"

"One that says not to cross you. Like you know where the alligators are and that no one will ever find the body."

"O-kay," Terrance said, amused because he'd lost track of the number of times he and the guys had joked about there being gators and no one would find the body if they needed to hide one. It was a running joke.

"Yeah. I saw it that night with those guys. They didn't know what hit them. And then when you smile, all that goes away and you look like this kid who's fifteen years old and just got told his story was the best in the class." Terrance growled. "You don't like anyone to see that part of you."

"I work as a bouncer. Nice guys aren't particularly good at that job. I'm supposed to intimidate. That keeps people on their best behavior."

"You're not a bouncer now. And there isn't anyone here who's going to cause trouble. You've tried to make me comfortable, so you should do the same thing too." Ashton leaned over the table. "Let me see the man you keep hidden under the tough-guy veneer, and I can try to let you see the real me as well." He flashed another of those smiles, and Terrance found himself completely disarmed. The twinkle in Ashton's eyes was completely charming.

"Okay. What do you like to do besides work molten glass?" Terrance asked.

Ashton shook his head. "Nope. What do *you* like to do? Tell me something most people don't know about you." He leaned over the table with a slight grin.

"Like what?" Terrance asked.

"I don't know. Maybe that you like pink ice cream. Or that you spend your nights knitting in front of the television." Ashton gasped dramatically. "I know. You spend your free time making soap in your bathtub."

Terrance gaped at him for two seconds before laughing. "Very funny."

"I can see you bent over the tub, stirring up lavender and God knows what to make some fancy soap." He leaned closer, sniffing. "I think I can smell a hint of it."

Terrance groaned. "I use simple soap with no fancy, froofy crap in it… and you know it." He winked and paused. "Look, you better not tell anyone. But in the evening when I'm watching television…." He glanced around. "Adult coloring books."

Ashton grinned. "How adult are they? Like dirty coloring books with guys with huge…?"

Terence shook his head. "Not *that* kind of adult. God, now I know how your mind works. Not that it's a bad thing." A chuckle escaped before he could stop it. "But you know, those intricate coloring books. I use colored pencils and things." His cheeks heated. He'd never told anyone about them. Terrance kept the books in a drawer in his bedroom in case one of the guys stopped by. That way no one would find them. "They're fun to do, and it passes the time."

"I knew it. Remember when you saw my work…? I knew you had an artistic eye."

Terrance nearly choked on his water. "I do not. I like what I like, but I have no idea how to compose anything. The books I color even have suggested coloring templates on the back, and sometimes I just fill them in with their suggestion. Other times I go on my own." He shrugged. "I don't think I have any real talent. Not like yours." Ashton was not only talented, but incredibly gifted with the way he could not only work the glass but make the pieces stunningly beautiful and eye-catching. A craftsman and an artist, a deadly combination. "I told you my secret, now you tell me yours." He ate the last few bites of dinner and set his fork down, waiting for Ashton to spill the beans.

"Well… a secret." He sighed and grew paler for a moment. "I like to… well… during the summer when I was a kid… sometimes my friends and I would sneak into one of the county pools after dark and go skinny-dipping. We would climb the fence and swim for a few hours. We almost got caught once. I managed to grab my clothes, but my friend Joseph wasn't so lucky. He climbed back over the fence after us and ran bare-assed toward the woods… and kept going. I swear he ran halfway to Kenosha before he stopped. We tried to find him once we'd dressed, but it seemed he'd run all the way home. I heard his mother barely batted an eyelash when he came in buck naked. But she did make him go back the following day to get his clothes." Ashton chuckled softly.

It was Terrance's turned to lean over the table. "Do you still like skinny-dipping?" He kept his voice low and deep, loving the shiver that ran through Ashton. God, that was sexy, adorable, and hot. "I'll take that as a yes."

Ashton glanced around. "Sometimes it's fun to be naughty, but I don't want to go around climbing fences and breaking into pools any longer. I'm too old for that shit." He sat back. "I'm also too old for games. I've had plenty played on me, and I don't like it."

"I see." Terrance wondered at the source of that admission. "Frank?"

Ashton nodded. "He loved to play games, and most of them weren't a great deal of fun. When I told him the story about almost getting caught, he wanted to see if we could reenact the incident." He shivered. "I told him no, and we ended up having a fight about it. But I wasn't going to do it, and that was one of the few times he actually backed down." Once again Terrance noticed that Ashton rubbed his wrist.

"Did he hurt you?"

Ashton tugged his hands under the table once more. Terrance waited, and eventually Ashton put his hands where he could see them. Terrance gently took Ashton's hand, running his finger over the palm and down to the wrist. "What happened?" he asked as the pad of his thumb rubbed rough skin.

"He cut me," Ashton said. "It was one of his games… and the moment I realized I had to get the hell out or I wasn't going to survive. He cut the top of my wrist, and I had to have stitches and bandages for a couple weeks. Frank was nice the entire time, but I knew I had to get the fuck out of there. I didn't have anyone I could ask for help. My friends had all melted away because of Frank, so I planned and started hiding as much cash as I could get my hands on. That part was surprisingly easy because there was a lot of it around the house and Frank seemed to spend it like water a lot of the time."

That comment told Terrance a lot about Frank. Spending a lot of cash and throwing it around was a definite sign of recklessness. Guys like them didn't generally want to draw attention to themselves and their activities. Yet a huge amount of spending, especially today when it was so much easier to follow patterns—even if the money was cash—was taking a big chance.

"So you left just about everything behind and made a run for it," Terrance said.

"Yeah. I took what I could of my equipment and got the hell out of there. It was all I cared about. I hoped I could find somewhere safe where I could start work again and figured a quiet area like this would be a good place to try."

Terrance kept the wince off his face as the irony of the situation slammed into him. Ashton had run away from a mobster and come to Florida to get away, only to run into yet another one. He couldn't help wondering how Ashton would react if he knew the truth. Granted, Terrance and the guys had given up that life for the boring straight and narrow—though come to think of it, given their antics over the past few years, maybe it wasn't boring. They just had longer amounts of time between excitement.

"Sorry. No matter how I try to talk about something else, everything leads back to him. It's like I'm on some roller coaster and I keep returning to the beginning over and over again and can't get the hell off."

Terrance signaled the server and asked for the check. He paid and then stood, with Ashton doing the same.

"I understand if you just want to take me home and go do something else," Ashton said.

"Why? Do you want to go? I had thought that now that the sun is down, we could go take a walk through one of the parks." A low rumble in the distance brought an end to that idea—the weather this time of year could change on a dime. "Maybe we should head back toward the key. If it's better there, we could walk on the beach."

Ashton nodded, and Terrance took his hand. "I'm not boring you to death with all this talk about... you know who?"

"Just relax and don't worry about it." He was doing his best to try to get Ashton to relax. He'd caught a glimpse of Relaxed Ashton for a little while, but as soon as Frank made his reappearance, that door had snapped shut. It was a little frustrating.

They left the restaurant, the air having grown heavier in the time they'd been inside, and by the time they reached the bridge, they were in a downpour. Fortunately it didn't last long, and when they reached the key, the clouds had parted and the sun was setting. Terrance pulled into a park near the waterfront, pointing the front of the car toward the Gulf of Mexico. The storm was now behind them, and the evening seemed more promising. He shut off the engine and got out of the car, waited for Ashton, and then took his hand once again.

"What about the other people?" Ashton asked.

"Like they're going to give me shit," Terrance told him. "Come on."

The sand was damp from the rain, and the waves rolled onto shore in a regular pattern. They walked far enough away to be out of the water as seagulls floated on air currents above. A couple down the beach threw sticks for their dog as it romped on the sand.

"I always wanted a dog," Ashton said. "A good-sized dog like that one. Not too big, but not tiny either. One you can play with and run with." He smiled, and Terrance squeezed his fingers lightly.

"Me too. I could never have one growing up. It wouldn't have been fair to the dog anyway. Our neighborhood was pretty rough, and there were plenty of dogs. Most of them were cooped up in somebody's backyard, barking all day and snarling at anyone who got close." They drew closer, and the dog raced over with a stick in its mouth. He dropped it in front of Ashton, who picked it up and threw it down the beach. The golden-haired dog barked happily and raced off, running back along the beach to its owner.

"My foster father was allergic to animals, so there weren't any allowed in the house. They had friends with dogs, and I used to play with them when we went over, but always outside. I thought of getting a dog a while ago, but I can barely care for myself." He shrugged, and Terrance got the idea that Ashton had been putting his life on hold the same way that Terrance had. Neither of them had been living. Sure, Terrance had his friends, but still, it was like he had been holding his breath for the past few years, waiting for everything to fall apart. Ashton was probably the exact same way.

The sun dipped below the horizon, and the colors against the remaining clouds darkened to oranges and reds. Terrance watched Ashton as the sky continued to lose the light, the shadows lengthening until they began to disappear into their surroundings. "I love the beach at the last of the day," Terrance said softly.

Ashton turned to him, and the waves provided background music as Terrance caressed Ashton's cheek and then drew closer, their gazes locked. He didn't want to go too quickly and scare Ashton, so Terrance paused with his lips an inch from Ashton's, waiting for him to close the distance.

When Ashton did, it was with more force than Terrance expected. Ashton wound his arms around Terrance's neck and kissed hard, taking surprising possession of Terrance's lips. The energy, the need, seared through Terrance's mind until the flowing waves receded to nothing and the sand dropped away. Terrance was floating for a few seconds, a feeling he had never experienced in his entire life. His feet were always planted firmly on the ground and his eyes on everything around him. But at this moment, he was lost and nothing mattered but the way Ashton's lips, touched with a slight salt spray, gave Terrance more pleasure than his most spirited past lover.

"God." He inhaled when Ashton pulled away, his consciousness dropping back to the present. He blinked as though disoriented and smiled at Ashton, sliding his arm around his waist, pulling Ashton closer.

"Yeah…," Ashton breathed in agreement. "Wow."

Terrance didn't move, holding Ashton in his gaze before guiding him off the beach and back toward the car. He didn't want to let him go once they got there and only reluctantly pulled away so Ashton could get inside. Then Terrance slid into his seat behind the wheel and without another word drove Ashton to his place, his left leg bouncing with excitement as he navigated.

"Is this okay?" he asked after pulling in.

As an answer, Ashton got out and hurried around to Terrance's side of the car, where he pulled open the door. Terrance got out, and Ashton stood next to him, holding his arm as he unlocked the door and went inside. Once they were alone inside, Ashton pressed against him, trying to climb him in his excitement.

Terrance was hard as a rock, tugging Ashton to him. Damn, he hadn't expected Ashton to be such a firebrand, but he loved every second. It seemed that once Ashton got past any similarities to his ex, he turned into this ball of energy. Terrance took a step back against the onslaught and ended up against the door, the panels pressing into his back. He held Ashton tighter and returned his impassioned kisses with ones of his own. "Damn, I…," Terrance said as he pulled away for a break to catch his breath.

"What? Is something wrong?" He could already feel Ashton tensing.

"God, no. I wasn't expecting you to be so… forceful." He smiled.

Ashton shrugged. "You thought I'd be shy and demure?" He giggled slightly. "I guess I can see that. But I think I figured out that you're you and that…." He turned away. "Frank would never do anything so artsy as adult coloring books."

Terrance gasped. "You mean to tell me that all this energy, this hotness, is because I told you about the coloring books? Damn… tomorrow I'm going to get twenty more if they turn you on like this."

Ashton patted his chest. "It wasn't the coloring books but the fact that you told me something like that about yourself. Something vulnerable, or at least telling me something that you don't want other people to know." He rested his head against Terrance's chest. "There's nothing wrong with coloring or anything artistic."

"I know. But the guys would tease me about it." Damn, that was as much of an admission as the coloring books. He hated being teased. In general, the guys could get away with it, but he hated it and often bit back his words when they did.

"I see." Ashton held him. "I used to be teased a lot. I was a foster kid, and when the others found out, the taunts were fast and cruel. I got used to ignoring them. It was the only way I could get through it. Eventually they moved on and found someone else to vent their cruelty on."

Terrance closed his eyes and held Ashton to him. Growing up, he would have been one of the kids doing the picking, the taunting. That way no one dared get on *his* case. Not if they knew what was good for them. "This is the strangest conversation to be having here at the door, and one I wouldn't have suspected we'd be having just a few minutes ago."

"Maybe. But maybe sometimes it's good to have a few minutes of breathing time." Ashton stroked his fingers over Terrance's smooth cheek. "Come on." He took Terrance by the hand. "Which way?"

"Are you sure this is what you want?" Terrance had never asked a question like that before. The guys he was with were all after one thing, and Terrance had been more than happy to oblige. But this seemed different—*Ashton* was different.

He received a nod and a smile. "I know I seem kind of helpless and afraid, but I'm not usually like that. I'm stronger than I think I am. I got away from Frank, and that took guts." He took a deep breath. But…." Ashton stopped. "I know what I want. It's been a while since I was with anyone, but I'm not a child."

"No, you're not," Terrance agreed. "But you don't have to do this just because you think you have to or to prove something." He tugged Ashton into his arms. "I'm not trying to talk you out of anything. Lord knows…." He wiped Ashton's blond hair out of his eyes as he swallowed, trying to get rid of the dryness that had taken over his throat. "Every time I see you, I want you. But that doesn't mean I should act on it."

"Why not? I may work with glass, but I'm not fragile."

"No. I don't think you are. But that doesn't mean that we need to rush into the bedroom. Not if you aren't ready." This conversation was becoming more unbelievable by the second. Why in the hell was he hesitating around something that Ashton clearly wanted… something he had thought about at all hours of the day and night? Here it was being offered, and he was resisting. It didn't make any sense.

Ashton took a step back, opening the door to his bedroom. Terrance snapped his mouth shut and followed him inside, then shut out the rest of the world. He had already gotten a hint that Ashton was adventurous, but the fact that he pushed Terrance to the side of the bed, got him sitting, and then backed away, swaying his hips to some inaudible music, told him even more.

"What are you doing?" Terrance asked.

Ashton stopped. "I'm doing a little tease. You know."

Terrance growled and pulled Ashton right in front of him. "How about I tease you for a while." He lifted Ashton off his feet and manhandled him onto the bed. "Now you stay there, and I'll do all the teasing you can stand." He slipped his hand under Ashton's shirt, smooth skin flowing under his touch. Damn, he was hot and rippling with energy. Terrance adored the feeling, letting his fingers roam until they encountered a small nipple. He flicked the bud, and Ashton hissed softly, arching into the sensation. That was so hot, and he did it again and again until Ashton squirmed beneath him.

"Ter… rance," Ashton whimpered just before Terrance tugged the T-shirt off of him, then pressed him back down on the bed. He was pale and smooth, with little pink nipples that stood at attention as Terrance rubbed them. From the way Ashton whimpered, they were sensitive. "Stop teasing. It's not fair."

Terrance leaned close. "It's only mean if I don't let you tease in return." Ashton shivered as Terrance sucked right behind his ear. This wasn't one of those control situations. He just wanted to short-circuit Ashton's mind and make him forget his own name.

"Do you want me to hold the headboard?" Ashton asked.

Terrance paused. "Is that the kind of thing you like?" He hadn't seen that coming.

Ashton shrugged and then shook his head.

Terrance didn't want to ask if Frank liked that sort of thing. He got an idea of what their relationship had been like. "Then touch all you want." He met Ashton's gaze. "I want to feel your hands on me, and I want to delight you. Whatever your experience was, I don't want to control you. Be happy, laugh, talk—the dirtier the better. Whatever makes you happy." God, the sudden fear in Ashton's eyes sent a stab of pain through him. Sex and fear should not be companions.

When Ashton smiled, Terrance leaned closer once again, letting his hands roam over his smooth skin. Then Terrance paused and sat back, pulling his shirt off over his head. He took Ashton's hands in his and placed them against his skin. Ashton pulled him closer, his studio-rough hands a delight against Terrance's chest. There was something extra special about being under Ashton's work-roughened hands, like he was part of Ashton's art in some way. He groaned softly, and Ashton sat up, stroking harder.

"Do you like that? Frank always said my hands were too scratchy." Ashton snapped his lips closed. "Sorry."

"Frank was a complete fool. Your hands are sexy." He took them in both of his and lightly kissed his fingertips. "They're part of you, and that makes them special. How about you stop worrying about what fuckin' Frank wanted and just relax?" Ashton didn't move. "Look, you and I don't have to do anything tonight." He sighed and shifted so he sat next to Ashton on the bed. "We will have plenty of time to take things further. But you aren't ready. I can see Frank in your eyes and feel his presence in the room, and that isn't good for you." He didn't let go of Ashton's hands because he wanted to stay in close contact with him.

"But—" Ashton began softly.

"No. It's okay. Don't feel bad for a second. It's okay if you aren't ready and need a chance to work through your feelings." He didn't know exactly what those were, but Ashton had issues. Terrance wasn't going to pressure him into something he wasn't ready for.

"Okay… I guess." His cheeks reddened.

Terrance climbed off the bed and pulled his shirt back on. He handed Ashton his before guiding him out to the living room to find a movie.

"Do you want me to go?"

"No." Terrance patted the sofa next to him. "I have a number of movies, and you can choose what you want to watch." He figured that just spending some time together might help Ashton become more comfortable. He reached to the table and pulled out the single drawer to show Ashton what he had. There were plenty of action movies, but Ashton found a copy of *Love, Simon* that Daniel had given him as a kind of joke for Christmas. He'd said at the time that he thought Terrance needed a little romance. Terrance had tucked the Blu-Ray disc into the drawer unopened, but he put it in the player for Ashton.

"Have you seen it?" Ashton asked. "I wanted to but never got the chance."

Terrance shrugged and settled on the sofa, pressed Play on the remote, and waited for Ashton to get comfortable.

The movie started as the air-conditioning kicked in, and within seconds Ashton leaned against him. Terrance extended his arm around him, and they sat quietly as the movie played.

By the time Simon was being manipulated through his coming-out angst, Ashton was more relaxed, and Terrance had him in his arms, holding him as they watched.

"Do you want something to drink?" The movie was interesting but not really his thing. He had nothing in common with any of these kids and their families. A suburban life was about as far from Terrance's experience as the moon.

"Thank you," Ashton said quietly, yawning and blinking as he sat up. Terrance retrieved a couple beers from the refrigerator and handed one to Ashton as he sat back down. "God, I'd give anything to have had the kind of problems these kids had."

"Did people know you were gay in high school?" Terrance asked.

"They might have suspected, but I didn't come out or anything. And I didn't go to any school like that one. I did graduate high school, though. My foster parents were big on education and said that it was my only chance to have a better life. I struggled in school, and

Mom spent many hours at the kitchen table helping me with homework. Dad read a lot, and he helped me with writing and things like that." Ashton sighed. "I miss them so much sometimes. They cared about me." He twisted off the top of the beer and took a long drag on the bottle. "What about you?"

"My mother told all three of us that if we didn't graduate from high school, she'd beat us black and blue. She wasn't very big, but none of us messed with her. So all three of us finished school. It may seem dumb, but Mama knew we'd all drop out if we thought we could get away with it." Terrance sipped his beer. "I can still see her standing in the kitchen, a rolling pin bouncing in her hand. She was one strong woman. And I miss her too."

Ashton set his bottle on the table, turned, and hugged him. Neither of them said a word. Terrance held Ashton in return and closed his eyes. He never thought much about his feelings about his mom, but sitting with Ashton, he understood his loss as his own washed over him. Terrance wasn't going to cry. He was supposed to be strong, and he was damned well going to stay that way. But in the darkness, there was no one to see, and maybe a tear did escape, but he wiped his eyes and sighed softly. "Do you want to watch the rest of the movie?" He hoped his damned voice didn't break as he reached for the remote and started the movie once again. Not that he paid much attention to it.

Ashton had settled in, and Terrance basically ignored the rest of the movie, his focus centered on Ashton. Eventually Ashton pulled away to grab his beer, and Terrance ignored the small wet spot on his shirt. He hated the fact that Ashton had been crying, though he fully understood.

When the movie reached its happy ending and the boys kissed on the Ferris wheel, Ashton sat up and put some distance between them. "I should go on home."

Terrance had finished his beer and switched to water a while earlier. "I can take you." He shifted himself, getting his legs working and gathering his wallet and keys. Then he locked the apartment and opened the car and drove to Ashton's.

Terrance didn't let on that he was looking around the place for anyone hanging around just in case Ashton was being watched. It seemed safe, and he got out to see Ashton to his door. "I had a good time, though it was different from what I expected."

Ashton nodded, hanging his head slightly. "I'm sorry about that. I guess I thought I was over him, but then he showed up, and it threw me. I thought I could move on, and then…."

Terrance lightly touched Ashton under his chin to lift his gaze. "Nothing to be sorry for. I like you, and that isn't just because I was looking forward to taking you to bed. You're interesting and really talented and fun to talk to. And there's no hurry. You and I have plenty of time." He leaned closer and kissed him. "I'll call you, and we can go out again when I have a day off and it works for you." He smiled and backed away, waiting while Ashton went inside, before returning to his apartment.

Once he was alone inside, he pulled the coloring books out of his nightstand, took them to the living room, and settled in to try to keep his mind occupied. But it returned to Ashton again and again and refused to settle.

Chapter 8

ASHTON SPENT as much time in the studio as possible. Long hours working with glass were some of the happiest times he could think of. He wanted to get three additional pieces completed in case he was admitted to the show. Ashton knew he had his hopes up about getting in, and had gone as far as to send pictures of the additional pieces he wanted to include.

He closed the annealer door and turned off the rest of the equipment. The room grew quiet, and he sighed, pulled off his protective equipment, and set it aside. His clothes were plastered to his skin, and he pulled them away just to get the air moving around his body.

Stepping out of the studio, he locked the door and turned, nearly knocking into Terrance. "Hi.... Did I forget something?" He smiled and tried to remember if they had set up a date and he had forgotten. The past few days he had been so focused on work, he hadn't had a chance to think about anything else.

"No. I sent a few messages and you didn't respond, so on my way home from work, I passed by and thought I might have heard you working." Terrance stepped back, and Ashton hurried toward his apartment with Terrance behind him. They both breathed easier once they got inside the air-conditioning.

Ashton grabbed a couple bottles of water and drank a whole one and half of the second before remembering to offer some to Terrance.

"I found your mail in the box," Terrance said and handed it to him.

Ashton thumbed through it and stopped at the one from the arts guild. He paused and then pulled it open, unfolding the letter is his quivering hand. He blinked and read the letter again to make sure he'd read it right. Ashton lifted his gaze from the letter, smiling. "They want to include me in the fair. It says I have to bring all my own shelving as well as a tent if I want one." He should have thought about all that, but it hadn't occurred to him until now. "I don't have any of that stuff."

"The Driftwood has one of those collapsible canopies. We can check to see if they'll let you use it, and maybe some shelves for the back or side of the booth and a few pedestals for your showpieces. The hardware store had some displays made out of Plexiglas that they used a couple of years ago to display some of that flexible coating spray. They got them in as part of the promotion, and they've been in the back gathering dust ever since. We could build wide bases for them to make then sturdy, and I bet we could light them from inside and up into your pieces. That might be really cool." Terrance was almost as excited as Ashton.

"What about the chandelier?" Ashton mused.

"We'll need to build a frame to suspend it from and then light it. I could do that pretty easily." He rubbed his chin as he thought. "We can also make some light boxes to put under the other pieces to make them glow if you want. Maybe we could sell the boxes at an additional cost or something."

"Wow. You seem to have a lot of ideas. Do you go to art shows?"

Terrance snorted. "Are you kidding? I work a lot and usually spend my extra time with the guys. Do we really seem like the art fair kind of guys?" He seemed to realize what he'd said and grew quiet.

Ashton dropped his smile. He knew what Terrance meant, but seeing his discomfort was kind of rewarding even if was mean to think it. But flustered was a good look on the huge man.

"Not that there's anything wrong with art fairs and things like that, but none of us really have been to that sort of thing before." Man, he really stuck his foot in his mouth that time.

"And what kind of people go to art fairs?" Ashton put his hands on his hips, waiting for Terrance's reaction.

Terrance shrugged. "Ones with a lot more money than I have, that's for sure. I expect that the things at those kinds of places are rather expensive, and while I might have some disposable income at the moment, I can't afford to spend thousands of dollars on things to hang on the wall."

Ashton could understand that. He didn't have any extra money either and had been living on what he had been able to scrounge and take with him.

But he had learned that he was better off than a lot of people. Ashton had gotten away and was building something of a life on his own, but damn, it had been hard getting used to not having some of the nicer things. The furniture in his tiny apartment wasn't his. It came with the place. And while he'd bought a few things, his place, like his life, felt a lot like it belonged to someone else—like he was only borrowing it. Ashton hated that feeling, but maybe from what Terrance had told him, he might understand that.

"I guess what I'm trying to say and not swallow my foot at the same time is that there weren't a lot of art shows in my part of Detroit." Ashton liked that Terrance thought enough to try to explain.

"I get that, and I like your ideas. I was thinking that I could either get or make some raw wood shelves… out of sawn logs with all the great grain. It would be something natural and would go along with the floriform pieces. I wanted to include some handmade pieces that were more affordable as well as the individual art pieces. That way people who don't have a ton of money could still have something handmade to take home. But I want to display them in a special way and not on a tree or something."

Terrance rubbed the back of his neck. "How about a metal sculpture? Maybe not a wood tree, but a sculptural tree that could sit on one of the pedestals. Though I'm not sure how to make something like that, but maybe one of the guys could. Over the years, I've learned there isn't much that we couldn't do among the group of us."

"That would be awesome if…." Ashton trailed off as Terrance's phone chimed. He pulled it out of his pocket and swore softly. Then he typed and swore some more at the answer. "What is it?" Terrance's expression told him it wasn't good news, and a chill settled over him.

"Richard. He said that Frank is back in town and he has someone along with him." Terrance seemed both angry and afraid, with the fear lasting but a second before it was gone. "He says to come to his and Daniel's condo in an hour and he'll meet us there."

"I should just get out of here. If Frank has come back, then he's truly found some way to track me here, and he isn't going to just let me go." Ashton paused a second to try to think. "Maybe I can talk to him and convince him that I'm not interested in him and that I want a life of my own." Even as he uttered the words, he knew they were completely futile. If Frank had followed him here, then he wanted something… and it sure as hell wasn't to wish Ashton well and let him go on his way.

"Do you really think he'll be at all reasonable?" Terrance asked.

Ashton shook his head. Reasonableness wasn't one of Frank's strong points. Selfishness, control, willfulness, and a good case of stubborn ass were what the man was made of.

"No." He turned and was already looking through the small apartment, cataloging what was his and what he needed to leave behind. It didn't take him but a few minutes to remember that other than his clothes and a few pieces in the bedroom, the rest belonged to the landlord. Mostly he needed to pack up his work and his tools.

Shit, he had pieces in the annealer, and all the equipment was too hot to do anything with. The thought of leaving it all behind and starting over from scratch was too much to deal with. Starting in a new place was one thing, but leaving everything was quite another. "I have to get out of here."

Terrance's expression hardened. "What you need to do is get yourself something else to drink, have a shower, and then we'll go to Richard's in an hour to see what he has to say." He sighed, and while Ashton knew he was right, it still didn't ease any of his discomfort. If Frank found him, there was a good chance that the nearby alligators would be well fed and that Ashton would never be seen by anyone ever again. As hard as it was for him, he needed to trust Terrance, at least for now, and see if there was any chance that he could ever feel safe again.

TERRANCE STAYED with him, but that didn't diminish Ashton's nerves, at least not at first. He did like the company, and eventually Terrance tugged him onto the sofa and encircled him in his strong arms. Terrance didn't say a word; he just held him. Ashton could almost feel Terrance's anxiety, but he didn't know where it came from. Still, it was nice having someone concerned about him, even if he didn't know why Terrance seemed so intent on keeping him safe.

Ashton knew Terrance liked him, but that alone didn't account for the way he acted. There had to be something else behind it, and Ashton was more than a little curious about what it was. Terrance seemed to understand a lot of Ashton's life and what he was feeling. Maybe Terrance had experienced something similar to him. He wondered if there wasn't an ex-boyfriend out there who had made Terrance feel small and useless. Ashton stifled a snort at the idea. He was willing to bet that Terrance had never felt small in his whole life. No, there was something else going on with him, and it drew Ashton's curiosity.

"We should go and see what Richard's found out," Terrance said softly.

Ashton didn't want to move. As long as Terrance held him, he felt like nothing bad could get to him. Why that was true, he had no idea, but Terrance was strong and yet gentle, gruff sometimes and yet caring. His outside said "don't fuck with me," and yet on the inside he was intense and loyal. Ashton wondered if he would ever get used to the dichotomy of this man.

"Okay," he agreed, but he stayed where he was.

Terrance chuckled. "You need to get up."

"I don't want to." He nestled closer, and Terrance guided his face upward and met his lips with a kiss. "Now I really don't want to." That simple touch sent a wave of heat running through him, and the doubt and reticence from the other night seemed very far away. "If I go there, then I have to face what's wrong. If I stay here with you, the crap that's waiting for me can stay out there for a little while longer." That was probably a stupid attitude, but he was so tired of looking over his shoulder.

"Maybe, but it doesn't change any of the facts. If Frank is here, then we need to figure out what we're going to do."

His choice of words wasn't lost on Ashton. "We?"

"Yes. Now we should go."

Ashton sat up and Terrance did the same. They got their things together and left the apartment. As

Terrance drove toward the condo where Richard and Daniel lived, Ashton settled low in the seat, worrying the entire time about what awaited him.

"COME ON in," Daniel said without the brightness that Ashton usually associated with him. He always seemed happy. "The boys are over at Tucker's for the evening." He motioned to the living room, where a tray of snacks and drinks rested on the coffee table. Daniel gave Terrance a hug and then hurried into the kitchen. When he returned, he set a steaming dish of some sort of dip on the table next to the tortilla chips. It smelled of onions and maybe cheese of some type. Not that it mattered. Ashton's stomach rumbled and he took a small bite, careful because it was still really hot.

"Frank is back in town. Alan told me when I came in this morning that he had to ask him to leave the bar yesterday. Alan isn't a fan of the asshole, and he didn't appreciate him bothering all of his patrons," Richard reported, disappointment in his voice.

Daniel humphed. "It seems our diversion worked for a while."

"Yeah, it did." Richard patted Daniel on the shoulder. "The real issue is that Alan said someone was with him, and I checked the security video." Daniel turned his computer screen, and mumbled under his breath.

"Who is that?" Ashton asked, turning to Terrance.

"He's…," Terrance began and then cut himself off before grabbing a beer and taking a drink. "That is Carlo. He's my version of Frank."

Richard frowned for a second and then schooled his expression. "That's the asshole of the century?" He turned to Ashton. "They had a fling of sorts a number of years ago that ended terribly." Sometimes the three of them reminded Ashton of little boys with how they picked on one another, and yet stood firm when there was trouble.

"What are we going to do? None of us wants any trouble from the likes of him," Terrance warned.

Gerome scoffed. "Yeah, that's true. But at least you had the good sense to keep your liaisons with that weasel to yourself."

"Okay, then let me rephrase that. What are the two of you going to do about them?" It was clear that they all wanted both Carlo and Frank as far away from here as they could get. But what made Ashton curious was why Terrance wanted to stay out of sight just as much as he did. It didn't really make a lot of sense, but Ashton kept his curiosity to himself. He figured if he watched, listened, and went along, the guys would be more likely to let clues slip.

"We aren't sure," Gerome said, taking a bite of the dip. "We could confront them, but it wouldn't do us much good. It isn't like these guys are going to be frightened away." He turned to Daniel. "Can we lay another trail? Though I doubt that's going to work for long. They returned here for a reason, and we need to figure out what it is." Gerome was nervous, his gaze fluttering around the room. Richard seemed keyed up as well. They had something to lose. Whatever was going on, it was more than an ex-boyfriend situation.

"I'll give that a try," Richard said. "I could be wrong, but if they've been to the Driftwood twice, they'll be back again. I'll try to see what I can figure out, especially if the drinks are free and they keep coming."

"And Frank?" Ashton asked. "He doesn't drink much, and he won't imbibe enough to feel out of control." It was one of the things that always scared him the most. Frank always stayed in control, so his bad behavior could never be chalked up to alcohol. It was all him, all the time.

"Then I'll have to see what I can do," Richard said. Ashton wondered what he had in mind. The others seemed to understand, and no one inquired further.

"That's one course of action. I'll see what I can find out electronically." Daniel sat next to Richard and took a bite of his dip.

Ashton tried a little more, but he wasn't very hungry. "Is that all we can do? I mean, can't we call the police and ask them for help?"

Daniel leaned forward. "What are they going to do? Frank and Carlo haven't done anything here. There's limited police presence. Though I can see if there are any outstanding warrants. If there are, I could tip off the police and get them to take some action. Otherwise our hands are tied behind our backs as far as the authorities are concerned."

Terrance shrugged. "The authorities aren't going to be able to do much."

"Why? Frank has a record. I know he does. He spent a night in jail six months before I left." Ashton wasn't sure what he could do to help.

"Unless there's a warrant, there isn't much the police can do."

"I'll see what I can find out," Daniel said, going to his computer.

Ashton followed him with his gaze. "How will he know?"

Terrance lightly patted Ashton's knee. "Daniel has ways of finding out things."

Ashton rolled his eyes. "Well, if that isn't enigmatic and avoiding the question." He was getting tired of people keeping secrets. It might be for his own protection, but he deserved to know what was happening. He turned to Terrance, who shrugged and shook his head. Ashton looked at each of the others, but they didn't seem to be forthcoming either.

Finally Daniel turned in his chair. "I have a gift with electronics," he said. "They sing to me." He smiled and turned back to the computer, typing away.

"Are you a hacker?" Ashton asked.

"I used to be, okay? Now I stay on the straight and narrow for the most part. But I do occasional favors for friends and people who deserve it." Daniel gave him a quick smile. "Don't worry about it. Whatever I'm doing is for your protection."

"But why?" Ashton didn't really know them. It wasn't like they owed him anything, and they hadn't been friends with him for years. "Why stick your necks out for me?"

Terrance, Gerome, and Richard all looked at each other. Daniel huffed and rolled his eyes dramatically. "Sometimes you three can be real dicks, you know that?" He scowled at them before softening his gaze. "Because it's the right thing to do." If Daniel had been closer, he might have whapped each of the other three on the back of the head. Sometimes it was funny how the smaller guy commanded the others. "If these two are causing trouble, then that means that all of us are going to end up paying for it. This is a small community out here, and trouble—when it rears its head—seems to gravitate to the Driftwood. It's the place on the main drag where everyone congregates. All of us want to keep things peaceful and safe." He turned back to the computer and went to work, while the rest of the guys seemed more intent on either eating or holding one of those silent conversations that only people who had known each other for years seemed to be able to have.

Ashton took another bite. The dip was amazing, but his stomach roiled and he couldn't eat any more. What in the heck was he getting himself in the middle of? Frank had shown up again with someone they said was Terrance's ex. Ashton was willing to believe that, but he didn't think it was the whole truth, and that was what scared him. Should he just keep his mouth shut or ask what was really going on?

In the end, he thought it best to continue down the path he had already chosen and keep quiet and listen. But damn, sometimes that was nearly impossible.

"You could just scare them away?" Ashton offered. "Those biker guys I encountered that first night I met Terrance might do the trick." Things were getting too anxious and the room stuffy and close as everyone listened to Daniel type. "Get those guys to scare them away." Of course he was joking.

"I don't think that will work," Terrance said. "Because they aren't here."

"Aha," Daniel said. "Carlo is wanted in Ohio and Michigan. There are warrants for him in both states." He picked up the phone and made a call to the local police to explain whom he'd seen. "Yes, I'm sure it's him, and he's been making trouble in the area. He was last seen at the Driftwood."

"Beachcomber," Gerome said with his mouth full. Fortunately he didn't spray food everywhere as he talked.

"He's staying at the Beachcomber… and please be careful. I think I saw this guy on *America's Most Wanted*." Daniel hung up and grinned. "That should take care of Frank's little companion, and I bet that once the police are involved, old Frankie Boy will head for the hills." He grinned, but there was no humor in it.

"Does Frank have a record?" Ashton asked.

"I was just looking for warrants, and there are none outstanding." He shrugged. "I wish we could find out what these guys know and what they're after. Is it just a coincidence that Carlo is here? Or is he looking for something in particular?"

Richard stood up. "I'm going to head back to the Driftwood and see if there's anything I can learn there." He stood and leaned over Daniel, and the two of them shared a kiss. "I'll text if anything happens." He stroked Daniel's cheek gently, the motion so intimate and loving. It sent an ache through Ashton, and he couldn't help looking at Terrance, who smiled and patted his hand. "I know it's a long shot, but the Driftwood is also information central. If there's any gossip, I'll hear it, and if Frank returns, I'll do my best to get what I can out of him." He left.

Ashton wished to hell that there was something he could do. He felt helpless letting others fight his battles for him.

"Okay, what else?" Terrance asked.

"Nothing," Gerome pronounced. "Both of you need to stay the heck out of sight. If they don't find any trace, they'll give up and move on. What we need to do is wait them out, and that means you lay low."

Ashton groaned. "You sound like one of those guys in a mobster movie."

"It's true," Gerome added. "When do you need to work at the hardware store?"

"Saturday. I have tomorrow off." Terrance seemed resigned to what Gerome was telling him.

"Good. I suggest you and Ashton here find somewhere comfortable and spend the next couple of days together. Let Richard and me do the heavy lifting so we can see what's going on and figure out a way forward." He ate some more chips, and Ashton wondered how he could be so calm about all this. "Work on some more of those amazing pieces of yours," Gerome added. "We've sold four of the ones we've brought in, and we need some more to replace the stock. As I suspected, the tourists and even locals have loved them."

Ashton grinned widely. "Really?"

"Yeah." He flipped through his phone. "I'll forward you the order, but we have some special requests from a few customers as well as another order for the store. That should keep you busy for a while. Terrance should be able to help you. He's pretty good with his hands." Gerome smirked.

Terrance growled. "And you have a smart mouth. It's too bad Mama and her bar of soap are no longer with us." He sneered, but Gerome laughed it off.

"Dude. She was something. None of us dared swear around her or she'd threaten us with that bar of Ivory." He chuckled, but there was sadness in both Gerome's and Terrance's eyes, and it lingered until Gerome cleared his throat. "Just stay out of sight, whatever you do."

"I COULD try to help you in the studio," Terrance offered after they left Daniel and Richard's.

Daniel had plied them with enough food once Ashton's stomach settled that he was fuller than he could remember being in a long time.

Ashton had been planning to work on something else, but now he had orders and needed to get the work done. The money would be good too. "Are you sure? It's going to be really hot." He nudged Terrance with his shoulder. "Especially with you in the studio." Okay, so he wasn't really subtle. It was something they could do and stay out of sight. Hours sitting at home in front of the television, watching the hands of the clock go around, didn't hold much interest.

"Of course. I don't know much about glass, but I can help you like I did before." They pulled into the driveway, and Terrance parked behind the shrubs that ringed the yard by the road. At least they would be out of direct sight from anyone driving by.

The sun was setting as they went into the studio. Ashton turned on his equipment and let it heat up while he got the rest of his supplies together, adding the specific clear glass he wanted to use. The ovens would take time to come up to temperature, as would the furnace.

"What can I do to help?"

Ashton was used to doing things on his own, so he finished up and sat down at one of the stools. "Everything is ready. We just need to wait for the heat to do its job. In the meantime, I can draw up some ideas."

"How can you work in this heat all the time?" Terrance asked.

Ashton opened one of the windows on the side of the studio, away from the street. "You get used to it, I guess. Even when it's cold out, the studio is warm. The furnace and the annealer put out heat, and there's little you can do about it other than choose something

different as a living, and I don't think I could do that."
He checked the glass, which was coming along. It
would probably be another fifteen minutes before it
was the right temperature.

"What are you going to make?" Terrance drew
closer, peering over into the well of melting glass at the
base of the furnace.

Ashton closed the door to keep the heat inside.
"The items that Gerome wanted for the store. It will
take a couple of hours to make them. They aren't hard
to do, and they're things I've made in the past." It
would still take all his concentration, because any time
your attention wandered in the studio was a chance that
you could get injured. "You need to watch and be cau-
tious. Your help will be appreciated, but you can stay
out of the way if you want." Working with material that
was hundreds of degrees wasn't for everyone, and he
didn't want Terrance to feel obligated.

"I helped before."

"Then put on this protective equipment. I don't
want you to get burned." It had happened to him and
would happen again, but the aprons and gloves had
saved him from more accidents than he could list. He
handed Terrance the items he needed. The apron was a
little small on him, but it was the best he could do. Once
he was set, Ashton put his own gear on and checked the
furnace before getting to work.

Slow and steady, methodically, he made the pieces he needed and got them into the annealer. It was like
an oven in the studio, but the movements were familiar,
and with Terrance's help, he finished three of the pieces
before so much sweat ran down his face that he couldn't
see any longer. At that point he finished his last piece, put
it in the annealer, and set his tools aside.

"Is that it?" Terrance asked. He pulled off his gear, clothes sweated to his skin. Ashton was soaked through, but Terrance looked like he had been caught out in the rain. "I hope so. I think I sweated out a gallon."

"Yeah." He set the equipment to cool down and made sure the annealer was on the correct setting before hanging up the safety equipment and opening the door. They stepped out into the night, and Ashton led the way inside. "Take off your clothes and I'll get them in the washer." He grabbed a couple waters out of the refrigerator. "Drink the whole thing to start with and then we can switch to Gatorade."

"Beer." Terrance downed his water.

"No. Beer is a diuretic, and we need to drink things that will help us retain fluids." He threw away the empty bottles and handed Terrance a Gatorade, turning away while he drank and then began removing his clothes.

"I'm not shy," Terrance told him with a chuckle, and Ashton couldn't help turning around as the planes of Terrance's chest appeared from under his shirt. Ashton's throat went dry and he sipped his drink, unable to turn away even if his mind told him he should. Terrance reached for his belt, unfastened it, and pulled it off. His pants followed. Terrance peeled them off, revealing tree-trunk legs that rippled with muscle.

"You need to drink some more. Your body needs to rehydrate." Ashton gulped some more of the ice berry drink to cover the fact that he couldn't take his eyes off all Terrance's glistening skin or the bulge in his black boxer briefs.

"And you need to get out of your wet clothes." Terrance's voice was husky and deep, filled with desire. Ashton almost turned to see who else was in the room, because that kind of passion couldn't be aimed in his direction. But they were alone, and all Terrance's über-masculine wiles were aimed in his direction.

Terrance stepped closer. "Do you need help?" The smile was hot and disarming at the same time.

Ashton shook his head, pulling off his shirt and kicking his shoes to the side. His socks followed, and then he stood there in his wet jeans, unsure of himself.

Terrance slipped his arms around him, turning Ashton until his back pressed to Terrance's chest. He leaned against him, closing his eyes and letting himself feel for a few seconds. Terrance unsnapped his jeans and pulled them open before sliding them down his hips.

The fabric didn't want to move, and Ashton giggled as Terrance tried harder. Finally, his clingy skin released the fabric and Terrance peeled them down his legs. Ashton danced from foot to foot to get the jeans off and left them in a soggy pile on the floor, then turned to Terrance, who encircled him in his arms. "What now?" Ashton asked.

"We're a soaked mess," Terrance told him. Then he slotted their lips together, and Ashton forgot about sweat and wet clothes, his work, and the fact that he was nearly naked. His attention centered on the heady taste of Terrance's lips and the way they took charge of the kiss. He wasn't forceful, just firm and sexy as hell. A moan filled the room, and Ashton realized it came from him. Winding his arms around Terrance's neck, he held on and pressed into the intensifying kiss.

"Terrance…," Ashton said softly when they broke the kiss. "I need—"

Before he could finish the sentence, Terrance lifted him off the ground, and without thinking about it, Ashton wound his legs around Terrance's waist. Terrance's hands supported Ashton's butt as he walked the short distance to the bedroom.

"Fuck," Terrance groaned as he laid Ashton on the bed. Ashton bounced slightly, and then Terrance climbed on with him, prowling over him like a huge, sleek cat. Ashton couldn't break his connection with Terrance's gold-flecked eyes and drew him closer, kissing him deep as Terrance slipped the last bit of clothing down his hips and off his legs. He shivered in the cool room, but it had nothing to do with the temperature. Terrance's hands left ripples of excitement that raced through his muscles as they glided along his side and then up to his arms, guiding them up over his head, while Terrance's mouth left his and explored his chest. Ashton quivered with excitement as little jolts of energy burst out wherever Terrance touched. A nipple surrounded by wet heat, Terrance's tongue licking down him like a damned lollipop, swirling in his belly button before continuing to blaze a trail. Ashton closed his eyes, repeating over and over… asking, begging Terrance not to stop. "Is this what you want?"

That had to be the dumbest question he had ever heard. "Yeah," he breathed as Terrance took him slowly, sliding his lips over the head of his dick and then moving slowly down until he was buried inside. Ashton lifted his head—he had to see Terrance take him. It was too good to pass up, and holy hell, his cock slid between Terrance's full lips, sliding, retreating… Terrance was taking all of him. What an amazing feeling and sight. He closed his eyes and fell back on his mattress, trying to control himself and losing the battle.

He had fantasized about Terrance for days, ever since he blew it the last time they were together because of his nerves. He was ashamed that had happened, but

Terrance seemed to understand, and now he was thrilled that Terrance seemed to think he had been worth the wait. God knows it had been for him.

As Terrance pulled away, Ashton's head throbbed and he gulped for air.

"What are you doing to me?"

Terrance drew closer, until his lips were inches from Ashton's, his hot breath sliding over Ashton's skin. "I'm going to make you forget your name and scream in passion until you're hoarse." Terrance took possession of his lips, sliding his hand between Ashton's legs, cupping his balls and teasing at his opening.

Ashton spread his legs, whimpering at the overlapping sensations. This was wonderful, making him shake with anticipation. "Terrance, don't tease me."

"Oh, I won't. It isn't teasing if I follow through, and I have every intention of doing exactly what I promised." Terrance kissed him and then backed away briefly before swallowing Ashton down once again.

"Terrance… don't stop." God, he'd beg for this to continue forever.

Terrance took his time, playing Ashton's body like it was a fine instrument and Terrance knew every nuance. Which he did. Ashton had never been driven to such heights before. Terrance seemed to know exactly what he liked and how he wanted to be touched. "I'm…." He was losing control, hips rocking, but Terrance didn't back off for a second. With a final warning, Ashton tipped over the point of no return and tumbled into his mind-numbing release.

Ashton lay still, breathing deeply, floating in his own thoughts before slowly returning to the present. Terrance lay over him, smiling. Ashton put his arms around his neck and tugged him down into a kiss. "You know, if we need to keep out of sight, and if this is how you expect to spend most of that time… I think I could really get used to it."

Terrance hummed softly. "You think so?"

"Yeah." He grinned. "I mean, what a way to spend the time." He hugged Terrance tighter, running his hands down his muscled back. God, Terrance was all bunched power and hard as a rock. "But I think it's only fair that you remove the last of your clothes. It seems I'm at a bit of disadvantage."

"I see." Terrance's weight lifted away, and he stood next to the bed and dropped his boxer briefs before kicking them aside.

"Holy shit," Ashton whispered.

Terrance grinned. "Come with me. We need to get cleaned up." He winked, and Ashton's imagination raced ahead with all of the possibilities.

He slipped off the bed and went to the bathroom, with Terrance right behind him. Ashton started the water in the shower and wondered how they were both going to fit. Terrance figured it out. He stepped under the water first and then tugged Ashton in and pulled the door closed, keeping him in his arms. The water coursed over both of them. Terrance grabbed the soap, lathered his hands, and proceeded to wash him.

Ashton sighed, wetted his hair, and held his head under the water as Terrance stroked his skin. He leaned back against Terrance's chest and let him have his way. Terrance rubbed and washed as Ashton's fervor rose once again. He sighed, and once Terrance's hands stilled, he took his chance and turned around to wash Terrance's back.

They had to move carefully because of the lack of room. Ashton pressed Terrance against the back wall as he washed him. "You like that, don't you?"

Terrance nodded and groaned deeply, the sound resonating off the tile. He was strong and solid. Rubbing his furred chest was like washing sculpted stone, and yet he whimpered softly as Ashton tweaked his nipples and then pressed right to him. Terrance ran his hands down Ashton's back, cupped his butt, and held him closer. "It feels good to be clean."

"Only to be clean?" Ashton asked, and Terrance shimmied his hips slightly. Ashton hissed at the jolt of pleasure, while Terrance did the same.

"Oh no. Being with you has its own pleasures," Terrance whispered, pressing them both back under the water before turning it off. Ashton got out first and grabbed their towels, handing the biggest one to Terrance, who wiped himself down. Ashton forgot what he was supposed to be doing. Terrance was gorgeous even as he dabbed the wetness from his hair, arms flexing with each movement.

"Do you want something to eat?" Ashton hung up the towels and opened the bathroom door. "I have a few snacks in the kitchen. I can get us something."

"Just something to drink," Terrance answered, and Ashton hurried to the refrigerator for two bottles of water before scampering back. "I love watching you like that."

"What? You have a thing with my butt?" He grinned when Terrance nodded. "That's good. It's my best asset." He cocked his eyebrow, and sure enough Terrance groaned at his little joke.

"That's was pretty bad."

"I know. But I do have a small butt, so…." He took Terrance's hand and guided him to the sofa. Sitting down next to him, Ashton leaned against Terrance and turned on the television. What was on wasn't really important. He found an old movie to watch as Terrance's hands slowly wandered over him. There wasn't the urgency from earlier, at least on his part, and Terrance seemed more than willing to be patient. Ashton sighed and held Terrance's hand. "Are you always like this? So willing to wait for what's to come? I would have thought you would be more impatient."

Terrance chuckled. "As a general rule I am. I don't like to wait for anything. But then sometimes, the best things are worth waiting on." He drew Ashton nearer, and Ashton wound his arms around Terrance and rested his head against his bare chest.

"I don't think I've ever been worth waiting for." Frank was always pissed as hell if Ashton left him waiting, even for just a few minutes, though Frank thought nothing of being late by twenty minutes or more and Ashton was just supposed to wait quietly and say nothing. It had been really frustrating, and it had taken him longer than it should have to figure out that Frank didn't really care about Ashton's time. All that mattered was Frank's.

"Hey," Terrance snapped, and Ashton jumped slightly at the tone. "Forget about Frank and the asshole way he treated you. He isn't worth spending your time and energy on. He didn't treat you the way he should have, and that wasn't your fault. It was his. The guy clearly has problems, so don't measure me and everyone else by him." Terrance hugged him tighter for a second. "On second thought, go ahead and compare me to him all you want. It'll make me seem like the stud of the century." Terrance puffed up.

Ashton snorted. He liked it when Terrance tried to be funny. There were times when he could be so serious and intimidating, but his humor was disarming, and when he smiled, he appeared more like a naughty teenager.

"That's a deal." He settled with Terrance and turned toward the television. Not that he really watched the movie, especially once Terrance kissed his shoulder and then moved on to his neck. Ashton stretched to give Terrance room, closing his eyes and whimpering softly at the jolts of delight. He stiffened, wondering what Terrance would do next. He was surprised when Terrance got up off the sofa. Ashton put his arms around Terrance's neck, and he lifted him into his arms, hands supporting his butt once more. When Ashton wound his legs around him, he snapped his hips, Ashton's cock sliding along Terrance's skin. He groaned as Terrance carried him toward the bedroom.

"What about the TV?"

Terrance growled and continued toward into the other room. Ashton forgot all about it as Terrance set him down on the bed and climbed on with him. "Do you have stuff?" Terrance whispered.

Ashton motioned toward the bedside table. Terrance reached for the drawer and pulled it open, found his stash of condoms and lube, and placed them at hand.

Terrance had been so patient, so Ashton expected him to move faster now, but he showed no sign of it, taking his time to prepare him and drive Ashton crazy. He was learning that what he needed to do was lie back and let everything happen at Terrance's frustratingly mind-blowing pace. There was no rushing, no hurry, just pleasure on top of passion, again and again. When Terrance entered him, Ashton groaned and held on tight, looking deep into Terrance's eyes and letting him take him on a trip to ecstasy.

Chapter 9

"WHAT DID you find out?" Terrance asked the following morning. He'd left early after kissing Ashton goodbye and telling him he needed to handle some things at his place. Then he quietly went to his car and out onto the street, where he took a few extra turns to ensure he wasn't being followed or watched.

"I worked until after two and…." Richard schooled his annoyance.

"Sorry," Terrance said, still in his car. "I thought you weren't working last night."

"I stopped in and we were shorthanded, so I ended up staying." Richard sounded like he had just gotten to sleep. "I was going to call you when I woke up. Carlo has been taken into custody by the police. He and

Frank were in the Driftwood last night when the police received a tip. They arrested him there, and he was out of commission. He was more than a little drunk at the time." Richard chuckled. "Anyway, the guy didn't say much when he was drunk, but he talked enough. Carlo was here to try to find someone. He didn't say who, and though I can assume it was you, I'm wondering if he wasn't also here to help Frank find Ashton. It isn't clear. I asked how he knew where to look, and Carlo said that a friend saw their quarry while he was on vacation… or at least he thought so."

"Shit," Terrance swore.

"Yeah. This is getting a little too close for comfort. Fortunately Frank seemed as spooked as we hoped when Carlo was arrested right in front of him. The police checked him out too but didn't take him in. Apparently they played up a line that they had just met each other at the bar and had been talking." Richard, of course, knew that was a load of crap they were feeding the police, but he wouldn't have been able to say anything without arousing suspicion.

"What do we do?" Terrance asked.

Richard seemed to yawn, and Terrance waited. "You need to sit tight. With Carlo out of the picture, it should be safe enough for you to return to normal activity, but we need to be sure he's being transported and will be out of here. They arrested him on outstanding warrants, but if those don't hold up, he could be released. So we wait a little longer to see if he gets transported back. Then we need to take care of Frank, and he's going to be as riled up as a tormented bees' nest. He was pretty pissed last night."

"Okay. We can ask Ashton to stay out of sight for a while longer, but we still have the problem that Frank may be connected back to Detroit." That was the major fear. "Do you think we can scare him off? Guys like that only respond to power and force." Terrance was already thinking of the things he'd like to do to him. Hell, he'd love to scare Frank enough that he wet himself.

Richard paused. "I doubt it. Frank seems like the kind of guy who's been around the block. He was angry that Carlo was arrested, but he kept his cool and didn't cause any trouble or give the police any reason to take him in too." He sighed. "If you were to ask me, I'd say he was a cool cucumber. So scaring him is out." He groaned and spoke softly, probably to Daniel, and then returned to the call. "Frank will give up and go back to his life eventually as long as he doesn't find any sign of Ashton. What I'm worried about is whatever Carlo was after. Because you know damned well that if Garvic or anyone there gets wind of us, they aren't going to give up. Carlo out of the picture means they'll send someone else. We got lucky this time because the only person Carlo knew was you. What if they send someone who knows all three of us?"

Terrance was well aware of that. The Garvic family would give just about anything to find and eliminate all three of them. If that happened, then Tucker, Daniel, the boys, and even Ashton were in danger. They'd kill everyone just to send a fucking message. "What do we do?" Terrance couldn't let that happen.

"I'm not sure right now. Let me think about it and we'll get together. Until then, stay out of sight. With Carlo gone, we don't know if someone else is going to be sent in his place or not. Lay as low as you can."

He hung up, and Terrance tossed his phone onto the passenger seat. He wished to hell he knew what the fuck was going on. What they needed were eyes and ears back in Detroit, but they had nothing and no way to get them. Flying blind sucked.

He pulled out and onto the road to his apartment. Terrance stayed out of sight as he went inside and packed a few things in his bag. Remembering that he'd left his phone in the car, he dropped the bag on the table and went out to get it.

"I've been looking for you," Frank said from where he leaned against the driver's door.

Terrance closed the apartment door behind him. "Why?" He narrowed his gaze. "I don't know you." There was no way in hell he was giving Frank any information he didn't have to.

"That doesn't matter. I know you." Frank crossed his arms over his chest, trying to look more intimidating. Terrance wasn't falling for it, even if he wondered what the hell Frank thought he knew. "You're the bouncer sometimes at the Driftwood. Some of the guys there said that you would know the people who came in. The bartenders there weren't helpful, even when I greased the way, which tells me they know something and aren't saying. One of the customers was more helpful." He straightened up, lowering his arms. "I need some information. I'll make it worth your while."

"I see. And exactly what sort of information are you looking for?" Terrance wished he had the other guys here for backup. His heart raced as he wondered how much Frank knew and what kind of trouble he was bringing with him. He kept thinking that if Frank figured out who he was, they would all have their lives turned upside down… again. He did his best to keep calm and his head cool. "I don't know how I can help you." The best he could do was play along and see what he could find out.

"I have information that someone who was close to me is here in town. I've been looking for him for the last couple of years. He disappeared, and his entire family has been devastated that he left. We've been desperate to find him." Okay, that was a huge load of bullshit. Terrance leaned closer, pretending he was interested. "We got a lead that he might be in this area. When I asked around the Driftwood, I was sent on a wild goose chase. I don't like being lied to, and I don't know why they would do that unless they had information and were refusing to give it to me." The set of his jaw said that Frank was more angry than worried. It was clear that he didn't give a shit what happened as long as he found Ashton.

"I see." Terrance nodded.

"You might have seen him. It's your job to watch people." He pulled out a picture and pressed it into Terrance's hands. It was an older picture, but most definitely of Ashton. His hair was different and the smile on his lips was forced. There was no carefree happiness in this picture. It was a front. "Have you seen him?"

Terrance took the picture, looked it over, and slowly shook his head. "I don't think so." He was careful not to try to say too much. "I'm sorry." He handed back the picture. "The community here isn't all that large, and most everyone comes to the Driftwood at some point. But I don't think I've ever seen him." He figured he needed to stop. The less said at a time like this, the better. "Are you sure he's here?" Maybe he could find out something.

At first Terrance wasn't sure Frank was going to answer him. "I got a clue from a friend who thought he saw him a few months ago. We weren't sure, and I needed some time to get away. We're worried about him, and we want to find him and hope he'll come home." The song and dance was really played quite well. If Terrance didn't know differently, he'd have believed him.

He shrugged. "I'm sorry I can't help you." He smiled, and Frank moved away from the car. Terrance pulled open the door as his phone rang, Ashton's name showing on the display. He reached for it, ended the call, and put the phone in his pocket. "I hope you find him, though."

Terrance closed the car door and did his best to ignore Frank, who left the drive and got into his car, which he had parked by the side of the road. Terrance's heart didn't start beating again until Frank had pulled away. Then he calmed down and went back inside before returning Ashton's call.

TERRANCE WAS super careful when he left his apartment. He drove down the key and to Lido Key to the south. He made a few turns and stops before returning north. He wasn't followed, and he slowed down as he approached Ashton's, went past, and looked around the area to ensure that Frank's car was nowhere nearby. Then and only then did he turn around and go to Ashton's, where he made sure to park his car as out of sight as possible.

"Where were you?" Ashton asked, agitated and jumpy as he opened the door. "You called and said you were on your way over, but then you didn't come." He stepped back, and Terrance came inside with Ashton closing and locking the door.

"Did something happen here?" Terrance asked, but Ashton shook his head.

"No. I thought something happened to you. It only takes a few minutes to get here, and that was half an hour ago." He sat down, and Terrance sighed. It seemed Ashton was worried about him.

"I'm fine. But as I was getting ready to leave, I had a visitor. Frank was by my car. He wanted to ask me if I'd seen you at the bar. I told him I hadn't and tried to get some information. It seems that someone the two of you knew saw you down here and told him. That's why he's here." Terrance picked up the phone and called Gerome.

"Yeah…?"

"I met Frank today. The guy is a real piece of work. Listen, he's looking all over. Be sure to take all of Ashton's work in the store and pull it off the sale floor for a while. He paid me a visit at home and he thinks Ashton is here. If he stops in the store, he might recognize Ashton's work."

"Damn, I never thought of that. I'll take care of it today. The boss isn't going to be happy. Those items are some of the best-selling ones in the store lately. And if you're with Ashton, tell him I'll have a nice-sized check for him tomorrow." Gerome said he had customers and had to get off the phone.

Terrance hung up and relayed the message to Ashton.

"Damn, that was a way for me to make money, and now that's gone," Ashton said, slumping on the sofa. "Fucking Frank can't find me, but the asshole manages to take away my ability to make a living."

"It won't be for long, but I didn't want Frank to see your work and recognize it." Maybe he should have stayed out of it. It was in Terrance's nature to watch out for people he cared about. He did it with Richard and

Gerome, and now he was doing the same thing with Ashton. But maybe Ashton didn't want Terrance to watch out for him.

"I know, and I understand. But I don't have many resources left. The money I managed to put together is dwindling quickly, and with the rent on this place and the studio, I'm not going to be able to last too much longer. The check that Gerome has for me will help, but even it's not going to keep me going for very long." Ashton shrugged. "I'll have to figure something else out. I have the show coming up, but if Frank isn't gone, I won't be able to do that, and then I'll really be up a creek without a paddle." He seemed so defeated.

Terrance wanted to help him, but he didn't have the resources for that, at least not at the moment. There were millions hidden offshore, but there was no way he could get to any of it. "The guys are trying to figure out where Frank is staying this time. It isn't the same hotel. I went by there, and his car wasn't in the lot. He'd be stupid to stay at the same place." Terrance smiled and hummed. "Or maybe he is."

"What are you talking about?" Ashton asked.

Terrance shrugged and shook his head. If Frank was in the same place, then maybe it was time that the Unwelcome Wagon paid him a visit. He didn't want to explain to Ashton what he had in mind—it would bring up questions he didn't want to answer—but he had to do something to try to help. "I'm just thinking."

Ashton stared down at his feet, shuffling them slightly. "Look, I know you and your friends have some kind of past together. There are things that you don't want to talk about, and I get that. But you're scaring me a little." He bit his lower lip. "You have that same look that Frank got whenever something was about to happen that I wasn't going to like."

Terrance sat next to him. "Don't worry, okay?" He took his hand. "I know things are rough right now, but you aren't alone. I'm trying to figure out how to help you and get Frank to give up and go home." Without putting himself and the guys in a visible position so guys like Frank didn't figure out who they were— that was the sticking point. Whatever they did had to be done quietly. But first he was going to have to find Frank.

"Frank is stubborn as hell," Ashton told him. That was probably true, but so was Terrance, and he now had the upper hand. After all, he knew who Frank was, and the guy was far from home. Maybe a good push would send him right back there.

"It's okay," Terrance said, having made up his mind on an initial course of action. "It's going to be okay. I'll do what I can to keep you safe." He hugged Ashton. Terrance expected Ashton to agree.

"I don't need you to keep me safe," Ashton countered forcefully. "What I need is a way to make a living and go on with my life. I don't want to be holed up here in my apartment for God knows how long until Frank goes home. And what makes you think he'll go home? The guy is stubborn, and when he makes up his mind, he sticks with it."

"That may be true. But he doesn't know you're here. All he knows is that someone he knows might have seen you. That's all." Terrance tried to remain reasonable. He understood Ashton's frustration—he felt it as well, especially with Carlo in town. At least he was apparently on his way back to Detroit. But that didn't mean that someone else wouldn't follow or that Frank might not have more contacts to draw on. What they needed to do was get rid of Frank so they could all get back to their lives. Ashton could move on with his art and make a living. Everyone would be happy once this threat was gone.

"That doesn't change much. I still can't go out in case he sees me." Ashton got to his feet and paced the floor of the small apartment. "I know you're trying to help… and none of this is your fault… it's just frustrating as hell." He sighed. "I should have been a lot more careful with the people I let into my life." Terrance wondered if that meant Ashton was thinking that he should have been careful about letting Terrance into his life as well.

"I won't let anyone hurt you if I can help it," Terrance pronounced.

Ashton nodded and swallowed, but he didn't say anything. Still, Terrance worried that Ashton was putting him in the same category as Frank.

Terrance took his hand as Ashton passed by, then tugged him gently into his arms. "I swear I won't purposely hurt you. I'm not a selfish prick like that Frank." God, he used to be, though. He hoped he had put that shit behind him. Terrance wanted to be more than he'd been in the past. In Detroit he'd been the muscle, the one to do what Richard and Gerome needed him to do. They were the planners and the businessmen. He was the enforcer and the threat that kept everyone in line. But he wanted to be more than that. Ashton had already fallen under the influence of someone like that, and Terrance wanted to be more… to be strong and good enough to deserve someone like him.

"I didn't say you would. But all of it is…." Ashton screwed up his expression and seemed to stutter a little, trying to get his thoughts out. Then he jumped back up and began pacing again. Terrance sat quietly and let him sputter, let him burn off energy. When Ashton stomped out of the room to his bedroom, Terrance pulled out his phone and dialed Richard.

"What is it?"

Terrance explained about the visit he'd had earlier and described the car Frank was driving. "Do you think we can find him? Figure out where he's staying? I think we need to pay him a visit." If he found out where Frank was, he could arrange for some unfortunate events to befall him.

"What do you have in mind?" Richard asked.

"I'm not sure yet. But we need to find him. I was thinking of going out to look. He's either at one of the hotels or maybe at a marina if he's staying on a boat this time."

"Where are you now?" Richard asked.

"With Ashton. He's pretty upset and acting like a caged tiger at the moment." Terrance caught Ashton's gaze when he returned, and he winked at him and got one in return. "I was thinking that you and I would go out looking a little later. See what we can find." He also thought that a little dinner and being out of the four walls would be good for Ashton.

"Okay. I'll ask Daniel to see what he can dig up for us. Maybe there's something he can discover," Richard said. "And I'll put the word out to Gerome. Between us, we'll find him." Richard paused. "But Terrance, don't do anything without talking to the rest of us."

Terrance ground his teeth, already on edge. "I can take care of myself," he hissed.

"Duh," Richard countered, and Terrance sighed. "But this isn't about you or me, it's all of us. So we act together and we act smart, right?" He was so damned reasonable.

"Yeah." Richard was right, but it still chafed that he felt the need to caution him. They had always been a team.

"Good. Let's get together tomorrow and see what we can come up with. I'll order from the Driftwood and we can meet here. Hopefully we'll have something to talk about and we can eliminate this once and for all." That was Richard. He was all about keeping all of them safe. Not that Terrance didn't feel the same way. But Richard was the leader, and he tended to think more about them all as a group than just himself. Maybe that was why he was so good. Terrance trusted him and Gerome with his life.

"Fine. But all this acting so civilized is a real pain in the ass." In Detroit, he'd have found Frank and made sure that the problem was taken care of right then and there. This skulking in the shadows rankled him, even if it was necessary.

"What did Richard say?"

"That we'll meet tomorrow. And I thought that after dinner, we'll see if we can find Frank's car." He stood and went to Ashton. "I think it's time that we try to see what we can do. I'm tired of sitting here and waiting for something to happen. I bet you are too. So what do you say that we go out and have a look? Check the hotels and marinas for his car. It was a dark blue Honda Civic with a cracked front bumper. It was rented from Coastal Rental, and there's a sticker in the front and back window."

Ashton nodded. "Were you a cop or something?"

Terrance chuckled. "For now, let's go with 'or something.'" He stepped away. "Do you have things here for dinner, or should we go out?"

"I have pasta and salad," Ashton answered. He pulled out a box of pasta, a bag of salad, and a jar of pasta sauce. "Do you want to help? I think there's a little hamburger in here." He searched in the refrigerator and came up with the smallest package of ground meat Terrance had ever seen. He felt bad taking what might be the last of Ashton's food, but he wasn't going to turn down what he'd offered or make him feel bad. Everyone had their pride.

Terrance got out a pan to brown the meat. "Do you have any spices?" he asked. Ashton shrugged. "No problem." He browned the meat while Ashton got the water on for the pasta.

"I know it isn't much, but…."

Terrance patted Ashton's shoulder. "You know, when I was a kid, Mama served us the same thing for dinner, only she didn't have the hamburger. Mama was Italian, as you can probably guess, but she worked all the time. She said that jarred sauce was an affront to God, but that since she didn't have the time to make it herself, God was going to have to look the other way." He smiled, and Ashton laughed. "I grew up with next to nothing, and there were plenty of times when I went to bed hungry." He took the meat off the heat and drained the fat into a can. Then he popped open the sauce, added it to the pan, and put it on the stove to heat.

"But that was then…."

Terrance went behind Ashton and slipped his arms around his waist. "There's nothing wrong with being poor. Lots of us come from nothing, and sometimes things are tough. But there's no shame in it. Never has been. So don't feel bad about anything. We all do the best we can, try to build a future and make the hard times toughen us up so we're ready for the good. That's what Mama used to say, and she was the best person I ever knew." There were times when he wished to hell that his path in life had been different and that his mother hadn't had things so hard for so many years. But he'd helped support her and had made her life better, at least for a while.

"I remember my mom saying before she died, 'Whether you're rich or poor, it's always nice to have money.'" He chuckled. "I always thought that was kind of dumb. But I think I get it now." He leaned back. "You can have a rich life or a poor life… and money isn't required for either one."

Terrance sighed and held Ashton a little tighter. "It could also have been your mom's sense of humor." He rested his chin on Ashton's shoulder.

"Maybe." Ashton turned down the water as it began to boil, and Terrance moved away so he could finish the pasta. Terrance stirred the sauce and then used the bowl that Ashton pulled out to finish up the salad.

Their meal was simple and tasted better than it probably had a right to. Maybe that was because they had made it together, or maybe jarred sauce had improved since he was a kid.

"You really want to go out and try to find Frank?" Ashton asked as he scraped the last of the salad from the bowl onto his plate and added a dash of squeeze-bottle ranch dressing.

"Yeah." Terrance set his fork down on the empty plate. "Sometimes you have to do something, and if we can find him, then we have a leg up. Knowing where he is can help us keep an eye on him. That way he doesn't show up unannounced once again. And we'll know when he leaves." He leaned slightly over the table. "I need to ask you something. Frank is obviously here looking for you, but it's been two years, and he should have gotten over his heartbreak and loss by now." He winked, and Ashton rolled his eyes dramatically. "Do you really think he's the kind of person to go to all this trouble… unless there's another reason?" This had niggled at the back of his mind for a while.

"What do you mean?"

"Would he be here to look for you if that was the only reason? Or would he come here on say… business… and then spend some time trying to find you?"

"I don't know. He might have come here to find me and then decided to do some business since he was here." Ashton shrugged. Not that the order mattered. It made sense that a guy like Frank would try to maximize his efforts. "Why?"

"There have been some activities here that aren't very good for the community or anyone who lives here." He didn't go into detail about how they had put an end to a drug smuggling racket. That was too much information and would get Ashton more curious about them.

Ashton nodded. "Frank would always be on the lookout for a way he could make more money. That's his number-one motivator—cash. The more there is, the more interested Frank will become."

Terrance sat back. "That's what I was thinking." Mainly because in their old life, it's what the three of them would have done. Even if they went on a vacation, they were always looking to make a score, and Terrance knew there were plenty of places on the key to do just that. He gathered the dishes and carried them to the sink. Ashton had already set some of them to soak, so they washed up and put things away.

The sun was setting by the time they borrowed Richard's car. "Where are we going?"

"I thought we'd start at the southern end of the key and work our way north. We can check out the hotels and marinas, anything with a parking lot, to see if he's there. Then if we find him, we figure out what he might be up to."

Ashton buckled himself in with a shrug. "Okay. If you think it will help."

Terrance pulled out of the parking spot. "Finding him is step one. He thinks he's hunting for you, but he doesn't know that he's now the prey."

Chapter 10

ASHTON SQUIRMED in the seat, trying to get comfortable. Night had completely set in, and they had driven through every parking lot, hotel drive, and marina for the past two hours with no luck. The few times they thought they might have seen the car, it wasn't it. Ashton covered his mouth while he yawned and blinked. "There's nothing here."

They didn't have far to go and they would come to the bridge at the north end of the key. They could continue across and onto the mainland, but then the possibilities opened up greatly and they weren't likely to find the car. Their only chance was in the next few places ahead. Ashton was getting tired, but Terrance seemed to have almost infinite patience.

He made the right turn into the marina and slowed as they passed through the parking lot. "Is that it?" Ashton asked, pointing.

"No. There's no rental sticker," Terrance answered as he slowed to take a better look, then continued on. This was getting old, but Ashton figured they might as well check the last places before heading on home. He was tired and his backside ached from the old, uncomfortable seat.

Terrance turned back out onto the main road and into a small hotel parking lot. They passed through quickly without stopping. Nothing there was even close to the car they were looking for.

They approached a final marina on the right. Terrance turned in and Ashton pointed. "Right there," he said. The dark blue car even had the rental sticker in the back window. Terrance pulled in and left the engine running, got out, and checked the front of the car before hurrying back inside.

"That's definitely it." He pulled out and back onto the road.

"What do we do now? He could be visiting someone," Ashton asked as Terrance turned into a small store parking area and shut off the lights. The stores were closed for the night, though there was one other car a few spaces over.

"You stay here, please. I'm going to go see if I can find where he is." Terrance was already getting out of the car. Ashton huffed and sat back for about two seconds before he opened his door. "What are you doing?" Terrance snapped in a whisper.

"What are *you* doing? You can't go in there alone. What if something happens, or if someone comes here?" he added softly but firmly. Ashton had no intention of being a sitting duck waiting in the damned car. He scampered behind Terrance, and they headed across the lot and toward the foliage that separated the parking area from the marina property.

"What if we see him and he recognizes you?" Terrance asked as he stopped just shy of the green verge. "Remember, he's the guy who's been looking for you."

"He's seen you too," Ashton countered and stepped off the concrete. He was tired of sitting around waiting for everyone else to see to him. Terrance had been right—it felt good to do something, and he'd be damned if he just sat on the sidelines. "You coming?" He looked over his shoulder and then continued on through until an arm encircled his waist.

"Good God. You want to get yourself hurt?" Terrance tugged him back. "If you're going to come along, you need to stay in the shadows. And for goodness' sake, if anything happens, hightail it back to the car and stay there. Whatever you do, don't let anyone see you." Terrance held him closer. "I don't want anything to happen to you. Okay?"

Ashton nodded—like he had much choice with the big guy holding him like this. Though if he had an option, they'd be somewhere much more private when Terrance had him in his arms and they would be a lot less dressed. He pressed back, and Terrance growled softly into his ear.

"Let's go." He released him, and Ashton let Terrance take the lead, both of them using the darkness as cover. "Stay right there and watch." Terrance pointed to the shadows. "If you see Frank, duck deeper into the shadows and text me. Then as soon as you can, go back to the car."

"What if he's in there?" Ashton asked.

"Then it's my job to find him." Terrance flashed him a glare, and Ashton stepped into the shadows and pressed to the side of the building. He could see part of the parking lot as well as the entrance to the secure marina area. Terrance turned and strode off toward the docks like he belonged there, barely pausing at the gate before swinging it open. Ashton didn't want to think about how easily he'd gotten past. Maybe in his rough past, Terrance had gotten what he needed by stealing or something. As Terrance disappeared from sight down the docks, Ashton checked the quiet surroundings with no one about. The only sound was the lap of the water and the soft bump of boats against pilings.

He wondered exactly what kind of life Terrance had had before coming here. Detroit a few years ago had been a tough city. He understood that there had been changes and that the city had come a long way, but Terrance's behavior and the stories he told made Ashton wonder just what kind of guy Terrance had been… and who he was now. Terrance knew what he was doing as far as getting into the marina, and the way he strode down the dock like he owned the place showed confidence and even bravado in the situation. Clearly Terrance had done things like this before, and Ashton wasn't sure how he felt about that. It reminded him too much of Frank.

Footsteps on the gravel drew Ashton's attention, and he pressed closer to the building, holding his breath as a figure carrying grocery bags and a cooler appeared. It definitely wasn't Frank, but Ashton didn't want to be seen in any case. He was relieved when the man passed by. Maybe coming along wasn't such a good idea and he should have just stayed in the car. The air was still sticky, and he wasn't doing anything just hiding in the shadows. Ashton figured he might as well head back and wait when footsteps sounded once again. A phone rang and was answered almost immediately.

"Yeah."

That single word sent a chill up his spine. Ashton would know that voice anywhere, and it was one he hoped he'd never hear again.

"Yeah, I got everything set." The footsteps paused, and Ashton held his breath. He was so damned close that if Frank took another step and turned his head, he'd be able to see Ashton. "Tomorrow night. I know where it is. I'm heading there now. I got cash, and we can do business." His voice silenced and the footsteps sounded again. Ashton didn't dare move, berating himself for how stupid he was until Frank was out of sight. Then he pulled out the phone Terrance had given him, sent a text, and made his way back to the car as quietly as he could. Once inside, he locked the doors and slunk low into the seat to stay out of sight.

He wanted to find out if Terrance was okay, but if he called, he might give him away, so Ashton sat still and waited. He didn't know how long Terrance was going to be, but as the minutes ticked by, he started to wonder if something had happened.

The driver's door handle clicked, and Ashton jumped, then opened the door when Terrance peered through the window.

"Let's get out of here," Terrance said. He pulled the door closed and started the engine.

"Did you find out where he's staying?" Ashton asked.

"Yeah. On a boat called *Dreamscape*. I'm glad you texted because I was able to follow him." Terrance pulled out of the lot, and they headed toward home. "But you should have just stayed here."

"If I had, I wouldn't have overheard Frank. He has some deal going down tomorrow, on the boat it seemed, and he said he had the cash." Ashton was pleased, and Terrance nodded. "But it could be a different boat, though he said he was heading there now."

"Okay. So we know where he'll be all day tomorrow."

"Not necessarily." After all, Frank could go anywhere he wanted.

"Oh yeah. It's going to take him most of the day to get his tires fixed. I put small holes in one of them on my way out. It isn't going to be really noticeable, but by morning his tire will be flat, and it's going to take time for the rental company to replace it." He flashed a smile. "Yeah, it was probably petty, but we need to know where he is and to restrict his movements." He turned back to the road and began making calls before he started the car moving.

"Ashton and I found him, and I made sure he'll stay there," Terrance told Richard when he answered. "We're in the car on the way back to my place." Terrance turned to Ashton. "Unless you need to work tonight."

Ashton thought about it but shook his head. He'd already had enough excitement and wasn't at the top of his game.

"It seems something is going down tomorrow."

"Okay. What do you want to do?"

"Not sure yet. We'll figure it out tomorrow. At least for now, we have him contained."

"But not for long. Still, we know where he is and where he'll be for a while." Richard grew quiet, and Ashton glanced at Terrance. "We'll see you both tomorrow." Richard ended the call, and Terrance continued on down to his apartment building, parked, and turned off the engine. The humid heat immediately began working its way into the car.

"You going to be okay?" Terrance asked. "You did real good, by the way."

"And you didn't seem to have any trouble with the locked gate." It was Ashton's way of feeling him out.

Terrance wriggled his fingers. "I'm a man of many talents."

"And not all of them exactly legal." Ashton got out of the car and waited for Terrance. "Are you going to tell me about these special skills of yours?"

"Rough neighborhood." Terrance led the way inside and closed the door. "I don't go around robbing convenience stores. But sometimes I need certain skills to make sure my friends and family stay safe." His expression grew darker for a second, and he seemed more closed off than Ashton could remember.

"Fine. I grew up tough too, but I can't pick locks and shit." He was determined to press. "Frank could do stuff like that too, and he…." Ashton swallowed.

"Yeah. I know he's an asshole. But I'm not him." Terrance kicked off his shoes and sat down. "And yeah, I can be an asshole too sometimes. Sorry, but that's the truth. I'm not perfect, Lord knows." He shook his head. "My mama would tell you that and then regale you with stories to prove her point. But I don't go around hurting people unless I have to in order to protect people who deserve it."

"You make yourself sound like Robin Hood or something." Ashton somehow doubted that was true, though Terrance would look good in a pair of green tights. He had great legs.

"Nope. I'm just a guy who's trying to take care of the important people in my life." He sat back, and when Ashton came close, he tugged him down onto his lap. "Do you think we could talk about something else? Like maybe how sexy you are." He pulled Ashton's collar open and nipped at the skin he exposed.

Ashton wanted to ask more questions, but his train of thought derailed, and he groaned softly. "Terrance," Ashton whimpered. "We should talk about stuff."

Terrance chucked. "Then you talk—I'm going to do this." He popped another button on his shirt, and Ashton groaned at the heat from Terrance's mouth on his skin.

"It isn't fair," he countered as more buttons opened, and then Terrance spread open his shirt and slipped it off his arms.

"Who said I had to be fair?" Terrance sucked at a nipple, and Ashton swallowed a groan. "I could stop if that's what you really want me to do, and then you and I could talk about all kinds of serious things. Global warming, maybe the state of international affairs." Terrance licked again, sending a thrill racing through him. "We could talk about the state of the Gulf and what needs to be done to make sure it stays ecologically sound."

Ashton wound his arms around Terrance's neck. "You know, you're starting to prove that asshole comment."

"Oh, I am, huh?" Terrance growled, and Ashton felt himself giggle. He hadn't done that in years, but Terrance's teasing left him jubilant. He tried to remember the last time he had had someone in his life that he was this comfortable with—free enough to let go—and it was almost impossible. Ashton had learned a long time ago to be regimented and circumspect in how he reacted to everyone. He rarely had the confidence and security to take anything or anyone for granted. Frank had only reinforced that notion. "Come on. I can strip you down right here and lick you all over, or we can go to the bedroom, where you'll be more comfortable."

Ashton swallowed hard and climbed off Terrance, jumped out of his reach, and hurried to the bedroom. He heard Terrance behind him and tumbled onto the bed, turning onto his back as Terrance came in after him with desire shining in his eyes. Damn, Terrance was sexy. Before Ashton could get to him, Terrance grabbed his legs, holding his feet. "Get these off," he growled, and Ashton undid his pants. Terrance peeled them down his legs and dropped them on the floor.

The intensity in Terrance's eyes was heady as all hell. For a second Ashton felt his cheeks heat at the fact that he was naked and Terrance completely dressed. But then Terrance rolled him onto his belly, then slid his hands up his inner legs and thighs, pressing his legs apart.

"What are you…?" Ashton mewled as wet heat touched his opening, and then he groaned when Terrance's tongue probed him. "Oh God, you're…." He shook as Terrance repeated his motion. Ashton couldn't help pressing his legs farther apart, pushing back, giving Terrance more access. This was… it…. His head spun as he tried to get his head around what Terrance was doing to him. God, it….

His thoughts sputtered even as his body seemed to know what to do, and he pressed back, desperate for more. Terrance slipped his hand between Ashton's legs, wrapping his fingers around his cock and stroking slowly, adding pleasure on top of ecstasy. "You like that?" Terrance asked, voice muffled, fingers gripping him harder.

"Uh-huh," he managed to breathe, his legs shaking with excitement. Ashton had never thought about this, and he'd had no idea what he had been missing. The openness—the way Terrance took him and the way he gave himself completely over to him... it felt like lying out under the stars without a care in the world, only with the most mind-blowing sensation... ever! He didn't know what to make of it all until Terrance pulled away and slowly rolled him onto his back. "Wha...?"

Terrance tugged his polo shirt up and over his head, displaying a powerful, lightly furred chest to Ashton's gaze. Ashton could take in that view forever. He sat up and tugged Terrance down on top of him. God, he loved the feel of Terrance's skin on his.

Ashton worked open Terrance's pants, pulling at the denim to get the waist unbuttoned and the zipper down. Once he had access, he slid his hands inside, cupping Terrance's powerful buttcheeks. Terrance thrust against him, rutting slowly as Ashton worked the jeans lower.

"You need to get these off," Ashton growled, doing a pretty fair imitation of Terrance when he got worked up.

Terrance sat back and then climbed off the bed, pushed his jeans down, then stepped out of them and the rest of his clothes and stood next to the bed, cock jutting in Ashton's direction.

Ashton shifted on the bed, raising his head and sliding forward to take Terrance's cock between his lips. Terrance stilled, and Ashton slid deeper, taking all he could. Ashton loved Terrance's rich, musky, male taste, the head of his cock sliding over his tongue.

Terrance softly petted his head, rubbing his hair as
Ashton paused for a second. There was no pressure in
Terrance's touch, and that helped him get past his initial
resistance. Frank had always had to be in charge and
held his head.

"Damn, you're good at that." Terrance stilled as
Ashton took him as deeply as possible.

Terrance pulled away and bent down, kissing him
hard before climbing onto the bed. Ashton wasn't sure
what Terrance had in mind, and he hesitated until Terrance pressed him back on the mattress. Ashton quivered with anticipation and wasn't disappointed when
Terrance returned the favor, sucking him deep. Ashton
moved his hips, and Terrance sucked harder, only en-
couraging him. Terrance let him take charge, and it was
kind of heady, especially with the way Terrance drove
him to distraction. Within minutes, Ashton was breath-
less and silently begging for more. He tried to talk,
but every time he tried, Terrance stole his words away
again and all that came out was a whimper.

He clutched the bedding in an attempt to keep himself under control and nearly failed. This was too much
for him to take. "Terrance… I…."

Terrance paused a second, and Ashton breathed
deeply, regaining some of the control. He had been seconds from losing it, and dang it, he wasn't ready for this
to be over. "It's okay." Terrance brushed the hair off his
forehead. "I want this to last too." He nuzzled Ashton's
neck, lowering himself on top, pushing Ashton against
the mattress. "Am I too heavy?"

The solid weight was delicious, and he held on to
Terrance tightly, shaking his head, then returned the
kiss that sent him reeling once more. Terrance rocked
slowly, Ashton holding him, and together they built

more tension and pressure. Ashton rolled them on the bed until Ashton lay on top, Terrance's hands cupping his butt. "That's better."

"Yeah. I like being the one in charge."

Terrance chuckled and squeezed lightly. "I may be the one on the bottom, but I'm still the one in charge." He kissed Ashton again. "And you like it. I can feel just how much each time you tense and your cock throbs between us." He stroked his finger over Ashton's opening, and Ashton quivered. "See, I know what you like, you sexy thing."

"Yeah." Ashton pulled away. "You're the one that's sexy."

"That's the beauty. We both think the same things of the other. That's what's great." Terrance put his finger over Ashton's lips, and Ashton sucked on it. "Did anyone ever tell you that you talk too much?"

"Maybe." He smiled. "And maybe you can give me something better to do with my mouth."

Terrance held him tighter. "Now you're speaking my language."

Ashton scoffed. "Now it sounds like you're the one doing too much talking." He stared into Terrance's eyes. He loved that view and could get lost in those brown eyes forever.

"Oh, it is?" He closed his lips over Ashton's and the talking ceased. Not that Ashton regretted it for a second. There were so many more interesting things they could do with their mouths besides talking, and he intended to explore each and every one of them.

Terrance seemed intent on taking his time. Ashton had no reason to argue. Something about the big man and his gentle touch turned him on. There was no force or muscling; instead, Terrance was solicitous, putting

Ashton's pleasure before his own. That was almost a foreign concept to him, or at least it had become one the last years he'd been with someone. His throat felt rough and every inch of his body on fire, desiring one more touch, one more taste. He couldn't get enough of Terrance and wanted to make him just as happy, show Terrance as much joy as he was being shown.

"What do you want?" Terrance asked in a husky voice that resonated in Ashton's chest. It was probably the first time anyone had asked him that question when it came to intimate moments, and he wasn't sure how to answer. He didn't want to disappoint Terrance and say something that he didn't want. The end result was a few blinks and silence. "Don't go quiet on me now. Just say what it is that will make you happy." Terrance nipped at the base of his neck.

"I want you," Ashton whispered and wondered when he'd lost his voice. When had his ability to just say what he wanted, what he thought about in the middle of the night when no one was there, become so hard to vocalize? "I want… this…." He pressed his body to Terrance's.

"Just this?" Terrance asked and snapped his hips with a grin. "We can do that."

"Yes… I mean, no… I mean…." He growled. "I want you like last time. I want everything, like you were doing a little while ago." He snapped his lips closed.

"You liked me rimming you and you want more?" Terrance smirked. "Then just say so. I'll give you anything you want, sweet cheeks."

Ashton snorted before he could stop it. "Are you being mean?"

Terrance flipped him on the bed and rolled him over, sliding his rough hands over Ashton's backside.

"Never." He teased him, gliding his fingers over the sensitive skin, adding fuel to the fire that had begun to cool and rekindling the heat inside him. "Remember, you asked for this." He spread Ashton's legs wide and leaned over him, tugging Ashton's hips upward, bringing his lips and tongue to the skin, damn near sending Ashton into orbit. Holy hell, he had never thought *that* could be so sexy and would feel so good. And the way Terrance stroked his cock at the same time, doubling the intensity…. He whined and pressed back, rocking slightly, with Terrance following right along.

Terrance added his fingers, kneading his flesh, tongue spearing him, other hand stroking. It was overwhelming and all Ashton could possibly think about. This was someone who knew about pleasure. But at that moment it allowed Ashton to think, hope, for the first time that maybe it was more. That he might be special. And Terrance reinforced that thought with mind-numbing pleasure that continued until Ashton couldn't take it any longer and came hard enough he felt like he would pass out.

ASHTON RETURNED to himself slowly, with Terrance holding him as he caught his breath. The sheets were soft and Terrance was warm next to him. "Are you okay? You were sort of out of it for a while."

"Yeah, I'm fine. But…." He blinked and tried to remember exactly what had happened. "Did you… oh my God, I was so selfish."

Terrance slowly ran his hands up and down Ashton's arm. He nuzzled closer and hummed softly into his ear. "Everything is just fine. You were so sexy that I came when you did. Just relax and let yourself bask in the glow." He pulled him closer, and Ashton relaxed, sighing and closing his eyes, letting contentment wash over him.

"How do you do that?" Ashton asked.

"What?" Terrance tensed a little.

"Make me feel safe and totally content at the same time. I'm here with you and, well…." He paused. There was no way in hell that he wanted to bring up Frank at a time like this. "Everything is just so nice."

Terrance chuckled. "This is how things should feel. At least that's what Richard and Gerome tell me. I've never experienced this sort of thing firsthand before."

Ashton rolled over. "So, I have to ask. Do the three of you sit around and talk about your feelings a lot? Because I just don't see that. I mean, you're great guys, but sitting in a living room with your feet up talking about feelings and relationships seems like a stretch." He patted Terrance's chest.

"Okay. You got me. What we really do is sit around with our feet up. You have that part right. We drink beer and belch. One belch for 'I feel crappy,' two for 'I'm happy,' and three is for 'I had great sex last night.'"

Ashton wondered for a second if he was telling the truth and then burst into laughter. "Now that I can believe. We can call it the belch code, and if I drank that much beer, I'd definitely go for the three belches. But what's four?"

"I drank too damned much, so don't get between me and the bathroom." Terrance didn't miss a beat.

Ashton groaned and lay back down, smiling. "You're too funny sometimes." He liked that about Terrance. That he could be funny and didn't think Ashton was being stupid when he tried to make a joke. Terrance seemed to get him, and few others ever did. That was both surprising and attractive as hell. "But you didn't answer my question, not really."

Terrance sighed. "Sometimes we all sit around and talk about stuff. When Richard found Daniel and Coby, it was a shock to all of us. It had only been the three of us for so long, and then he had Daniel, and when Gerome found Tucker, along with him came Cheryl and Joshie. I got to be an uncle for the second time, and I realized things weren't going to be the same for any of us. They had partners and children to take care of and love, even if they aren't their own."

"I don't understand the thing with Tucker and Cheryl and Joshie," Ashton admitted.

"Yeah, well, that's different. Tucker, Cheryl, and Joshie were homeless living in tents, and they sort of took care of each other. Gerome met Tucker and at first tried to help them, and then Cheryl got sick and nearly died. Gerome helped Tucker take care of Joshie and… well…." He sighed. "I think once we grow to care for someone, we don't let them go. Gerome really came to love Joshie, and Richard helped Cheryl get a job. She's building a life for her and her son, and Joshie calls all of us uncle."

"And you like that," Ashton said. There was something more than merely attractive about a man who loved children. In Ashton's limited experience, children were pure, and if there was a reason to be afraid of in Terrance or any of the guys, they'd sense it. On the boat, the boys had been nothing but joyous, and it was clear that all of the men loved those boys—including their Uncle Terrance.

Ashton closed his eyes, fatigue catching up to him but not overwhelming him enough that Ashton could stop wondering exactly what this meeting at Richard's

was going to be about and what they planned to do
about Frank.

ASHTON WORKED most of the day. It was
hot, but he wanted a few more things for the show, and
it was the only thing that kept his thoughts from running in circles between all this business with Frank and
the upcoming show, which he hoped to hell the crap
with his ex didn't put in jeopardy. Ashton worked alone
this time. Terrance had left a while ago, and it was either go stir-crazy watching television or work—and the
glass centered his mind.

Now he had three pieces in the annealer and he was
about as dry as the Sahara, so he began the shutdown
process and took off his safety equipment. He hung it
up before checking that the annealer was on the prop-
er setting to go through its gradual cooldown process
and then left the studio. Ashton went to the apartment,
where he drank two glasses of water and downed a Gatorade to rehydrate before hitting the shower and dressing once more.

He checked the time and peered out around the
drawn curtains for Terrance's car. He pulled in just as
Ashton was about to let the curtain fall back into place.
With a smile already in place, he opened the door for
him and practically tried to climb him as soon as they
were alone inside.

"I'm happy to see you too."

"I got a follow-up call this afternoon. I missed it,
but they left a message making sure I got their letter
about the art fair," Ashton whispered. "They want to
include me in the Sarasota Regional Art Fair as well
as another they are planning in the area. It's going to

be wonderful, and my work will be seen by thousands of people. And since it's juried, they will be giving out various prizes and ribbons." He was so excited. This was what he had been working toward for a long time. It looked like what he wanted most was going to come to pass.

"That's awesome," Terrance told him. "You deserve it."

"But I need to make some more pieces, especially with another show. What I figured is that I'd bring the best ones with me and then have pictures of the others available so if someone wanted to look, they would be able to. People have been known to sell pieces that way." He could hardly sit still. "It's going to take a lot of work, but I really want to finish the chandelier and maybe develop a companion smaller lighting piece to go with it. I have so many ideas running through my head right now."

"That's wonderful." Terrance hugged him tightly. "I'm so thrilled and I hate to bring you down, but we need to go to Richard's so we can figure out how to get rid of Frank."

Ashton groaned. The last thing he wanted to think about at a happy time like this was his asshole ex. But hopefully with the guys helping, they could get rid of him and Ashton could be safe and able to move ahead with his life. "Okay. Let's go." He said the words but didn't let go of Terrance. He liked the way he held him and how solid he was. Ashton felt like he was safe and nothing was going to happen to him as long as he stayed right here.

"I could pick you up and carry you to the car."

"Or the bedroom," Ashton growled. If he could convince Terrance to take him in there, he was pretty sure that it wouldn't be long before he forgot all about Frank—and everything else—and got lost in Terrance.

"That's so tempting," Terrance agreed. "But we have to go meet the guys. Richard knows where we are, and if we don't show up, he'll come find us to make sure we're okay. And if you and I are blowing him off to do the horizontal hula, he isn't going to be happy, and he'll make sure I have all the crap jobs at the Driftwood for the rest of my life." He shuddered. "And I don't want dishpan hands."

Ashton chuckled. "We wouldn't want to subject you to that." He pulled away and got his things. "Let's go and get this over with."

"Don't you want to get rid of Frank?" Terrance asked.

Ashton knew he was trying to help, but he was so tired of Frank dictating everything in his life that he wanted to scream. But Terrance was right, they needed to go, and he nodded and grabbed his keys.

AS WHAT seemed to be the usual, there was plenty of food and everyone seemed happy—talking and laughing as though there wasn't a threat somewhere out there. Ashton had no appetite, but he ate a little anyway because he knew he needed to.

"Okay, boys," Cheryl said once they had eaten and were getting ready to settle on the floor. "Why don't we go out and see what kind of shells we can find on the beach?"

"I'll go with you," Tucker offered, and soon enough the boys half skipped out the door, heading down toward the water.

"Okay, we don't have a lot of time," Daniel said with Richard sitting next to him.

"What did you find out?" Richard asked.

"We know where Frank is staying—on the *Dreamscape*—and the car he's driving," Terrance reported.

"And that some sort of deal is happening on the boat tonight. Knowing Frank, it definitely isn't a Boy Scout meeting," Ashton said nervously.

"Okay. So we know where he is and where he's going to be. We don't know what sort of deal he's up to," Richard interjected.

Ashton smiled. "No. But he did say he had the money."

Terrance, Gerome, and Richard all shared one of those looks that Ashton had noticed before. "Are you all thinking the same thing? If he has the money, where is he keeping it?" Gerome asked. "It has to be close to him. It could be in the car or hidden on the boat. I doubt if he'd let it out of his sight."

Ashton leaned forward. "Do you really think Frank, or anyone, would keep any amount of cash just hanging around?"

"Okay. But where would he get any amount of cash down here? This isn't his territory. He must have either brought it or gotten it from Carlo." Richard stood and paced a little. "There are a number of possibilities. Maybe Carlo was down here to do a deal and now that he's out of commission, Frank is stepping in to take control." He sighed. "I wish to hell we knew more about all this. But one thing is for sure."

"Wait. I didn't think about it until now, but Frank said something about 'acting for him now.' Whatever that means."

Richard smiled. "The *him* has to be Carlo, because he's now out of the picture. Frank's doing the deal in his place. If this deal goes south, Frank is probably going to be in a hell of a lot of trouble, especially if the money that he happens to be using is Detroit money." He once again shared that look with the others, like they were communicating something between them or talking around something that Ashton didn't know.

"They always do that. Just don't worry about it," Daniel told him before turning to Richard. "Do you want Ashton and me to go out to the beach, and that way you three could be alone? From the way you're looking at each other, it looks like the circle-jerk is going to start any second."

"Stop it," Richard said without heat. "I'm just trying to figure out what all this could mean."

"Why not call the police and tell them what we know and let them handle it?" Ashton asked.

Terrance took his hand and tugged him down. "Because we don't know anything concrete. Yeah, we think Frank is up to no good, but we have no idea what, and if the police investigate it, Frank will hide whatever he's doing and nothing will come of it. Then Frank will be on his guard."

"But if he does his deal, won't he just leave?" Ashton asked. "That's what we want him to do."

"If Frank makes a lot of money here, do you think he'll leave and never come back? Or will he make regular trips here to conduct business?" Gerome asked.

Ashton groaned. If Frank could make a dime, he'd return to Antarctica on a yearly pilgrimage. "Okay, you have a point. But how do you guys know all about this stuff? Terrance says that you aren't cops or anything like that. And you grew up in Detroit." He held the gaze of the others. "What kind of things did you do there? You certainly weren't Boy Scouts either." He crossed his arms, glaring at all three of them. "I've had too many people lie to me and push me to the side to let it happen again."

It was Daniel who answered. "No one here means you any harm, and we're doing what we can to help you. Please just accept that and keep it to yourself. Sometimes the past is best left there, and this is one of those times. Whatever happened in Chicago is your past, and some of it you don't want to talk about, right? It's too painful or whatever, but it is in the past. And you can't change it." Daniel nodded. "We all have a past. I do. So does Tucker and so do each of the guys. But that doesn't mean we aren't the people you know us to be right now."

Ashton swallowed hard. There was definitely something they didn't want him to know, and it ate at him even if what Daniel said made sense. "But—"

"Curiosity is good, but sometimes it gets us into trouble," Daniel added.

"You know, then?" Ashton pressed.

"It doesn't matter what I know or don't. I trust Richard, Gerome, and Terrance. What's important is, do you trust them?" Daniel seemed to be able to get to the heart of the issue with ease. "That's a decision that you have to make, and you need to do it with the limited information you have and what you know about them." He set down the glass he was holding.

Terrance held his gaze, and Ashton knew this was the moment of truth. If he walked away, it was likely that he wouldn't see any of them again, and the thought of walking away from Terrance was too much. It was difficult for him to trust anyone after Frank, but he had to remember that Terrance and the guys weren't Frank. They'd invited him to go fishing when they barely knew him, and they'd opened their group to him and even helped him when he needed it. The biggest thing was that they didn't ask for anything in return. He had been wondering, since they weren't police, if they were criminals like Frank. But then, none of them acted like Frank, and they sure weren't assholes like him. Ashton didn't know what to think about anything they might have done.

Terrance and the guys didn't act like any of the criminals he knew. They lived in modest places and worked for a living. There was no flashy spending, and they genuinely cared for each other. Sure, they picked on each other, but they also had each other's backs, and because of Terrance, that seemed to extend to Ashton now. Hell, the guys were planning something—Lord knows what—just to try to help keep him safe.

"I think you're right." He turned away. "I think it's best if I just go out and take a walk on the beach with the others."

He swallowed hard. Terrance had already put himself in harm's way for him, and that should be enough. Whatever happened between them, he needed to trust that they were doing it to help him. And that needed to be enough… for now. He went to the door and pulled it open, stepped outside into the sun, and headed down the path to where he saw the boys and Cheryl and Tucker a distance off. He walked faster to try to catch up.

Chapter 11

TERRANCE WATCHED Ashton go, and his belly did a little flip, but he wasn't quite sure why. Maybe it was the fact that he was leaving.

"It will be fine, big guy," Daniel told him. "He's got to figure things out, though for now, it seems he's willing to give you the benefit of the doubt. And given some of the things he seems to have gone through, that's saying something." Daniel's gaze shifted to the group. "What are you going to do?"

"We need to put an end to this deal, and the easiest way would be to get on that boat and see if we can find the money. If that disappears, there can't be a deal, and if the money happens to belong to someone other than Frank, then he'll be in huge trouble and they'll want to get their money back… one way or another." Terrance grinned evilly. "We know the boat and his car." Terrance groaned. "Shit, I flattened his tire so he wouldn't have the chance to go anywhere."

"Don't worry about it. The tire could be fixed." Gerome got up. "Tell me where he is and exactly where the boat is. I'll go check to see if he's there and message back. If Frank is gone, then you can board the boat, and I'll—"

"We'll all go. I know what he looks like, and he knows Terrance and me already, so we're going to tag-team the guy and try to keep out of his line of sight." Richard ate a little more and wiped his mouth before getting up. "Gerome, do you want to go down and see if he's there? Pretend to be looking for a friend or something and you can't quite find the boat."

"Will do." He stood and headed for the door. "Tell Tucker that I'll call him later and that I promise to be careful." He left, and Terrance sighed.

"Okay," Daniel said. "Now that you know what you want to do, I need to say something." He had one of those expressions that told Terrance he was in for a talking-to. "Ashton is a real nice guy, and I can tell he likes you. But you need to be gentle with him. He's been hurt, and bad, and it's hard for him to trust. That he did this evening is a testament to his faith in you."

Terrance nodded. "I get that."

"Good. Don't fuck it up," Daniel told him flatly. "I mean it. He needs a chance to really build trust. Frank was an asshole, and he hurt him badly. That's really apparent to me. Maybe not to the others, but he's almost timid sometimes, and then once he gets wound up, he's strong and will stand up for himself. But we all have a secret, you know that. We can talk around it all you like, but he knows there are things none of us will talk about. That upsets him because secrets mean that he's going to get hurt." Daniel patted his shoulder. "You need to decide how you really feel about him."

Terrance wasn't sure how he felt about being analyzed like this, but if he got up in Daniel's face, it was likely Richard would rearrange his. "I know how I feel about him."

"Yeah… okay. But does *he* know how you feel about him? I'm sure the two of you have had sex and that you're compatible in the bedroom and all that. So he's aware of the hotness that is you. But does he know your heart? That's what you need to show him." Daniel cocked his head slightly. "And he deserves to see it."

"Yes, he does," Richard added as he came back in the room.

Daniel rolled his eyes. "Like you're one to talk. There were times when I wondered so much about you too. You liked me, but you kept your heart to yourself for a long time. You all do that. It's part of how you protect yourselves." Daniel's gaze flashed back to Terrance. "But if you want someone to love you, then you have to show them something you don't let anyone else see… and I'm not talking about what you have in your Calvins. Though I suspect he's probably already seen that." Daniel snickered, and Terrance turned to Richard for help.

"Are you saying I should tell him about us?" Terrance asked.

"No," Richard interjected quickly.

Daniel shook his head. "I'm not. At least not yet. But you need to understand that he's aware that you're keeping things from him. So you need to deal with it. Even if it's just to tell him… hell, I don't know what you should tell him. Be as honest as you feel you can and hope it's enough. But let him know that you care for him and that what you aren't telling him has nothing to do with your feelings or with him." He sighed. "Sometimes this whole thing sucks."

"Yeah, I know it does. According to the rules, we aren't supposed to tell anyone, even you," Terrance said. "But we all agreed that if we trusted people enough to share our lives, they needed to be able to make an informed decision. But I just met Ashton, and I can't tell him yet."

Daniel and Richard nodded. "True. But he's already curious, and you're going to need to try to allay his fears somehow. And understand that he'll be looking at everything you do for clues." That really sounded ominous.

"So be careful and understand what you're getting into," Richard added. "This impacts all of us."

If there had been heat in Richard's voice, Terrance might have gotten angry. He knew the risks as well as everyone else. If they shared the secrets of their past and Ashton betrayed them, then all of them would have their lives uprooted and it was likely that they would be separated. After they had all gone to see his mother, it had taken a great deal of negotiating for them to stay together. They wouldn't get a second chance. The thought of never seeing his "brothers" and their families again sent a ripple of fear up his spine.

"I'm going to tell Ashton that we all have a rough past that we are trying to put behind us and move forward living better lives," Terrance said. "It's the truth, and something we've all tried to live up to." It hadn't been easy a lot of the time, but as a group, they had helped people and done some good while keeping their heads down, and so far out of the line of fire. There were still members of the Garvic organization that would love to find them to teach them all a lesson, and if that happened, none of them, including their families, would be safe.

"Yes. Be sure to take the time to reassure him. He's going to need that."

Footsteps sounded outside the door just as their phones both chimed. It seemed that Frank's tires had been repaired. The car was not in the lot, and the boat seemed deserted.

"I'll answer. You and I need to get going," Richard said, and they stood as the others all came back inside. Terrance tugged Ashton into a tight hug before he could pass him. "I'll be back later. I promise. Please stay here with Daniel and the others." He didn't want Ashton to be alone because he'd worry otherwise.

"Play LEGOs with us," Coby offered, pulling Ashton over almost as soon as Terrance released him.

Ashton smiled, and Terrance took in that sight. He loved that expression on him. Terrance hadn't seen it often, but leave it to Coby to interject some pure childish innocent happiness. "I'll see you later." Terrance left the condo, closed the door after him, and joined Richard at the car.

"One thing we need to try to find out is the kind of relationship Frank has with the Garvics," Richard told him as he started the car. "I don't like any of this. I keep thinking we're walking into something we know little about and that we can all get burned in a big way." Still, he pulled out of the drive, heading toward the marina. "Shit…."

"What?" Terrance asked.

"Call Daniel and ask him to track down the *Dream-scape*. See what sort of information he can find out about her. I wish we had the registration information. But ask him to look into it. Maybe he'll get lucky and it will tell us something. Lord knows Frank has to have some sort of connection to the owners if they're letting him stay there."

"Okay," Terrance agreed and made the call. Daniel wasn't sure what he could do with just the boat name, but he said he would see what he could figure out.

Terrance put his phone away and forced himself to relax as Richard made the turn into a small parking lot just down from the marina. "How do you want to handle this?" he asked Richard.

Gerome tapped quietly on the window. Terrance lowered it, and Gerome leaned in.

"Okay, he's definitely not here, and the nearby boats are quiet. I checked for cameras and there don't seem to be any. Since he doesn't know me, I'm going to act as lookout. I saw him at the Driftwood so I know what he looks like, and I have the description of his car." Gerome pulled out a pack of cigarettes. "I hate these things, but I'll text if I see him and then ask for a light to slow him down. Don't take very long, and then we can get the hell out of here."

The sun had set and the last light of the day was fading away. Lights, probably on sensors, were beginning to come on to illuminate the dock entrance, but they didn't extend the entire way down. Gerome stepped back, and Terrance opened his door and joined Richard on the other side. "Let's go." He had no idea what they were going to find, but they had to look. Maybe they'd get lucky.

Gerome stayed behind as he and Richard made their way to the entrance of the dock. It took Terrance seconds to open the gate, and they let it close behind them. He thought of jamming it to slow Frank down when he returned but decided against it. There was no need to draw any accidental attention to themselves.

The two of them went right for the boat. There was no need to play any games. Act like they belonged and no one would think anything of them. A few bells clinked occasionally as the sailboats and motorboats rocked lightly in the gentle waves that sloshed around the pilings.

"That's it," Terrance said rather softly.

"Cool. He told us to wait for him," Richard said in a normal conversational tone before both of them stepped onto the boat. Richard sat down, and Terrance went right for the locked door to the cabin. He picked it with ease and went below.

The place was a mess—not like someone had been there to search before them, just that there were dishes in the sink and trash hadn't been taken out. The seats were covered with stuff. How could anyone spend five minutes in this mess? Terrance was tempted to pick the place up, but he got to work checking all the cupboards and hatches instead.

"Find anything?" Richard whispered down.

"No. At least the mess will cover that we were here." He checked the seats of the fold-down table and found them filled with jumbled supplies, but nothing incriminating. He pulled open the refrigerator and checked inside quickly, and was glad to close the door once again. Who knew what he could contract from what was growing inside? It was too small to hide anything in anyway.

Working his way clockwise through the space, he checked all the crevices he could find before turning his attention to the bed in the bow of the boat. The first thing he did was take a picture of the jumbled mess. Then he slipped his phone into his pocket and lifted the mattress and pulled the bedding back before returning it to the jumble it had been. Then he lifted the top of the under-bed storage and checked inside it. The space beneath was shallow, dark, and difficult to access. He sneezed and was tempted to pull away, but he got out his pocket flashlight and shone the light into the space.

He got another whiff of dust and God knows what. Terrance concentrated on his task, leaning as close as he dared. The space was filled with cast-off junk that probably hadn't seen the light of day in years. He was about to lower the cover back into place when he re-alized that the dirt wasn't even. All of the items were dusty and grimy, but some looked partially new, espe-cially the bottom of the cast-iron frying pan, which was jet-black. It should be gray with all the dirt.

Terrance shifted to that end and poked through the things, careful not to shift them too much. He found a white plastic grocery bag under some cruddy floats and pulled it into the light, along with a second one. Terrance peered inside, checked for a third, and then put everything back as best he could and set the top back into place. He checked his phone and shuffled the bedding back into place, then returned the clothes and a shoe to where they had been.

He turned and was about to pick up the bags when his eye caught a scrap of white paper. He tried to re-member if he had seen it before.

Terrance wasn't sure, but he lifted the bed a little and placed the scrap under the edge before lowering it again. He had been here longer than he intended.

He grabbed the bags and headed for the steps to the deck. "Let's get out of here," he said quietly.

"Okay. I guess he isn't coming." Richard took one of the bags before stepping off the boat and back onto the dock. Terrance's phone dinged, as did Richard's, and Richard pulled his out. "He's coming," Richard mouthed as he headed down the dock toward the entrance.

Terrance's heart sped up as they walked quickly, passing the T of the dock and continuing down the other way. This end of the dock had more occupied boats, and at the moment they were sitting ducks and easily seen.

A few of the boats had dock boxes. Terrance passed one, then moved over and stood on the other side of it and motioned for Richard to do the same, but it wasn't possible. It would provide some level of cover. Terrance leaned on it, pulling out his phone to use as a prop as he watched the dock entrance.

Frank's figure entered the gate and strode down the ramp to the water level. At the T, he paused, looking around. Terrance held his breath, still pretending to look at his phone as Richard, a little farther away, raised his hand in greeting. Frank did the same and then turned toward the *Dreamscape*.

As soon as he was out of sight, Terrance strode back down the dock toward the entrance, trying to look as though he belonged there, with Richard right behind him.

Terrance half expected a cry to rise up at any second as he passed through the gate and then out into the parking lot.

Gerome was already in his car, and he pulled out as soon as they passed him. Terrance took the big heavy bag from Richard, and they slipped into Richard's car with Terrance placing the plastic bags at his feet. "Let's get out of here."

"What's in the bags?" Richard asked. It said a lot that he hadn't even looked.

"Money. A lot of it. You felt how heavy they were. The bags are packed with stacks of bills. I didn't get a good look, but it's enough to buy a hell of a lot of whatever Frank was after." He sat back, relieved to be away from there.

"Of course you know that we've kicked the beehive. Frank may not know that we were there right away, but he's going to find that his money is missing, and the anger is going to be felt all over the key like the repercussions of a bomb. He's going to be desperate to get his money back," Richard explained.

"Yeah, true," Terrance told him, and called Daniel. "Hey, bud, it's me."

"Yeah. I wasn't able to find out anything about the boat. There are a number of them with that name, and…."

"It's okay. Can you check if Carlo is out on bail? I understand he was going to be transported, but is he out and free?"

"Why?"

"Can you just check? Please?" Terrance breathlessly.

"Okay. But what did you do?" Daniel asked.

"It's fine. We're on our way back. Tell Ashton and Tucker that everything is fine. Gerome is probably

ahead of us, and we'll be there in five minutes or so."
He breathed a sigh of relief. "Thank you." He hung up.

"What are you thinking?" Richard asked.

"Well, I know I'm not that smart, but what if Carlo
is out on bail, and what if he was seen in the area again?
And what if we or someone could get that information
to Frank? I'm not sure how, but I can tell you that might
be just enough information to get Frank to put two and
two together and come up with the answer we want.
Can you imagine the fallout?"

Richard actually laughed. "That's simple and bril-
liant." He clapped Terrance on the shoulder. "But what
if he's still in Detroit?"

Terrance grinned. "Does it matter where he really
is? All that needs to happen is that Frank thinks he was
here. That may be just enough for Frank to believe Carlo took the money. And from there, the groups square
off in a fight between them that sets the two organi-
zations at odds. It's even possible that what's left of
the Garvic operation could be wiped out completely."
Maybe it was too simplistic, but Terrance knew how
these people operated, and if they viewed someone as
insulting their honor or their power, they were likely to
hit back hard.

Richard pulled into the parking spot but left the
engine running. "We need to figure out how to let Frank
know what we want him to know without him knowing
we're feeding it to him. That may take a little luck. It
has to seem like he's the one in charge."

"Okay." Terrance understood that but didn't know
how to make it happen. "One problem solved, and another opens up."

"Exactly," Richard said as he turned off the engine.
"Let's go inside and figure it out." He opened his door.

"What about the money?" Terrance turned to reach for the bags. God, what he could do with that cash. All of them. Their lives were hard, and they lived on very little. Their cars were all old, and so were their clothes. Terrance wasn't thinking of returning to the way they lived in Detroit, but damn it all, he could sure as hell make things easier for Ashton, who lived on even less than he did. The guys could get some toys for the kids… one of those Nintendo Switches that Coby kept asking for, and maybe…. He sighed.

"We bury it for now. I'll do it tonight, out back in the sand. That way it can stay there and will be out of sight. That shit isn't ours, and who the hell knows where it came from or who paid what for it."

"I was hoping that a little of it…."

Richard was already shaking his head. "Do we really want to do that? If we start spending, that could raise questions, and a little will turn into more… and then more. It's a slippery slope." He closed his door and locked the car. "Gerome is working to figure out how to repatriate some of the money we put aside. Besides, this is drug money, and we never dealt with that shit before. Do you want to now?" Richard held his gaze, and Terrance shook his head. Fucking hell, he knew he was right, but that didn't make it go down any easier.

"Should we put it in the trunk?" Terrance asked.

Richard turned around, grabbed the bags out of the back, popped open the trunk, and placed them inside before slamming the trunk lid closed. A few bills blew out, and Terrance chased them down. Six hundred-dollar bills. He looked at them, wondering when such a small amount of money came to mean so fucking much. Terrance turned to Richard.

"Put them in your pocket and pass them to Ashton when you can. I know he needs it and that his art isn't cheap to make." He stepped closer. "Make sure they're real first. If they aren't, then we will have to burn all of it."

God, he hoped they were real. Terrance shared a "thank you" look with Richard and handed him a pair of bills. "Get the boys each one of those video games they want, and I'll get this to Ashton." He wasn't sure how he was going to help him, but he definitely intended to.

They went inside, where everyone else had gathered. Ashton seemed relaxed and happy, talking to Tucker and Cheryl. When Terrance came in, Ashton turned and smiled. "Everything okay?"

"For now," Richard answered and sat next to Daniel.

"Can I have some fruit?" Coby asked.

Daniel got out some snacks for everyone, including crackers, cheese, grapes, and strawberries. The boys settled in to eat like they had been starving for days.

"You need to share," Daniel told Coby as he tried to stuff another strawberry into his mouth. "Just relax, there's plenty for everyone." Coby handed the strawberry in his clutches to Joshie. "Eat some cheese too."

Terrance slid his hand into Ashton's, and Ashton squeezed back. This was his family, all of them. He was Uncle Terrance to the boys, and he knew and trusted Daniel and Tucker because his brothers did. Even Cheryl had been integrated into the family. She didn't know about their past, but that didn't seem to matter. When Terrance was a kid, he used to love watching gangster movies, especially ones like *The Godfather* and *Goodfellas*. He saw a lot of himself in some of those characters—not that he aspired to be one of them, but sometimes he saw himself looking back from the screen. In those movies, gatherings were the family, the people around them they trusted. And it was like that for them. They went out together and spent their time together. They weren't related by blood, but they were still a family, and Terrance would do anything for any of them. This family was his world… except as he turned to Ashton, he realized that he was just as important. That Ashton was beginning to become his world within a world… if that was possible.

"Joshie, finish your snack. We need to get home. It's close to your bedtime," Cheryl said, and Joshie grinned and went to her. "Say goodbye and give everyone hugs." She was an amazing woman and a wonderful parent. Terrance wondered, though, when she would meet someone. Cheryl was attractive, and she deserved to be happy like the rest of them. He figured when that happened, either their family would expand or she would drift away.

"What are you thinking about?" Ashton whispered, handing him a cracker with some cheese on it.

"Family," he answered as Joshie made his way around the room. Terrance got his hug, and then Ashton received one too. Then Cheryl gathered their things and she and Joshie left. Daniel reminded Coby of the time, and they all got hugs from him too before he and Daniel left the room.

Richard took the lead and explained what they had found and their thoughts.

Gerome nodded his agreement. "What you're saying makes sense. Frank has been moving around the country in a supposed effort to find Ashton. He returns here and suddenly he's sitting on a pile of money. I doubt he carried it around in the trunk of his rental car."

"It has to be Carlo's money, and he likely asked Frank to complete the deal," Terrance said. "But now the money will come up missing, and Frank is going to be on the hook for it. Carlo and his people aren't going to be happy." He filled in their line of thought.

"True, and that's going to spread mistrust. But we need more than that… and some luck," Richard added. Terrance watched Ashton as he tried to keep up and squeezed his fingers lightly. "What I'm hoping is that Frank shows up at the Driftwood again. Maybe that will give me a chance to instill some doubt."

Ashton leaned closer. "Okay. Can I get a complete picture? You checked out the boat Frank was on and found a lot of cash." Terrance nodded. "And you took it. Which means Frank is going to be pissed as hell and God knows what else."

"It also means that whatever deal he was trying to do isn't going to happen," Terrance clarified as gently as he could. "And he's going to want to get the money back."

"Of course. So what? You wanna instill what *kind* of doubt?"

Richard leaned forward. "It's simple. We want Frank to be missing his money… and we want him to think someone else took it." He sat back.

"Your ex-boyfriend, Carlo the dickhead?" Ashton asked, and Terrance nodded. "Let them all chase their tails, and meanwhile we can get on with our lives." He smiled as he sat back. "That's pretty good. Frank is going to need to get the hell out of Dodge and back where he might have friends and support. Carlo is going to follow him, and all of us are left alone to live our lives safely." It wasn't that simple, but yeah, Ashton had the gist of it.

"That's pretty much it. But it hinges on Carlo being out on bail—probably a pretty good bet by now—and finding a way to cast suspicion onto Carlo without Frank knowing what we're doing," Richard explained. "Can you help us?"

"I…." Ashton's gaze shifted between them. "I have no idea what I can do. Frank has a huge ego, and since the money is missing, he's going to shit himself." Ashton actually grinned. "First thing, he'll tear that boat apart to find it, then call off the deal and move heaven and earth to find out who took it. His ego and reputation will be at stake, two things he holds very dear." He grew quiet as Daniel came into the room.

"Has Carlo gotten out on bail?" Gerome asked.

Daniel rolled his eyes. "I love you all too," he snapped back. "I haven't had a chance to look yet." He went to his computer to get started on his own particular brand of magic. "Fortunately, those records are public. You just have to know where to look." He continued typing.

"Let's say he is," Gerome said. "What's your plan?"

"I'd say that Terrance and Richard need to go back to work and hope Frank comes into the Driftwood. He's going to kick stones to see what he can find."

Terrance tugged Ashton to him. "And when he does, we'll let him kick over our stones, and hopefully we can lead him on a wild goose chase… straight to hell."

Ashton WAS quiet on the ride home. Terrance had a good idea that he had to be mulling things over. From his expression, the mulling was getting deeper by the second. "Secret agents?" Ashton asked. "You guys have to be secret agents."

Terrance chuckled. "No, we aren't secret agents or part of some international spy network. We're just three guys. What we've told you is true." He hated keeping secrets from Ashton, which was unusual because usually he didn't have any trouble with secrets. They kept all of them safe. "Our past is our past, and…." He was about to say that it had nothing to do with the present, but that would be a bald-faced lie. Under normal circumstances, weaving a set of lies was something he could do very easily. But he didn't want to do that to Ashton. Lying to him felt like lying to himself, and that really sucked.

He pulled into the parking area and came to a stop.

"We're at your place," Ashton commented as Terrance turned off the engine and leaned over the console.

"I'll take you home." He wasn't going to pressure Ashton into anything. He gently touched the underside of his chin with his fingertips.

Ashton slowly turned toward him but made no move to come closer.

Terrance could almost see the war going on behind his eyes. Ashton was trying to decide what he wanted. Terrance could only wait while whatever was going on in his mind played out. Not that he could blame him. Terrance would probably do the same thing if he were in his shoes, though he would be more bulldozer-y about it. "You're a thinker. You ponder what's going on around you and try to figure it out." Ashton smiled. "Richard and Gerome are a lot more like that than me."

Ashton nodded slowly. It was the first indication that he was actually not mentally far away and deep in his thoughts. "Yes. I get in my head sometimes…."

"I tend to be more a man of action. I don't spend a lot of time examining all sides of everything." Terrance leaned closer. "What I do is look at someone's actions to see what they tell me. It's all I can deal with."

"You were pretty good at figuring out Frank and what he might be doing," Ashton told him. "Is it because you understand his world?"

He was so close to the truth that Terrance didn't know how to answer for fear of giving too much away. "I understand where he might be coming from and his motivations. They used to be mine." He turned away, looking out the windshield toward the front of the building. "I didn't have anything as a kid, and I spent a lot of time trying to change my circumstances any way I could. It was what I felt I had to do." He swallowed hard. "Detroit was a rough place, especially if you grew up where I did. There weren't any opportunities for me to do what you do or to learn anything other than how to survive and claw your way to whatever you wanted. That's what I understood."

"But not what you know now?" Ashton asked, almost a whisper.

"It's all I used to know. Then we moved here, and Richard met Daniel and Gerome met Tucker, and they have very different lives. But more than that, they have kids, who deserve to have so much more than what I did. Those guys have changed all of us. But so have the boys." He gnawed slightly at his lower lip. "How could I be what I was and do what was right for Coby and Joshie?"

Ashton finally cracked a slightly smile. "Those two boys love you all."

"I like to think that as big as I am—and I know I can be as intimidating as all hell—if I wasn't good enough, they'd be afraid of me." Terrance didn't think he could take that.

"I can't argue with that," Ashton told him. "I just hate secrets. I know everyone has them, but Frank had tons of them, and he always shut me out. That's what initially told me that he was something other than what he seemed. Then things got worse."

The seat scrunched a little as Terrance leaned closer. "Look, I can't tell you some things, but I will say that there are things none of us can talk about. Maybe someday. But what we're doing with Frank is because of you. If I hadn't met you, none of us would have thought anything about him." Terrance swore under his breath. "God, I'm really terrible at this sort of thing. Frank is a bad person, and we all want him to go the hell away. But more than anything else, we want you to be safe. That's what's important to all of us... but me especially."

Ashton finally met his gaze. "I know what you're saying, and I'm aware that Gerome and Richard, as well as you, put yourselves in danger to try to help me." His gaze hardened. "I just wished I knew why they were doing this."

Terrance smiled. "Now that's the easiest question you've asked all day." He closed the distance between them and lightly kissed Ashton's full lips before deepening it, taking Ashton harder, carding his fingers through Ashton's soft hair. "They're doing it because I care about you. Just like I'd do the same thing for them." And he had, but now was not to the time to go into stuff like that. Not with his chest pounding and his head reeling just from the taste of Ashton's lips.

"You really are like Robin Hood. You help people in distress and ask for nothing in return." Ashton snorted. "I don't quite know what to make of that. See, everyone wants something, and each person has their own motivations for doing what they do. The problem is that I can't seem to quite figure out what yours are. It makes me nervous."

Terrance wasn't sure how to answer, and he thought of what Daniel had said. "What does your heart tell you?" That was what his mother used to ask him when he had a decision to make. He had a tendency to go with his fists first and think later, or at least he used to. But Mama... well, she had been very different.

"It's not that simple."

Terrance shrugged. "Maybe sometimes it is." He could hardly believe he was having a conversation about hearts and feelings, but then, that was what Daniel had warned him about. "I know you're trying to figure things out." He pulled his fingers out of Ashton's hair and took his hand instead. "I guess I'm expecting you to believe me and accept me for who I am when you don't have all the facts. Right now I can't give you all you want—for your own good... and mine. But I have to tell you that I care for you. That I...." Terrance swallowed hard. Why was it so hard just to say the words?

Ashton blinked at him, his lips slightly parted. He said nothing, holding still... waiting while Terrance fumbled over his own damned emotions, some of which he didn't even completely understand.

"I'm on new ground here. This isn't something I have ever done before or talked about before." How his throat could be so dry in one of the most humid places on earth was a complete mystery to him, but hell, it was happening right now.

"What is?" Ashton asked, his gaze steady. Terrance wished he dared use his hard-as-granite look to get Ashton to turn away, but if he did, that would be the end. Opening up was hard as hell, but he knew this was the moment. He needed to take the chance—to show Ashton some of that part of himself that he held down deep, locked away so he couldn't be hurt, and trust that Ashton wouldn't stomp on it the way life seemed to a lot of the time.

"I don't talk about my feelings and shit. It isn't something I do. I let people know how I feel with my body, with my hands if necessary. I show them, and I…."

"But you already did that," Ashton whispered.

Terrance's cheeks heated. Hell, he never blushed—ever—and here he was acting like a teenager. "I didn't mean like that."

Ashton squeezed his fingers. "I know what you meant. But maybe it's time you did a few things my way. It's okay to tell me how you feel. I can't read your mind and I don't know what you're thinking. As much as I'd like to sometimes, I think if I could, it might be closer to a Stephen King novel than an Amy Lane romance." He smiled. "You have to talk to me."

Terrance knew he was right, but it was still hard as fuck to do. "I know I do, and I…." He sighed. "I haven't said this to anyone since the day I called my mother to talk to her just before she passed away." He paused once again and felt a little lost—not because he didn't know how he felt, but because…. Oh, dammit. He'd seen things that would send most men running back to their mothers. He could do this.

"Terrance…."

"Okay. Here's the deal." He smiled, still looking into Ashton's eyes. "I like you. I, you know, *like*… like you."

Ashton snorted and grinned. "Is this high school?"

Terrance growled.

"Ooh, I got one of those."

"One of what?"

Ashton shrugged. "When you get all growly, I know I'm treading on thin ice. Just say what you really mean and stop beating around the bush."

Terrance bit his lower lip and then drew Ashton into another kiss. "I love you. That's what I've been trying to say."

Ashton smiled and kissed him back. "Was that so hard to say, you big lummox? Did it hurt to say that? Because let me tell you, it was wonderful to hear." He squeezed Terrance's hand. "And I love you too. Which is why the secrets worry me."

"Daniel explained that, or at least he tried to." Terrance opened his door, got out of the car, and waited for Ashton before going inside and back into air-conditioning. "I won't hurt you. I'd rather hurt myself than let anyone get to you, and that includes me."

"How do you know that?"

"Because I'm following the advice of my mom and listening to my heart. Right now, that's all I can do. I think it's all either of us can." Terrance stood inside living area with Ashton, afraid to move. The way Ashton looked at him was like he had just hung the moon. Terrance wanted to bask in that look for as long as possible, so he stayed still.

It was Ashton who took his hand and, without a word, guided him toward the bedroom, pulling him along behind. "I think an occasion like this should be celebrated."

"You know, Daniel is really great at arranging parties. Maybe we could let him know and he could put one together so we always remember this night."

Ashton snickered and kicked the door closed. "Somehow I don't think we want to be calling Daniel or anyone else, and if we want to throw ourselves a party, we can make it a party of two. No one else allowed, and we already have all the party favors we could possibly need."

Terrance really liked that idea. "I see. So how should I dress for this party?"

"That's just it. The party doesn't have a dress code. In fact, you might say it has an *un*dress code." Ashton's voice grew deeper and rumblier.

"I really love that idea." He tugged Ashton to him. "And I love you." There was very little need for additional conversation for quite a while.

Chapter 12

ASHTON'S PHONE rang, and he glanced over at it, then returned to his work. He finished the pale yellow flower petal, placed it in the annealer, and shut down the equipment. He was drained and needed something to drink before he passed out from the heat. As he headed inside, he returned Terrance's call.

"Hey." Ashton couldn't help the smile that tugged at his lips. For the past week, they had spent their free time at his place. Terrance's was bigger, but with the studio, it made more sense to be at Ashton's so he could work and prepare for the show. "How's work?" He checked the time and wondered why Terrance had been calling at this hour. Still, he was glad to hear from him.

"Were you in the studio?"

"Yeah. I just finished up. I think I have more pieces than they expect, and I'm not sure I'm going to have room for them all." That was a good thing.

"Well, we'll set up the booth on the first day, and as pieces sell, we'll arrange to bring in fresh ones to replace them. It'll keep the booth changing and make it more interesting. We'll also have pictures of all the pieces so they can be sold, like you said. I think it will be great." Terrance had become his cheerleader of sorts, keeping him steady when things threatened to overwhelm him.

"That isn't why you called," Ashton prompted.

"No. Frank was in tonight, and he seemed steamed beyond measure." There was no missing the pleasure in his voice. "You would have loved it. I saw him first and approached him, asking if he'd had any luck finding the guy he was looking for. He shook his head and turned away and went up to the bar. He spoke to Richard for a little while, and then when they finished, Frank practically sprinted out of here."

"Okay…." Ashton wasn't sure what Terrance was getting at.

"Richard asked Frank about the friend he'd been in here with earlier, and Frank apparently told Richard that he was out of town." Terrance chuckled. "Richard should get an Academy Award, because I could see from the other side of the room that puzzled look on his face." Obviously Richard had filled Terrance in on the conversation. "Anyway, he told Frank he thought he'd seen him just the other night and was surprised when Frank hadn't been with him. And that was when Frank raced out of there."

Ashton snickered. "So Frank thinks that Carlo returned and double-crossed him." That was pretty sweet.

"And it isn't like Frank is going to sit down and ask Carlo about it… and if he did, Frank wouldn't believe him anyway."

"Yup. I bet Frank will be out of here in short order and you aren't going to have to worry about him for much longer." Terrance sounded pleased with himself. Ashton was pretty pleased with him too. Frank was going to be chasing his tail for quite some time, it seemed. "We'll go by and check that he's gone tomorrow morning."

For the first time in weeks, Ashton felt like part of the weight on his shoulders was lifting. If Frank was gone, he could go back to leading a more normal life. It was like he could breathe again. Even as hot as he was from the studio, it was as if someone had opened the window to a crisp northern breeze. "That would be great."

"Yes, it will. Look, I need to go back to work, but I'll see you at your place once I'm done here. I have an hour or so and I'll be able to head your way. See you then."

Terrance ended the call, and Ashton set his phone aside and grabbed and downed a bottle of water before heading to the shower.

His legs shook as the water sprayed down on him. He was so keyed up and excited, he could barely stand still. Maybe he was finally free. Frank hadn't found him, and whatever he was doing hanging around the area had come to naught. Hopefully he'd be heading out in search of more lucrative prey, and Ashton could go back to building his life.

But at the moment, he had other thoughts racing through his head. Terrance was coming home soon. At times like these, it was impossible for him not to think about the big man. God, he was strong, and so many times, Ashton just wanted to climb the guy like a mountain, wrap his legs around him, and hold the hell on.

What continually shocked him was the way Terrance touched him, with such care. Oh, he used that strength, and one of the things Ashton liked best was when Terrance tossed him on the bed so he bounced before Terrance joined him, his eyes blazing with heat. Just the thought was enough to send Ashton's hand to his dick. He stroked, his eyes closed, leg shaking with unabashed excitement. Ashton had to stop himself from getting lost in his own fantasy. He was going to have the real Terrance home very soon, and he didn't need to get himself too excited with his mental one.

Ashton turned off the water and got out, dried himself, and put on a light robe. Then he cleaned up his tiny bathroom and returned to the kitchen, drank some more water, and settled into the living room to relax. He checked the time before he turned on the television. Terrance would be there soon, and he was excited.

"Terrance?" he asked when a thud sounded just outside the door. He stood, expecting the door to open at any moment, but instead, a bang made him jump and he hurried to the window to peer outside. A shadow moved near the studio and then disappeared—probably an animal. Moments later, headlights illuminated the area out by the road as Terrance's car slowed and then pulled into the area.

Ashton cocked his head as much as he could toward the studio, but he saw no one, just a raccoon racing for cover into the trees. Maybe that was the cause of the ruckus.

He relaxed and opened the door so Terrance could come inside. "Everything okay?" Ashton asked when

Terrance closed the door and stopped dead. Ashton looked down at himself and then up at Terrance once more, pulling his robe tighter. "Did I do something?"

Terrance stepped forward, engulfing him in his arms and sliding his hands under the robe. "You're naked under that thing."

"Yeah…." Ashton giggled when Terrance found a ticklish spot. "You expect me to wear a tuxedo under it? I could, you know. Just to tease you. But it would be awfully warm."

"No. I like you just like this." Terrance's voice grew rough and his hands slid upward, cupping Ashton's buttcheeks.

"Wait. I need to lock the door, and I have some snacks and things made up for you. When you get off work you're always hungry, so…." He cut off his words when Terrance growled and held him tighter.

"There's only one snack I want." Terrance lifted him, and Ashton wound his legs around Terrance's waist. It looked like it was going to be one of those nights. *Oh goody.*

Ashton bounced as Terrance plopped him on the bed. His robe came open, and Ashton shimmied out of it, lying naked on the blanket. Terrance slowly removed his shirt, pulling the polo over his head and stretching those normally bunched muscles. "I kept thinking of you all night…." He dropped the shirt on the floor.

"I see, and I was in the shower earlier and I thought of you." He smirked. "I thought of you a whole lot."

Terrance drew closer. "You did, huh? And what exactly did you think about? How I touch you, or maybe how I taste you?"

Ashton quivered. "Both," he whimpered, growing more excited by the second. "And I was good, you

know. I waited for you to come home." God, he liked
the idea of this being a home for them. But he mentally
cautioned himself not to make huge leaps ahead. He'd
done that with Frank, and look where it had landed him.
No. He needed to be careful and not rush into anything.
That was the best way forward. But he knew he could
repeat that all he wanted and it would do him little good
with Terrance just a few feet away, bare-chested and
already kicking off his shoes.

"I'm glad you were able to control yourself, because I really like it when you lose control... because
of *me*." Terrance's voice was now deep enough to be
called a growl, and it sent a shiver racing through Ashton. He watched as Terrance slowly pulled off the last
of his clothes and then stood naked next to the bed.
That was a sight he would never get tired of.

"Do you work out a lot?" Ashton asked as he slid
closer, running his fingers over the ridges on Terrance's
belly.

"Sometimes. Mostly I think I'm just lucky." He
crawled onto the bed, pressing Ashton back on the
mattress.

A bang from outside made Ashton go suddenly still.

Terrance got off the bed, grabbed his clothes, and
pulled them on. "You stay here. If I'm not back in a few
minutes, call Richard and Gerome and tell them to get
over here." He hadn't even put on his shoes before he
zipped out of the room.

Ashton got off the bed and pulled on his own
clothes. If something was going to happen, he wasn't
going to get caught naked.

Moving slowly, he left the room and sat on the
sofa, watching the front door.

Terrance came in and closed the door.

"Raccoons?"

Terrance groaned. "Yes, I think so. They were messing around in the garbage cans. I closed them well and put them around the corner where they can't be knocked over. Hopefully they'll move on now. Have you seen them before?"

"Before you got here, I heard something and saw one run away. I don't know, but I thought I saw a shadow. It could have been nothing, though."

"There was nothing out there but raccoons this time." He locked the door again. "There's nothing to worry about. We'll check that Frank is gone in the morning, and then you can go back to your life." Terrance sat down next to him. "I never thought of damned raccoons as such mood breakers."

"Yeah, me neither." Ashton got up and got out the cheese and stuff he had put together and set it on the old, scuffed coffee table. He then brought out a couple of beers and turned on the TV, switched off the rest of the lights, and cuddled next to Terrance. "I hate being afraid all the time. I left him two years ago, and he has no right to came back like this. Frank needs to leave me alone. Whatever happens to him, he deserves." He held Terrance tighter.

"Yes, he does, and the rug has been pulled out from under him. You don't need to worry about that guy anymore. He has much worse problems to worry about." Terrance reached for a few pieces of cheese and some crackers, made a sandwich, and handed it to him.

"You're the one who's supposed to eat." He pushed Terrance's hand back toward him.

"And you're going to need your strength later, so...." He smiled as Ashton nibbled on the crackers and cheese.

There wasn't much on television, but he found some reruns of *The Big Bang Theory* and they watched a couple of episodes, the scare with the raccoons fading away. Ashton really needed to stop worrying so much, especially with Terrance here. It wasn't like Frank was going to burst in and hold them at gunpoint or anything.

Ashton watched the television, his eyelids growing heavy. Terrance stayed where he was as one episode shifted to another. "Sweetheart, I think it's time to go to bed."

"Oh. Yeah." Ashton yawned. "I'm sorry. Give me a few minutes to wake up a little and…."

Terrance shifted away and got up. "Come on. Let's just go to bed. We can have loads of fun in the morning." He took Ashton's hand, turned off the television and the lights, and led the way to the bedroom.

THE FOLLOWING day, a thick bank of clouds obscured the sky, which kept the temperature down. Storms were probably on the way, but for now, Ashton was relieved and went to his studio to work during the rare break in the heat. He smiled with each step between the door and the one to his small studio, the tightness and ache a wonderful reminder of Terrance's wake-up call.

He'd had an email from Gerome that he wanted a few more pieces now that he was putting Ashton's work back on sale, so he figured he'd get that done.

Inside the studio, he turned on the equipment to let everything heat up and sat at his planning desk to get his head around what he wanted to do. His phone dinged with a message, and he smiled. It seemed that

Dreamscape, the boat Frank had been staying on, had been closed up and was locked up tight with parts of it covered. *Thanks for letting me know*, he sent along with a smiley face. Things were going pretty well along the lines of how they expected. Frank was gone, and the rest of it wasn't his concern. He opened the windows at the top of the studio to keep the heat from being trapped inside.

Of course. I'll see you tonight. I've been thinking and I have some stuff to ask you, Terrance replied, and butterflies danced in Ashton's belly. He wasn't sure if that was good or not, but Terrance almost immediately sent a smiley face, and Ashton felt better.

Stop by once you get off work, Ashton sent and then put his phone aside and checked on the glass. It wasn't yet ready, but his head was already racing. Instead of the things he wanted to do for Gerome, something else flashed in his mind, an inspiration, and Ashton hurried back to the desk to draw what his mind was conjuring. It was something like what he'd done when he had been so anxious, only this was open and lighter, a version of his happiness.

He checked the glass once more and grabbed a punty, swirled on a beginning dollop of glass, and set it to stay heated before setting up three more. Then he got the first one, starting with a small amount, heated it, and then blew in a little air to enlarge it.

Ashton continued working as quickly as he could, but not too fast, and the piece of glass on the punty grew as he added layers, each one adding to the weight and enlarging the piece with intertwined ropes of glass. He added clear leaves in a few places, the vines opening up, the piece growing and coming to life before his eyes. He heated it again, careful not to hit the edge of the furnace.

The piece was getting heavy, and he continually swirled it in the furnace as he heated it. Then he used his second piece to add one final layer, creating a short stem where he would add a small flower that he'd make as a separate piece. There were so many times he wished he had an assistant, but he couldn't afford one, so he had stands that he used to help hold things in place. Ashton set the nearly finished piece in the furnace for a final heat so he could work out a few details.

The door opened and closed behind him. "I wasn't expecting you until—" Ashton looked over his shoulder as he pulled his piece out of the furnace.

"I bet you weren't." Frank stood inside the door.

Ashton's heart skipped a beat and he nearly dropped the punty, but managed to keep it in his hand, placing it across two stands to keep it steadied. "What do you want?" Ashton asked, talking a step away from him. "What are you doing here?" He bit his lip to keep from running away at the mouth.

"I came for you, of course. Did you really think I was going to let you go?" He sneered, his upper lip curling slightly. Frank was a predator, and he resembled a dog with its teeth bared, ready to strike. Ashton's phone vibrated on the desk behind him, but Ashton didn't dare turn to see what it was. He kept his gaze on Frank even as he tried to put distance between them.

"It's been two years."

"And I've spent a lot of time and effort trying to find you. Imagine my surprise when I got word that you were here. I came down to try to bring you home and to tell you that I forgive you and want you back, and then you managed to set up that little wild goose chase." He slapped a fist into his palm and then slowly cracked his knuckles. "You'd think you didn't care about me anymore."

"I don't. Not anymore. You should just go back to Chicago and find someone else. I like it here, and you're a king there. So go and make yourself happy." Ashton bumped into one of the stands holding the glass and managed to keep everything from falling over. He pushed it out of the way and reached for the punty.

"Put that back," Frank ordered.

Ashton pulled his hand away and stepped around it, trying to put some distance between himself and the glass. There was a lot of weight there, and the pieces of glass would cool at different rates. It was only a matter of time before the stresses building up inside the piece became too great and it cracked and then shattered. That only added to his jangling nerves. "But—"

"Don't argue with me. You know what happens when you talk back." Frank stalked closer, and Ashton wished he could figure a way out of this. He was quickly getting boxed into the corner of the studio with the hunk of glass acting as a time bomb a few steps away.

"Ashton," Terrance said as he came inside. Frank turned, and Terrance immediately went on alert, ready to fight.

"I should have known there was something fishy going on." Frank's gaze bored into Ashton. "You and him? No wonder I kept chasing my tail. I bet that guy at the restaurant where you work is in league with you as well." He smiled. "Not that it matters now."

"Frank, just—" Ashton stammered.

Frank reached under his open shirt and pulled out a gun. "You"—he waved the gun at Ashton—"go over and join your boyfriend."

Ashton stepped around and away from the glass, which was already cooling much faster than it should. The piece was still hundreds of degrees.

"Are you okay?" Terrance asked quietly once he got close.

Ashton nodded, unable to take his gaze off Frank and the gun.

"Why are you doing this? Why not move on?" Ashton asked, doing his best to keep his legs from shaking. "You're surrounded by plenty of guys. You always were. They would all love to spend time with you and have you take them places. They would dote on you. Why me?"

Frank raised the gun, holding it aimed square at Ashton's chest. Ashton could almost feel the line of sight like a laser-pointed red dot on his chest. "Because you *left*. I've had to explain to everyone for two fucking years what happened to you. Some of the guys laughed at me. They weren't happy that I was dating guys to begin with. I had to break a few skulls to shut them the hell up. But then you fucking left, and I became the gay hood whose guy ran away."

Ashton might have felt sorry for him if he wasn't a crazy psychopath.

"Just leave and walk away. No one has to get hurt," Terrance said. "It's the middle of the day, there are people out and about, and my friends know where I am and will be coming here soon. You'll be trapped."

"Yeah. You and your friends from Detroit." Frank smiled, but it was filled with evil. "Did he tell you about his past? You left me, but they're worse than me. They're snitches. When things got a little hot, they turned on their friends. Well, call them and I can take out the trash. They'll be more than a little grateful for the information. There are things I owe, but this will even the score with Carlo." He might have rubbed his hands together if he could.

Ashton glanced at Terrance and then back at Frank.

"I see—he never told you. Yeah, he and his friends were part of the Garvic family in Detroit. That's why Carlo was here, looking for him. I didn't realize until just now. But it's all clear. They ran all the gay vices there. It was some operation they had… until they turned on their family." The gun shifted from Ashton to Terrance. "They've been looking for those guys for years now."

"Are you really so sure they actually care all that much any longer?" Terrance asked.

Ashton felt the bottom drop out of his stomach. So it was true. Terrance was a gangster, and the guys…. God, he could really pick them. Out of the frying pan and into the fire.

A tink drew his attention, and he took a step back. The glass was getting cooler by the second. The stress was going to become too much for the piece to handle.

"Oh, they care. You sent half of them to prison, so they aren't going to forgive and forget, no matter how much time has passed. They will hate you forever."

Ashton looked into Frank's eyes and saw nothing but the cold hard flint that had driven him away in the first place. There was no way to appeal to his better nature because he didn't have one.

"Once you're dead, I'll go after your friends." He grinned and his finger twitched on the trigger.

Ashton closed his eyes as what sounded like a shot rang out. He fell to the floor, pulling Terrance down with him.

Frank screamed, and Ashton chanced a glance before grabbing Terrance by the hand and racing out the door. A second, larger explosion followed as the rest of the hunk of glass exploded inside the studio. A second scream followed, and then silence.

Ashton picked himself up off the concrete, considering himself lucky that he hadn't been hit. "Are you okay?" he asked, turning to Terrance.

"Yeah. I got hit in the shoulder and it stings like hell, but I'll be okay. But what the hell happened?" He got up, his arm hanging by his side.

"The piece I was working on didn't have a chance to cool properly, and it exploded." He reached for Terrance's shoulder, but Terrance brushed Ashton's hand away and pulled out the shard of glass. Ashton winced for him, but Terrance barely reacted to the pain.

"I'll be fine. I need to check on our friend. Go inside your apartment and stay there." Terrance went back into the studio, but Ashton wasn't going to let him deal with his mess alone, so he followed him.

The interior of the studio was a mess. Bits of glass had flown everywhere; shards littered the concrete floor. Frank lay on his back on the concrete, covered in blood. Ashton turned away. "Is he alive?"

Terrance must have checked. "No. He took some large pieces to the head."

"I see." Ashton looked and wished he hadn't. Frank was covered in cuts and burns, with large shards of glass through his eye and skull. Ashton hugged Terrance and buried his face against his chest.

"Just go inside," Terrance said gently and called 911 for emergency help.

THE POLICE spoke with Ashton more than once. It seemed that when someone died on your property, there were a million questions. Did he know the glass would explode? Did Frank know? Why was he here? Had he really held them at gunpoint? Ashton answered all the questions with as much patience he could muster, while the whole time, what Frank had told him echoed through his mind.

But he kept the revelations about Terrance to himself. He wasn't sure why, other than they didn't seem pertinent to the incident. And if the truth be told, he wanted to give Terrance a chance to deny it or at the very least explain.

"Other than the victim, Mr. Vicardi was injured, but you weren't," Detective Ramone said. "Why is that?"

"Because I heard the glass cracking. I expected to be shot, but part of the piece shattered, and I got down, dragging Terrance too. I think the first large piece must have hit Frank, because he screamed, and then the rest of the piece exploded, and I think that's what killed him. I'm only saying that from experience and supposition. I didn't actually see the explosions or else I'd be where Frank is now."

"Did you try to warn him?" the detective asked.

"Yes. But he had a gun on me and didn't give me a chance," Ashton explained. "He and I dated back before I moved here, and he was angry that I left him. When we dated, Frank was much more interested in what he was doing rather than my art. He couldn't have cared less as long as I was where he wanted me to be."

"So he had no idea?"

Ashton shook his head. "He obviously didn't, otherwise he wouldn't be dead." Ashton's throat ached, and he began to shake. Someone had died right in front of him. Frank was gone forever, and he'd never need to worry about him. Part of him was horrified that Frank had been killed, but he was relieved too. Frank would have shot them both—there was no doubt in Ashton's mind at all, and he told the detective that. "Can I get some water?"

The detective had one of the other officers get him a glass of water, and Ashton answered the rest of his questions.

"Why did Frank come here after all this time?"

"Because I damaged his ego. At least that's what he said. Frank was always obsessive, and that's part of why I ran away from him. I think there might have been more to it, but I don't know. For someone to do what he did, there has to be something not right." Ashton took the water and drank, closing his eyes, just wishing this was over.

A knock startled him, and he nearly dropped his glass. A uniformed police officer joined them, spoke softly to the detective, and received a nod in response. He left, and then Terrance came in. Ashton wanted to rush to him, but he held back. The things Frank had said planted doubts. Mobster, criminal, killer? Did he really know who Terrance was?

"Are there any more questions for us?" Terrance asked. "If not, then we're going to lock up here and go to my place. The officer has the address. Lock up the studio when you're finished with it." Terrance took Ashton's arm and gently drew him to his feet.

"Yes. I think we have everything." The detective stood as well. "If we need anything else, we'll let you know."

"Okay. Thank you," Ashton said, too worn out to argue. Having someone die in the studio would do that to a guy.

The detective left, and Ashton got a bag. "Can you take me to Daniel's?"

"Why?"

Ashton sighed. "I need to think. He said you were a gangster in Detroit, and I don't know what to think, but he was an outsider too, and maybe he can tell me how he dealt with this. I know he's with Richard and all, but he'll tell me the truth. You told me you had a secret, but I thought that maybe you guys had been arrested for something. I didn't know. You knew stuff normal people didn't. But being part of organized crime—I know now that Frank was, and…."

"We aren't anymore," Terrance said. "You heard him. We turned evidence against them. That's why we're here." He sounded almost broken. "We turned on them because they were going to turn on us. We testified and sent a number of people to jail, including the bosses. It was a huge deal, and we got put in witness protection. That's why we're here and why we didn't tell you. We can't. But I wasn't—"

"It *feels* like you lied, even though you told me there were things you couldn't talk about. I knew there was something." Ashton sniffed and rubbed his eyes. "I spent months with Frank where I was scared all the time, and I finally had to run away from him. It took two years, but he found me again. Frank was sick, and I'm glad he's gone. There, I said it. I'm glad. But I can't do something like that again, and with what I know now, I don't know what it will take to stop me from feeling this way."

Terrance nodded. "I see." They got in the car and Terrance drove and made the turn off the main road toward Daniel's condo. "Then I'll take you to Daniel's. You deserve the chance to think things over." They pulled into the lot, and Terrance got out, went up to the door, and spoke to Daniel a minute. Then Ashton followed, and Daniel hugged him and guided Ashton into the condo, closing the door, leaving Terrance on the other side.

Chapter 13

TERRANCE COLLAPSED the box flat and placed it to the side. Then he opened another, continuing the task of filling the shelf with bug spray. Then he moved on to fill the other chemicals. The store seemed to have had a run on them lately, and the shelf had been nearly empty.

"Is this what you do all day?" Daniel asked as he approached down the aisle.

"Not usually, no. But the stock boy called in sick, and this needed to be done." He collapsed the last box and transferred everything to the rolling cart.

"Do you need that taken back?" Ned asked, and Terrance thanked him for taking it to the back room. He was new and very eager to please.

"Is there something you needed?" Terrance asked, turning toward Daniel. "Can I help you find something?"

Daniel rolled his eyes. "Quit acting like a total prat, at least with me. Ashton has been staying in our guest room for the past two days, and you haven't stopped by once. What the heck is going on?"

"You know what happened from him, I'm sure." Terrance had plenty of work to do. "He said he needed time to think, so I'm giving him all he needs. I'm not going to push myself on him or bug him. He doesn't need me trying to worm my way back into his affections." He needed something to do, because standing here talking to Daniel was only adding to his nervousness. For the past two days, he jumped at every noise outside the apartment and kept looking over his shoulder at work. When his phone chimed, he jumped to see who it was.

Daniel sighed. "So this is you being noble."

Terrance rubbed one hand in the other in frustration. "Look. That ex of his did a number on him. He tracked him down after two years because Ashton bruised the sicko's ego. And then Ashton found out about us." He lowered his voice to a whisper. "And that freaked him out. I have to show him that I'm not like Frank, and if that means staying away until Ashton decides what he wants, then so be it. And if he doesn't want me, then I'll have to live with it." He stood taller. "I won't badger him into anything. This is his decision, and he needs to make it without my interference." It had been so tempting to go over to Daniel and Richard's, barge in, and grab Ashton, take him into his arms, and never let him go.

"So you're afraid Ashton is going to think you're like Frank."

"I know that's what he thinks. He told me so on the way to your condo. That's why I left him there. I knew you would take care of him and see that he was looked after. Why, is something wrong?"

Daniel slowly shook his head. "Sometimes I swear the three of you don't have the sense God gave a gnat. Ashton had just seen his ex killed, and he had been part of it. The poor guy was in shock and he was scared. He heard stuff that upended his world, and the one person who he had been turning to as a rock decided to throw himself on his sword and leave him alone."

"What was I supposed to do?" Terrance hissed in a whisper. "Kidnap him? That's what fucking Frank would have done."

"No. I expected you to take him to my place and then stop by to ensure he knew you really cared. Maybe even offer to take a walk with him on the beach so the two of you could talk. Because, ya big dummy, he thinks you rejected him for rejecting you." Daniel poked his chest. "But *noooooo*. You stayed away and let Ashton worry that you were never that interested in him in the first place. He isn't dumb. He knows that Frank being gone eliminates the threat through him as well as Carlo. There is no one to report back to Garvic, so we're all safe. And he thinks that was all you really wanted and that the rest was an act."

"It wasn't," Terrance said with all the earnestness he felt. "I…. We took on Frank because we needed to be safe, but I was never… ever going to let anyone hurt Ashton. I stepped in before there was any threat from Frank to any of us. I did it because it was the right thing to do, and in the process I met and got to know Ashton."

Daniel nodded. "And now you're afraid you blew it and that he doesn't care." The way he rolled his eyes told Terrance just how stupid Daniel thought he was behaving.

"I know he cares, and that's the problem. He cares for me, but he didn't really know me or any of us. There was always this gulf between him and us because of my background. Now it's out in the open." He had expected that Richard and Daniel would tell Ashton the story, but it seemed they hadn't. Which was probably right. Ashton needed to hear it from him.

"Then go to him and explain things. Tell him the truth. Share that part of yourself with him, the good and the bad. Let him make a real decision with all the information instead of just what his imagination keeps showing him. Because if you don't and you let him get away, so help me, I'll…." Daniel angry was not a pretty sight. "Just get off your ass and make it right… for both of you." With that final pronouncement, he whirled around and left the store.

Terrance watched him go, wondering how in the hell all the people in his life seemed to be able to make these grand exits, leaving him on the outside.

TAKING DANIEL'S advice, when Terrance finished work, he called in an order to the Driftwood for dinner and went home to clean up and change. Then he stopped to pick up the food and went to Daniel's, where he knocked nervously on the door.

Coby answered it. "Uncle Ashton, Uncle Terrance is finally here."

God, what had everyone been saying?

"Do you want to see him, or should I send the big oaf packing like you said you wanted to do last night?"

Ashton hurried in, and Coby raced into the living room, climbed into one of the chairs, and turned on the television. "Well, are you going to send me packing?"

"Come on in. Richard and Daniel will be back in a little while."

Terrance brought in the food. Ashton seemed stiff.

"I brought something to eat," Terrance said, setting the bag on the table. "Richard said Coby was here, so I got him some macaroni and cheese. Are you hungry?"

Coby raced over and climbed into one of the chairs. "I'm hungry." He grinned, and Terrance handed him the Styrofoam package with his food inside and a fork. He dug right in.

"How about you?" Terrance asked. "I remembered that you liked the fish, so I got you that." He passed it to Ashton. "Look, I think you and I need to talk. But we can do that once Richard and Daniel get back."

Ashton shrugged. "I guess." He continued looking down at the tabletop. "I don't know what you want from me, and I don't know what I can give you."

"How about we just talk for a while later? There are some things I think I really need to tell you about." Terrance slowly reached across the table and gently touched Ashton's fingers. "I want you to know that you give me plenty. I don't know what you think I expect, but it's nothing more than what you want to give." He swallowed hard and locked gazes with Ashton.

"This is good." Coby smiled at Terrance. "Thank you for bringing me the food. Daddy says I need to remember to say that." He grinned again and began to eat once more.

"I'm glad you like it. I hope you both like it." He pulled out his own dinner. "I should have told you things earlier, but it isn't just my secret to tell."

Ashton pulled his hand away and slowly began to eat. "I know that. But I think I…."

"It's complicated. But I'll tell you all about it, I promise." That was all he could do at the moment. Terrance wasn't going to talk about such things in front of Coby.

Fortunately, as they were finishing up, Richard and Daniel came in. They brought their own food and joined them at the table. The conversation stayed general until the meal was over, and then Terrance asked Ashton to take a walk with him and they excused themselves for a little while.

"What did you want to say?" Ashton asked once they had reached the beach. They were alone with the sand, waves, and setting sun.

"I'm sorry. I wanted to tell you the whole truth, but I couldn't. However, I didn't lie to you, and I never showed you anyone other than the person that I am. I told you about my mother and the guys. We did grow up on the streets of Detroit. All that is true. But when we were teenagers, we started working for the family. We were good together—gay, tough, and hungry. Before we left, we operated the gay vices in Detroit. Clubs, guys, stores, stuff like that. We made lots of money. Until it ended." He paused and turned to Ashton. "We found out that the new boss was going to turn on us, so we did it first. The police rounded up a lot of our former associates, we testified, and then we went into witness protection and eventually got moved here."

"Is that really it?" Ashton asked.

"To make a long story, short, yes. Daniel and Tucker know, and that's it. Cheryl doesn't, and we are careful around her. Most of the time we don't think about it, and we focus on our lives here because they're the ones that matter." He paused. "See, what Frank didn't get was that we've changed, all of us. We're all a family. One we made ourselves. Richard has become part of the Driftwood. We have roots in the community now."

Ashton blinked. "Is that really all there is to it? Somehow I bet there's a lot more to it."

"There is. But that's the gist of it. We aren't criminals any longer. We lead normal lives and protect the people in them." He sighed.

"How do I know that?" Ashton asked. "I know you don't really lead those normal lives because normal people don't go around picking locks and breaking into marinas and boats."

"No. But normal people don't have guys like Frank and Carlo looking for them. So I do what I have to in order to protect my family, and I'd do it again."

"But how do I know?" Ashton asked.

Terrance shrugged. "I don't know what to say to that. You can't know for sure. I guess you have to trust me." He sighed. "I could tell you about the money that we found a few years ago when Gerome met Tucker, and how we used it to send Tucker to school and pay for all of Cheryl's treatments as well as set up funds for the boys to go to college. Or even the money we found on Frank's boat, the loss of which got him in trouble."

Ashton actually smiled slightly for the first time. "So that's what you did to send Frank over the edge."

"Yeah. But I didn't know he'd actually located you and would find you." He felt terrible about that. "I think he found you because of the studio. Maybe it wasn't just raccoons the other night." His thoughts were a jumble, and he took a second to get them in order, but they calmed just as soon as he took Ashton's hand. The anxiety of the past few days melted away, and he brought Ashton's knuckles to his lips. "I missed you."

"You did?" Ashton cleared his throat. "I missed you too. I thought that you'd decided I was just too much trouble."

Terrance leaned closer. "Oh, I have no doubt that you're trouble, plenty of it. It's a good thing that I like a little trouble in my life." He had missed that sparkle from Ashton. "And I love you."

Ashton swallowed and leaned slightly against him. "And I love you too. That's what scared me so much." They continued walking quietly, just the two of them. "What happens now?" Ashton asked.

"That's up to you. I went to your place and cleaned up the studio as best I could. All the glass that was left has been thrown away, and I cleaned up the blood and stuff. I wasn't sure about the equipment, so I put it away as best I could." He'd spent time there because being in the studio made him feel a little closer to Ashton. "I was thinking that if you wanted, maybe we could use some of that money that we got from Frank to get you a little larger studio."

"Is that what you do with things like that?" Ashton blinked and then shook his head. "I don't want anything from him. Use it for whatever you want, but don't spend it on me. I'll make things work out on my own." Damn, that only made Terrance prouder.

"Okay. It can stay where it is. But maybe you come stay with me and just rent a studio." God, it would be nice to have Ashton in his bed every night. That was something he could definitely get used to.

"But don't the rest of you need it?" Ashton asked. "There's a lot you could do."

Terrance nodded but thought again. That was probably true. Maybe they could find some worthwhile cause and make an anonymous donation. There were plenty of them. The money was tainted, just like everything else that had anything to do with their old lives. And like those lives, the money was best left buried. Their former selves were in the past, and the money somewhere behind the condo was another thing they didn't need to hang on to. "Come on. Let's walk." He squeezed Ashton's hand, and they started down the beach. They had a future to look forward to.

Terrance had spent a lot of time looking over his shoulder and wishing for the past, but as long as he did that, he wouldn't be able to see his future, and that was where he needed to be looking.

"Where are we going?" Ashton asked, and Terrance stopped, leaned down, and kissed him.

"Home." Looking straight ahead.

Epilogue

ASHTON STEPPED back, checking out his booth for a second before going back to work. The sun was just rising, and it was one of those late November days when everything seemed perfect. It was warm but not oppressively hot, and the breeze off the water freshened the air, waving the fronds in the palm trees overhead. He and Terrance had arrived as soon as the grounds opened. The canopy was set up, and Terrance was putting up the black shelves.

"This is where we planned it, but I think we should move them to the other side because of the ground," Terrance suggested, and Ashton helped him move them. They were steady, and Terrance lashed the edge of the shelf to the pole of the canopy for extra stability.

"Where do you want these tubs?" Gerome asked as he slowly wheeled up a cart. Each of the pieces had been well packed, and they all fit into the dozen tubs, three of which were still in one of the cars.

"Right here against the side. This is where my checkout stand will be. I figured we'd set that up last, so we can set them there."

Gerome unloaded them while Ashton helped Terrance with the shelves they'd made together. Each shelf had a lip that hung down slightly, with LED lights behind to illuminate the pieces. Once the shelves were in place, he began placing each work of art according to the layout he'd drawn out. Ashton carefully unpacked the pieces and set them out, the glass sparkling in the light. It was just as he'd planned it.

Terrance placed the three pedestals in front, each with lighting from underneath. Ashton was pleased he'd paid extra for the booth to have power.

Ashton unpacked and placed the final large piece before taking a last look at the booth.

"It's really wonderful," Gerome told him. "It's entrancing, and the light draws the eye."

"Thank you," he said softly. "Thank you both." He couldn't have done this without Terrance and his help with the shelves, or Gerome, who had gotten the pedestals and made them extra stable.

"No problem," Gerome said. "It looks like all you need to do is set up the display of ornaments and you'll be all set." He got out of the way, and Ashton brought out the last items and hung them on the palm tree display. Then he stacked the tubs and set up his little checkout stand. He was all ready and could hardly believe that he was here. Thousands of people would come through the fair, and he hoped they would buy his work.

"It's going to be okay," Terrance said, sliding an arm around his waist as he stood in the walkway. "It's beautiful, the work is stunning, and people are going to love it."

"I hope so." Ashton's throat was dry. He had worked for months on these pieces. The bookstand was in place with a portfolio of pictures of his other works, and everything in the booth was just as it should be. He had done everything he could to make this show a success. Now he just needed customers. That was the ultimate test.

"Hey," Terrance said softly. "I know so. Stop worrying." Terrance held him tighter, and Ashton nodded.

Things had worked out. He and Terrance had found a condo near Daniel and Richard's, and with Gerome's help, they had been able to buy it outright. It had taken some time to get the money together, but apparently Gerome could work magic. Ashton wasn't sure where the money had come from, but Terrance had assured him that none of it was from Frank. For now Ashton still had his small studio, but he was looking for a workable place closer to the condo. To top it off, Terrance had been promoted a few weeks earlier to be the manager of the hardware store. Wonderful things were happening all around. Ashton hoped today would add to that.

Their lives had meshed together—not perfectly, but it *worked*. Terrance's family had become his.

"Uncle Ashton!" Joshie called, half skipping as he held hands with Cheryl. "It's so pretty," he breathed.

"Now remember what we talked about. You have to keep your hands to yourself," Cheryl told him.

Joshie nodded very seriously. "I know. Everything is pretty and 'spensive."

"Where are the others?" Terrance asked.

"They're coming," Cheryl answered. "Daniel and Richard, with Coby and Tucker, were right behind us, but they got stuck in traffic." She turned, and Joshie waved. Sure enough, the rest joined them. Terrance's family—Ashton's family too now—gathered around them. It was perfect, and Ashton got hugs from everyone. The excitement from all of them infused him with energy. After a few minutes they wandered off to enjoy the fair while Ashton got in place to see what others thought.

THE SHOW lasted two days, and he swore his nerves were going to get the better of him.

"Hey, it's okay. You've done well," Terrance said to offer encouragement as Ashton rang up a pair of hand-blown ornaments halfway through the afternoon.

"But I hoped…," he said softly, looking over the booth. It seemed the same as it had when they set it up. None of the larger pieces had sold, and he wondered if his work just wasn't interesting enough. He thanked his customers, and they left the booth.

"Young man," a stunning middle-aged woman said gently. She was dressed in a beautifully cut outfit and carried a designer purse that cost more than most of the pieces in the booth. "Are you the artist?"

"Yes, ma'am. How can I help you?"

She hesitated. "I passed your booth earlier and I loved your work, but you were busy." She smiled as she looked over the pieces on display. "I'm trying to choose what I'd like, but I can't seem to do it." She stepped back and out of the booth. "I think I'd like… that." She pointed to the piece he'd done to encapsulate his anxiety. "It's so impassioned and full of emotion." Then she turned to the chandelier that they'd hung from a frame next to the shelf. "I'd also like that fixture for my beach house." She grinned, stepped over to the stand, and handed Ashton her credit card.

His hands shook as he rung up the sale, completed it, and then wrapped up the pieces. He gave her a tub to help in carrying them home. "Would you like me to help you to your car?" Terrance asked.

"That would be nice," she said and then handed Ashton a card. "I have a gallery in Sarasota, and I'd like to work with you. These pieces are original, and the workmanship is stunning. When the fair is over, give me a call and we can arrange a show at the gallery in a few months. My patrons are going to love your work."

"Thank you. I definitely will," Ashton said, clutching the card as though it were solid gold. "Thank you so much." He grinned, and Terrance hefted the tub and followed her through the show.

Ashton smiled and returned to his seat as the artist from the next booth poked his head in. "Was that Lauren Holler?" he asked.

Ashton nodded, still holding the business card.

"And she bought your work?"

"Yes. Two pieces." Ashton answered.

"Wow" was all he said. "Well done." He went back to his booth, and Ashton got to work taking down the frame that had held the chandelier and packing it away. He shifted his station to cover the empty space. Then he greeted the next patrons who entered the booth.

Ashton was busy with another small sale when Terrance returned just in time to help another customer take a major purchase to their car.

"I told you everything would work out," Terrance said as he returned with tubs of items to fill the now-empty spaces. Ashton set the new items out, and one was immediately purchased. "See, you're a huge success."

Ashton let himself be pulled into Terrance's arms. He was going to shake apart from happiness and excitement. "I never dreamed." Hell, there was so much he'd never let himself even think about.

"The fair closes in an hour," Terrance told him. "We'll need to pack up the work and bring it back with us. The setup we can leave for tomorrow." Ashton nodded but didn't pull away. "There's just one question."

"What's that?" Ashton asked, smiling at the amusement in his voice.

"Once we pack up, we need to get something to eat, and the guys asked if we were going to get together to celebrate your success."

Ashton stilled. "When did they do that?" They hadn't been back to the booth.

"Yesterday." And just like that, Ashton grinned. "I told them we'd celebrate as a family tomorrow night." Terrance leaned closer, his lips right at Ashton's ear. "Tonight it's a celebration for just the two of us."

That sounded perfect.

Read how the story began!

Bad to Be Good: Book One

Longboat Key, Florida, is about as far from the streets of Detroit as a group of gay former mobsters can get, but threats from within their own organization forced them into witness protection—and a new life.

Richard Marsden is making the best of his second chance, tending bar and learning who he is outside of organized crime… and flirting with the cute single dad, Daniel, who comes in every Wednesday. But much like Richard, Daniel hides dark secrets that could get him killed. When Daniel's past as a hacker catches up to him, Richard has the skills to help Daniel out, but not without raising some serious questions and risking his own new identity and the friends who went into hiding with him.

Solving problems like Daniel's is what Richard does best—and what he's trying to escape. But finding a way to keep Daniel and his son safe without sacrificing the person he's becoming will take some imagination, and the stakes have never been higher. This time it's not just lives on the line—it's his heart….

www.dreamspinnerpress.com

RICHARD MARSDEN—YES, that was his name now. It was always at the front of his mind that his old life was over. Everything had been stripped away, and the person and the life he'd had before were gone. And that included his real name. Well, now Marsden was his "real" name. At least it was supposed to be, but it didn't feel like it. Though to be fair, nothing about where he lived and what he did each day felt real to him. He doubted it ever would.

"I ain't never gonna get used to this shit," his brother Terrance grumped as he stalked into the empty bar, looking around. "You know what went down?" He came closer, stomping on the wooden floor. "A customer got in my face 'cause we didn't have the size flange that he needed, and I fucking had to stand there like a dope instead of ripping the fucker's head off."

Richard shot his hand out and smacked Terrance on the back of the head. "No talking about that stuff.

Not here—or anywhere, for that matter. And no street talk. Remember that we need to speak properly so we don't stand out." He rolled his eyes and then puffed up his chest, glaring hard at his younger, but built like a brick shithouse, brother in spirit. "And no ripping anyone's head off," he added in a hiss just above a whisper. "Sometimes I wonder what the hell is wrong with you."

Terrance inhaled, and anger flared in his eyes but then abated slowly. "At least he isn't dead." That was better.

Richard took a deep breath, inhaling the scent of fish, ocean water, and whatever seasoning the guys in the kitchen were using. The damned stuff had been stoking his appetite since he arrived an hour ago. "What are you doing here instead of being at work?"

"Break. I walked down to cool off," Terrance said.

"Okay. Go on back to the hardware store and finish your shift, because you are not to get fired. And don't draw any extra attention to yourself. Remember the rules." He crooked his finger and lowered his voice. "If you do decide to rip anyone's head off, remember that yours is next. You know I'll do it, and piss down your damned neck. Now go back to work, and no talking about…. Just keep your mouth shut. You know how to do that."

Terrance nodded and turned away, leaving the bar and smacking the door shut with a bang. Richard picked up his tray of glasses, shaking his head as he went back to work stocking the bar for tonight.

It wasn't that Richard didn't understand how Terrance felt—he very much did. Richard had spent the past four months stocking glasses and getting drinks, listening to guys who sat at the bar bellyaching over the fact that they thought their wives were having an affair or that things at work were going to shit. Richard could tell them all about things going to hell. It had happened to them—him and his brothers—and now he was tending bar instead of running an entertainment organization. Now that was the shits of epic proportions.

Richard finished stocking and stepped outside the bar for a breath of fresh air. They didn't open for another half hour, and he was ready.

The sun beat down on the empty parking area, the Florida heat wafting off the blacktop. If he looked carefully across the street and between the houses and palm trees, he could see the Gulf of Mexico, the water sparkling as the waves caught the light. To most people, this would be paradise. Richard knew that, and yet he missed Detroit and his home. Yeah, to most people Detroit was not the kind of place you missed. Richard could understand that. But it was the city he'd grown up in, his home, and he had been somebody there. He thought he was going places, in line for big things, and then everything fucking changed at the drop of a hat, and just like that it was gone.

The familiar white Focus with the ding in the front bumper pulled into the parking area and up next to where he was standing. His youngest friend and brother from a different mother, Gerome, lowered the window. "I saw you standing out here. You out to get sunstroke or something?"

Richard rolled his eyes. "No. Getting some fresh, water-filled air before I go back inside and pretend to be a bartender." That was it—his entire life was pretend. "And we gotta have the 'keep your damn mouth shut' conversation with Terrance… again." He was getting so sick of this. For the millionth time he wondered if anything was ever going to be normal again. The answer that he kept coming back to was that it wasn't.

Richard, Terrance, and Gerome had been friends and a family of their own making since they were twelve years old. They'd survived on the mean streets of depressed inner-city Detroit by their wits and having each other's backs. The three of them joined the Garvic organization of the Italian mafia when they were fourteen and worked their way upward fast. They were tough as hell and none of them took any shit from anyone—or had to—because everyone in the organization knew that to take one of them on was to engage all three of them. They were tough, smart, and feared. Richard liked that.

In the end, the three of them had made a great deal of money for Harold Garvic. Richard ran the gay clubs in Detroit and was the king of the gay mafia… so to speak. He ran the entire enterprise and returned a great deal of money, managing the legitimate club façade while laundering millions in cash. Terrance was the muscle and feared well beyond their group. No one messed with any of them because no one in the Garvic organization wanted to see Terrance come through their door. Gerome was the idea man. He dreamed up new ways to make piles of money, and together the three of them made it happen. Life was fucking sweet.

Then Harold Sr. died, and his prick of a son didn't want to be involved in "their" kind of business. Instead of letting the three of them have their little piece of the empire, he made his first and biggest mistake: Harold Jr. came after them. Now the Garvic organization was a shadow of what it was, their leaders were doing decades behind bars, and Richard, Terrance, and Gerome had different lives, living on Longboat Key in Florida, abiding by a million rules so the government could keep them safe. They were three brothers in spirit who were now trying to figure things out in a world where they didn't understand the rules.

"All right, I'll talk to him." Gerome nodded, seeming resigned, his words pulling Richard out of his good-old-days fog. Of the three of them, Gerome had had the easiest time. He had been placed at a gift boutique that sold upscale tourist items. The thing was that Gerome could sell anything. He had rearranged the place within the first two weeks, asked about new items, and all of a sudden he was in charge of the sales floor when sales started going through the roof. At least one of them was doing okay. "I'll handle it. See you later." He raised the window and pulled out of the lot.

Richard took a deep breath, pushing away the hurt to his pride that each and every day seemed to bring, and went back inside. He had work to do. He checked that the kitchen was all right, then greeted Andi as she came in through the back door.

"Everything okay?" she asked.

Richard wiped the moroseness off his face, plastering on a professional mask. "Sure. You all set?" He went behind the bar to cut limes and lemons for garnish, taking a second as she wound through the floor of tables that looked as though they had been through one of Florida's tropical storms and come out the other side. The chairs had seen the wear from hundreds of butts, and the walls, darkened with age and constant exposure to humid salt air, were decorated with mounted fish and old buoys, as well as pictures of great catches. The entire place seemed to have soaked up the scent of the sea, fish, and water.

"You know me. I'm always ready." She gave him a little swing of her hips and then turned away. Andi was one of the few people outside of the guys who knew that he was gay. She had made a play for him the first week he'd worked at the bar, and he had turned her down. To tell the truth, she was attractive, with shoulder-length black hair, a great figure, and intense eyes.

"Too bad you never go for a guy who would deserve you," he muttered and returned to work as the first patrons came through the front door.

The bar patrons were a combination of tourists and locals. A few of the people he saw all the time came in and took familiar places at the bar. Richard pulled beers and made drinks, started tabs, and took payment, the cash settling in his hand before going to the register.

That had been one of the hardest things to remember. In Detroit it was expected that he would skim a certain amount off the top. Richard and Gerome were masters of it, and he'd always been conscientious about returning a growing amount to Harold, which had kept him happy.

"Happy Wednesday," Tim, one of the regulars, said, and Richard's mind skipped a track for a second. He had completely forgotten, and now some of the gloom lifted from inside him.

Richard filled an order from Andi and continued his tasks with half an eye on the front door as he worked.

He knew when it was six o'clock because Daniel came into the bar.

Richard had no idea what it was about this slim man with intense brown eyes and surfer-length black hair hanging to just below his ears that drew him, but as long as Daniel was in the bar, Richard knew exactly where he was at all times, even when his back was turned.

Daniel took a place at the bar.

"You want your usual?" He was already pulling Daniel's beer without really thinking about it. Once Daniel nodded, he placed the beer on the scarred bar surface in front of him.

"The fish and chips, please," Daniel said in his soft voice. Then he flashed him a smile. Richard was determined not to allow his heart rate to rise, but the fucking thing did it anyway. He leaned over the bar just a little, almost as though Daniel had a gravity of his own and Richard was caught in it.

"Of course. I'll put your order in right away," Richard said and swallowed hard, licking his lips as their gazes locked for the fraction of a second. Then Richard remembered where they were and that this was not a gay club in Detroit, but the Cormorant on Longboat Key, Florida.

"Thank you," Daniel said without turning away. "I really appreciate that."

Richard had to break whatever was going on between them. Not that he wasn't excited, but damn, if he wasn't careful, someone was going to come in, and if they joined him behind the bar, there was no damned way they could miss how much Daniel got under his skin.

"Can I get another beer?" Mike asked from a few seats down.

Richard pulled himself away, poured the beer, and put in Daniel's order through the system. At least he could breathe for a few seconds.

Not that this attraction and the innocent flirting he did with Daniel on occasion were ever going to lead anywhere. They couldn't, not in a million years. It didn't matter how many times Richard wondered just what that lithe, compact body looked like under those worn jeans that hugged him like a second skin or the dark blue polo shirt with the tiny hole right at the collar where it sometimes rubbed at Daniel's neck.

Richard, Terrance, and Gerome were only here and stayed alive because they were doing their best to abide by the rules of the Witness Protection Program, and that meant they all needed to stay out of the public eye, not draw attention to themselves, and definitely not tell anyone anything about their past. But more than that, they had had to plead to be allowed to stay together. If they messed up, they wouldn't just be relocated, but separated as well. Sure, Richard could have a fling with Daniel and then they could go on their separate ways, but Richard knew that if he got a single taste of him, he'd want more. Daniel was like potato chips. One would never be enough.

He checked on Daniel's order with the kitchen and refilled glasses, telling himself he was going to ignore Daniel and do his job, keeping himself busy until he left. Daniel had a routine almost as regular as clockwork. Each Wednesday he came in a few minutes after six, had a beer, ordered fish and chips, and nursed his second beer until just before nine o'clock, when he said good night and left the bar. It had been that way since Richard's first week on the job. Richard had tried to talk with him on occasion, and other than his name and a little small talk, he'd learned nothing about him. Richard had cracked some of the hardest men, actually reducing them to tears when he was in charge of the clubs. But hell, Daniel could give lessons on keeping your mouth shut.

When Daniel's order was ready, Richard went to the kitchen to get it, returned, and placed it in front of him. Daniel reached for his cutlery and his hand brushed against Richard's. The gesture was completely innocent and accidental, and yet Richard nearly gasped at the shock that raced through him all the way to his bones.

"Thank you," Daniel said.

Richard nodded and turned away to go back to work, frustration building high enough that he felt it in his temples like the start of a headache, except this held a touch of the delicious and the forbidden, which only made him want it all the more, even though he told himself repeatedly that Daniel—or anyone at all—was off-limits.

ANDREW GREY is the author of more than one hundred works of Contemporary Gay Romantic fiction. After twenty-seven years in corporate America, he has now settled down in Central Pennsylvania with his husband, Dominic, and his laptop. An interesting ménage. Andrew grew up in western Michigan with a father who loved to tell stories and a mother who loved to read them. Since then he has lived throughout the country and traveled throughout the world. He is a recipient of the RWA Centennial Award, has a master's degree from the University of Wisconsin–Milwaukee, and now writes full-time. Andrew's hobbies include collecting antiques, gardening, and leaving his dirty dishes anywhere but in the sink (particularly when writing). He considers himself blessed with an accepting family, fantastic friends, and the world's most supportive and loving partner. Andrew currently lives in beautiful, historic Carlisle, Pennsylvania.

Email: andrewgrey@comcast.net

Website: www.andrewgreybooks.com

Read the rest of the series!

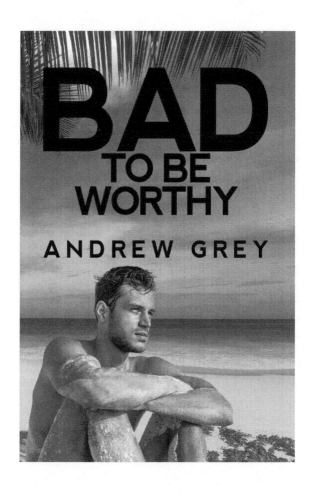

Bad to Be Good: Book Two

When a former mobster's past catches up with him, will it end the quiet life he's been struggling with, or transform it into something he couldn't have imagined?

Sometimes Gerome Meadows longs for the excitement of the life he left behind for Witness Protection. But when he stands up to a bully in a bar to protect a homeless man, his past comes very close to home—and it's no longer what he wants.

Tucker Wells has been living in a tent, surviving with the aid of his friend Cheryl and helping her watch over her son. When he winds up on the wrong side of an argument with some dangerous people, his already difficult life is thrown into turmoil. Gerome steps in to find them a temporary apartment, and Tucker is grateful and relieved.

Gerome never meant to open the door to trouble. His life and Tucker's depend on keeping his past a mystery. But as his desire to protect develops into something deeper, he and Tucker will have to evaluate what family means—and hope that their growing feelings pass unimaginable tests.

www.dreamspinnerpress.com

FOR **MORE** OF THE **BEST GAY ROMANCE**

dreamspinnerpress.com